Hart To Hart

Montana Promises
Book 4

Vella Day

HART TO HART
Copyright © 2015 by Vella Day
Print Edition
www.velladay.com
velladayauthor@gmail.com

Cover Art by Sloan Winters
Edited by Rebecca Cartee and Carol Adcock-Bezzo
Published in the United States of America
E-book ISBN: 978-1-941835-05-0
Print Edition ISBN: 978-1-941835-06-7

Prologue

DARKNESS WRAPPED ITSELF around Ellie Hart like a thin blanket, only tonight it brought little comfort. As she hurried to her car in Old Alexandria, Virginia, the hairs on the back of her neck stood up. If she hadn't left the art gallery to pick up more punch cups, she wouldn't have had to park so far away upon returning.

Brr. She tugged her wrap tighter across her chest to fend off the brisk November air. Wearing the bejeweled shawl instead of her fall coat had seemed like a good idea earlier in the day. Now? Not so much.

Ellie picked up the pace, but she wasn't able to go as fast as she wished. High heels weren't made for speed. The heavy footsteps about a half block behind her didn't worry her—at least, they didn't at first—but the street was too quiet tonight, and the thudding of the heavy heels echoed off the tall buildings.

What was up with the lack of pedestrians? It was ten on a Friday night. People in the Washington, D.C. suburbs were always about—but they weren't now for some reason. She chanced a glance behind her. Instead of some creepy man, two young girls stepped out of a bar and headed in her direction. Oh, well. Her imagination must be in overdrive.

Just keep going. Clutching her purse tight against her chest, she spotted her car in the next block. *Yes!* As she neared, that strange sensation of being watched crept up her spine again. She shook it off and dug her hand into her purse for her keys. It must be the residual unease from the strange phone calls she'd been receiving this past week. Heavy breathers were the worst.

She unlocked her car with the remote then stepped into the street to edge her way to the driver's side. Only then did she notice another Gerbera daisy hooked under the windshield wiper. She plucked it from under the rubber strip, hoping for a note this time, but didn't see one. Damn.

Had her ex-boyfriend, Brian, put it there hoping for a reconciliation? Or had it been Hilton, her co-owner of the gallery? Yeah, it must have been him—to thank her for the success of tonight's showing. But when had he placed it? When she'd dashed out to pick up more cups, the flower hadn't been there. Strange.

It didn't matter. On instinct, she brought the flower to her nose, but it didn't have much of a scent—at least, not enough to make a dent over the exhaust fumes. She slipped inside the car then locked the doors. Her hand actually shook so much she had to inhale to get the key in the lock. Damn. What was her problem? Too many late nights and too much caffeine? The stress this past month had been rather intense. Or was it that she'd agreed to teach an art class two nights a week when she really couldn't spare the time?

She started the engine and let it idle for a moment to warm up. The space in front of her was free, so she pulled forward— or rather, she tried to pull forward. It was as if she was driving through thick sand. Kerplunk. Thud. Kerplunk. Thud. *Shit.* She must have a flat. Ellie dropped her head back against the seat and groaned. She absolutely didn't need this. Not tonight.

She pushed open the door and jumped out. The streetlights

provided enough illumination to show both front tires had been slashed. "Are you kidding me? Freaking gangs."

This couldn't have come at a worse time. She was supposed to leave early tomorrow morning for a weeks' vacation to visit her daughter in Montana. Now, she'd have to postpone the trip a day or two to get the tires replaced. The added expense of changing the flight was the last straw. Ellie ran her hands through her short hair and tugged hard, trying to calm down. She failed.

She supposed she could call Brian to give her a lift home, but it might not be safe to leave her vehicle here overnight. Shit. She fished out the number for roadside assistance and slipped back into the car to stay warm. Once she gave the information, she locked the doors again and waited. With each minute that passed, her anger built. Who had left the flower? And why? And what ass saw fit to damage her car? Damn, she couldn't buy a break.

Chapter One

"MOM, I'M SO happy you finally made it," Charlotte said, giving Ellie a hug at baggage claim.

"Thanks, sweetie. Good to see you, too." It had been too long between visits.

Charlotte ran her hands down Ellie's arms. "Not to be rude, but you don't look so good. You're shaking; you look like death warmed over. What's wrong?"

Ellie chuckled. Had she been that blunt at twenty-three? "Way to sugarcoat it. I know I brought you up to speak your mind, but be kind. I'm just tired, that's all. I would have been in a lot better shape if some thugs hadn't slashed my tires." She wouldn't have told Charlotte about the incident had Ellie not needed to delay her flight by two days. Ugh.

"I get it. Do the cops know who did it?"

She hadn't reported it. "No. Things like that happen all the time in our area." Ellie checked the baggage claim belt and spotted her pink suitcase. When she grabbed it off the conveyor belt, Charlotte slipped it out of her hand. Ellie didn't argue. She was that tired.

"What you need is to rest this week," her daughter said.

"That and a hot cup of coffee."

"Coffee I can do."

The trip from Montana's Kalispell airport to Charlotte's cute one-bedroom bungalow was pretty, especially with the view of the mountains in the distance. Her daughter was smart enough not to grill her about what was going on in Ellie's life—yet.

"You can stay in my bedroom. I'll sleep on the sofa." Charlotte headed toward the hallway with Ellie's case.

"You'll do no such thing. I get up a lot in the middle of the night and don't want to disturb you." Of late, she'd been unable to shut off her brain. Between making the Davies-Hart Gallery a success, breaking up with Brian, and starting the classes, she was worn out. Sleep came in spurts.

They argued a bit, but in the end, Ellie won.

"Fine. I'll make some coffee."

Ellie smiled. "Now you're talking."

Charlotte fixed a pot and poured both of them cups. As soon as the first sip hit her stomach, the caffeine from the rich brew soaked into her veins. "Ah, I think I'll live."

Charlotte picked up her cup from the kitchen counter. "Let's sit in the living room. I want to hear what's going on with you."

Here it comes. Ellie followed her daughter. While the space was small, the living room was cozy with vibrant, rich colors, yet practical at the same time. Her daughter took after her artistically, which was why Charlotte now worked for an interior designer. "You've done a fantastic job with this place."

"Thanks. It's been fun."

Ellie plopped down on the sofa while Charlotte sat on the art deco style, lime green chair across from her. She set her drink on the coffee table. "So what has you so stressed out? And don't say it's the tire-slashing event."

"It's a long story." Ellie sipped more of her brew then began with her break up with Brian Lovett.

Her daughter's eyes widened. "You've been dating someone

and didn't tell me?"

Charlotte's indignation caused her to laugh. "Yes. You okay with that? I might be old and fat, but I'm not dead." She was only forty-five.

"You're not fat. You're...well-seasoned with curves."

Ellie groaned. Her ego was taking one hit after another. "Continuing with my story—I'd been dating Brian about a month, and things were going well, when Hilton suggested I offer an adult art class at the gallery a couple evenings a week. He believed it might bring in prospective buyers and possibly artists."

"How's that working out? Having a co-owner?"

"It's fine, but I'll get back to Hilton in a moment. The class began taking more and more of my time and I wasn't able to spend as much of it with Brian as I would have liked. The gallery is my livelihood and I had to put it first. He disagreed."

Charlotte leaned back. "If Brian were smart, he would have taken your class just to spend more time with you."

She smiled. "I actually suggested it, but he said his artistic side had never developed. He's a stock broker."

"Ah. I take it Brian broke up with you because of the neglect?"

That hurt. She and her ex, Vic, had split because he'd neglected both her and Charlotte. Vic never put up a fuss, claiming she was better off without him since his line of work was too dangerous. "I actually dropped him."

Her brows rose. "Are you okay with that now?"

"Yes and no. I like having someone in my life, but I'm not convinced Brian is the one."

"It sounds like you made a wise decision then."

When had her daughter grown up? "I like to think so. Then about a week later, I was feeling a little guilty and perhaps a bit sad about it, when a note suddenly appeared on my desk at work that said to meet *him* at the park that afternoon at twelve. It specifically stated where to meet—it was at our usual bench. But the note wasn't signed."

"You went, didn't you?"

Ellie nodded. "But I wished I hadn't. When I arrived at our park bench, Brian wasn't there. About five minutes later, a little girl about six came up to me with a half dozen pink Gerbera daisies. She said they were from a man and that he was sorry he couldn't be there."

Charlotte picked up her coffee. "That was sweet of him and probably cost him an arm and a leg given the time of year."

Ellie hadn't thought about the availability of those flowers in November. "It might have been, except when I called to thank Brian for the flowers, he said he hadn't sent them, nor had he written the note."

Her daughter frowned. "Then who did?"

Ellie shrugged. "I have no idea. I thought, perhaps, one of the students in my class had sent them. I teach six men and four women. One of them, Cal, has had a crush on me for a while. He has talent, but he's not ready to have his work exhibited, yet he doesn't see it that way. He's asked me out a few times, but he's too intense for me." She waved a hand. "Anyway, I casually mentioned the park incident to the group, but no one fessed up."

Charlotte sipped her coffee, looking lovely and mature. Ellie should have visited sooner, but the gallery was beginning to do well and she hadn't wanted to take the time off.

"Did you ask Hilton if he sent them?"

Hilton Davies, her gallery partner, had contributed the lion's share of the start-up money. Because of his backing, Ellie had agreed to be the face of the business—and do most of the legwork. "Even though I was a bit embarrassed, I told him. He seemed rather upset."

"Upset because another man sent you flowers or because this mystery man didn't show up?"

"I'm not sure. Hilton is a widower and thinks the two of us could have something special. I'm not convinced. He's a friend. A good one. But that's all."

"Ouch. Has he been persistent?"

"On and off. He's smart enough to back off when he can tell I'm stressed."

Charlotte looked off, her face unreadable. "Back to the tires. Didn't you say the night your tires were slashed, there was a Gerbera daisy on the windshield?" Ellie nodded. "Could this be some kind of stalker?"

Ellie laughed. "No."

"Mo-om. Think about it. An unsigned note, a mystery man, a random flower, slashed tires. Really? From the guilty look on your face, there's more. Spill."

Vic always said she was an open book and that she was a terrible liar.

Ellie held up her hand. Her daughter was smart. "It's nothing really, but I'll tell you so I can get some peace. A couple of weeks after the park incident, I began getting phone calls at night where the person would call but say nothing."

"A heavy breather?" Ellie nodded. "Why didn't you call him back?"

"I tried, but I got a recording saying the number was not in service. I know that wasn't possible, but it happened. This person is clever. I told Hilton about it and he said to go to the police."

"Thank God someone has sense. What did they say? Were they able to trace the call?"

Being grilled by her little girl wasn't pleasant. "I didn't go. I felt silly. Besides, what could they do?" Charlotte grunted, acting as if Ellie was too stupid to live. Hell, maybe she was. Denial had a way of distorting things.

"Arrest him? Or give him a stern warning?"

Ellie shrugged. "The phone calls stopped after that, and I thought everything was good. Then about two weeks ago, I found flowers by my apartment door."

"Gerbera daisies again?"

"Yes. I would have dismissed my unknown admirer until the emails and texts started."

"Emails and texts? My God, Mom. You act as if this is an everyday occurrence. If that had happened to me, I'd have gone to the police. What were you thinking?" Charlotte's mouth opened and her brows pinched. Her daughter looked so much like Vic that emotion swamped her.

"I guess I wasn't. The emails were from an unknown sender. The messages were innocuous enough. Things like, 'Did you enjoy Reynold's Restaurant?' Or 'Nice day for a run, I see.'"

"I'm guessing you had been to that restaurant and gone jogging?"

"Yes."

"Mom. You have to go to the police. Someone is stalking you."

Ellie blew out a long breath. "I was in denial for a long time, but don't worry. I finally came to my senses and hired a private investigator, but all he was able to tell me was that the person who sent the emails had been at a certain cybercafé at a particular time."

"Did he figure out the person's name?"

"No."

"Dad would have looked at the video feed."

A quick shiver tripped up Ellie's spine. Vic would have said it just like that. "Since when did you become an expert on your father's behavior?" He had never been around when she was growing up, and the resentment built until the two stopped talking years before Ellie's divorce.

Charlotte shrugged and glanced away. "We reconnected after the fire." Charlotte leaned forward. "He's changed, Mom."

Ellie didn't want to hear it. "Don't let him fool you."

"You should give him a chance. When he left the FBI, he was a broken man, but a good one."

God, she didn't need this. "I've moved on." At least she thought she had, until the notes and flowers started.

The light in her daughter's eyes dimmed. "Fine. Do you have any idea who might be doing all of this, assuming it's one person?"

"I don't interact with that many people. I can't imagine it being Hilton. He has no motive and nothing to gain from scaring me."

"And Brian?"

"He's my first choice, but if he wants me back, his method sucks. And then there's Cal, my kind of creepy artist."

"Mom." Charlotte lowered her gaze. "You have to call Dad now. If you don't, I will."

Chapter Two

I T HAD TAKEN a year, but Vic Hart had finally settled into Rock Hard, Montana, and was enjoying life. Leaving Washington, D.C. and the fast-pace of the FBI had been hard at first, but he'd seen the writing on the wall. With the distinctive burn on his neck and jaw from the fire, going undercover had become impossible. That meant he'd have to either push papers for the Bureau for the rest of his life or quit. He chose the latter. The good news was that he'd actually made friends in Rock Hard during his time there, making the transition to the small town life easier.

Once the FBI team, along with the Rock Hard Police Department, brought down the terrorist cell, Vic had returned to D.C. where his social life went from bad to worse. He'd tried connecting with his ex-wife, El, but she'd returned only one of his calls and that was to decline his dinner invitation. When he suggested coffee instead, she said she was busy and that she was seeing someone. He recognized the brush off for what it was. After what he'd been through, he didn't need any more emotional hits, so he backed off.

So, when El had called him this morning, he'd been stunned. In fact, he failed to live up to his nickname of Iceman, acting like a teenage boy having a girl ask him to his first prom.

Vic took a last look in the bathroom mirror and headed back to his office. Sharon, his secretary, was at her desk playing solitaire on the computer. When he'd hired her, she'd been rather conservative with mousy brown hair. Last week, she'd had it styled and streaked blue. He had to admit, he liked the new Sharon better.

He probably should suggest she work on organizing the files since business had slowed with the onset of winter, but he didn't want to lose her. She had her strengths. His main goal wasn't to make a big profit anyway. Between his pension from the FBI and the money he'd saved while he was in the service, he could afford to retire—he just didn't want to.

Before he reached the hallway, the bell above the front door rang. Jitters swamped him. El was here. He spun around. Had the five years since he'd seen his wife—or rather his ex-wife—been kind to her? His hadn't been.

El entered. Holy shit, but she was hot. He wasn't pleased about her downcast eyes, but the rest of her made him stand at attention. Her hips were wider than he remembered, but the extra weight was balanced well with her enlarged breasts. Even more positive was that her face had finally filled out. From all the worry he'd caused her when they were more or less together, she'd lost too much weight. He never was the type to like a woman who was all skin and bones. He wanted to be with someone who had womanly curves.

She looked good with the short hair, too. While he couldn't be certain, it looked as if there might be some auburn highlights in it, which went well with her warm skin tone.

Stop it. She's a client.

"Hello, El." Thankfully, Vic was able to keep his voice from cracking.

She glanced up, stilled, and studied him. "Vic."

Sharon glanced between them, and he held up a hand before she spoke. "I'll escort Ms. Hart into my office." Vic had a hard time not staring at his former wife. She was more beautiful than ever. "How's Charlotte?" he asked as he led her down the hallway.

"Fine, but then you know that since you speak with her all the time."

Shit. She was going to make it difficult for him. "Trying to make up for lost time, that's all." Once in the office, he pulled out the wooden chair across from his desk. He'd purposefully bought one that wasn't particularly comfortable so his clients wouldn't linger. Now, he could see a nicer chair was in his future. "Let me take your coat and hang it up."

El held up her hands as if his mere touch would scorch her. "I won't be staying long."

The jab pierced his heart. He honestly didn't deserve any better treatment. He'd been a shitty husband, putting country above his family. He dragged his chair from behind his desk and sat across from her, not wanting to put any more distance between them. "You mentioned over the phone that you've had a few misfortunes." Charlotte called it a stalker, but he wanted to hear what El thought. "How would you assess the threat level?"

It was nice to be able to use the lingo and not have to worry if his client understood.

"It's hard to say. I'm thinking it might be several different people. In any case, I want this to stop."

"Understood. How serious is it? Have you been physically harmed?" His throat tightened at the thought.

"There'd been no contact with me or my property until a few days ago when my tires were slashed—possibly by some local gang, so I'd have to rate this a yellow. It's not even orange because I've never seen this person nor has he threatened me bodily harm." She lifted her chin.

"Does this mystery man have a name?"

"How can he if I don't know who he is?"

"Sorry." Shit. He hadn't been thinking. Not having a clue as to the man's identity would make the search more difficult but not impossible. "Start from the beginning and leave nothing out. Do you mind if I record this?" He tapped his forehead. "Memory's going. Old age." His smile was not returned. Damn.

"Go ahead." El began her tale. With each word, his desire to punch something grew.

It wasn't so much what she told him, but the way she was fidgeting with the buttons on her coat that let him know this person was getting inside her head. Vic wanted to reach out and grab her hand for comfort, but he wouldn't. Clearly, his former wife was ill at ease around him, and he didn't want to make this worse for her.

"I'm very sorry, El. You said you confided in Henry?"

She blinked. "Do you mean Hilton?"

Shit. "Yes. Hilton." At least he hadn't called him hotel.

"I have."

"Any chance he's your flower-giving, tire-slashing man?"

El sat up straighter. "Absolutely not. He has no motive."

Vic could think of a few reasons why Hilton might want to scare her. One could be that he wanted to buy her out. El would say no, of course, because she loved the gallery more than life itself. The only option left would be to drive her out—make her leave town. On the other hand, it could also be that Hilton wanted to get into her pants, and if El had turned him down in the past, it might have pissed him off. Or perhaps she'd slept with him already and now he wanted more.

Don't go there.

Fuck. Maybe agreeing to take her case wasn't a good idea

after all.

"Who else might want to upset you? Although, the flowers imply this person wants you."

"One would think, but the creepy emails and texts suggest the person is merely watching me, trying to freak me out."

"Good point."

They spent a better part of an hour discussing her case and what she'd like him to do. With the sources he still had from his FBI days, he figured he could have this wrapped up in a couple of days. His best chance of finding this person would come from the emails, as he doubted he'd get access to any phone records.

It was still early in the day, yet El looked exhausted already. The fact she kept her coat on the whole time implied she was chomping at the bit to leave, but he wanted to be cordial.

"Where are you staying?"

"At the Park Hotel. I don't want to drive the two hours back to Charlotte's."

"Nice place." Vic was pleased she was doing well enough to afford the best. He glanced at the clock on his computer. "It's almost noon. Do you want to grab a bite to eat?"

El pushed back her chair. "Vic. Let's get one thing straight. I didn't come here to rekindle what we once had. If you must know, Charlotte insisted I let you handle my case. I agreed only because I trust you'll do a good job."

At least he'd maintained his integrity in her eyes over the years, but the rejection still stung. He pulled his business card from his desk, scribbled his cell phone number on the back, and handed it to her. "Call me in a few days to check on my progress." He smiled. "Unless you'd like me to call you."

If her body got any stiffer, he'd have worried she'd be unable to walk. "I'll call. And thank you. I'm sure you're busy."

El spun on her heels and strode out. The big question was

there anything he could do to convince her to stay?

✧　✧　✧

ELLIE COULD BARELY breathe. As she rushed to her rental car, cold air snaked down her lungs. She'd prepared herself to be put off by the burns on Vic's neck and jaw, but damn it, if it didn't make him look sexier. He'd lost weight, but given he'd played a homeless man for a while it was understandable. When he pulled out her chair, the sight of his muscles bulging under his cuffs along with his flat abs—something she'd always been a sucker for—took her back to the good old days when she ate lust for breakfast.

Stop it.

Vic never made her his priority when they were married, and men like that never changed—it was built into their DNA. He might not be part of the U.S. government any longer, but he had his own company, and Hart's Investigations had probably become his new mistress. Ellie had to let him do his job and find the identity of her stalker. Then she'd say thank you, pay him, and return to Charlotte's to finish her vacation—assuming he found the culprit quickly.

Her stomach grumbled. Needing food, but not wanting to run into Vic, she drove down the streets of Rock Hard looking for a place where he'd never frequent. The Happy Carrot Restaurant was perfect. Vic loved meat. Any kind of meat. He ate vegetables only because they were good for him, not because he liked the taste.

Not wanting to chance Vic finding her, she parked two blocks away and walked to the restaurant. By the time she stepped inside, she was chilled to the bone. It wasn't so much the dampness as the wind that sliced through her jacket and up her pant legs.

The walls were painted orange—not a big surprise there—and were covered in cute paintings of knife wielding vegetables battling cows and pigs. The artwork was surprisingly good.

Only about five people were seated. Once she was shown to her table, she ordered a coffee and checked the menu. Impressed with the selections, she decided on a robust salad.

The waitress returned with her coffee and took her order. While Ellie waited for the food to arrive, she checked her emails, expecting something from Charlotte. Her daughter would want to know how the meeting went with Vic. As Ellie scrolled through the list, one message popped out. The subject line read: *How's Charlotte?*

Her heart turned cold. "No."

A passing waitress stopped. "Ma'am? Are you all right?"

Ellie looked up. "Yes. Thank you."

As soon as the server left, Ellie flicked the screen to read the message: *How's the weather in Montana?*

Chills cascaded down her body. There was no signature. How did he know she'd come here? She placed her phone on the table and brought the cup to her lips, hoping the warmth would help stop her shivering. When liquid sloshed over the edge, slightly burning her fingers, she set it down. Fuck. Who was doing this? And why?

She hadn't pissed anyone off—at least not that she was aware of. Sure, Hilton was interested in a more intimate relationship, but he totally understood that she wanted to pour her energies into the gallery. She wasn't opposed to dating someone ten years older, but he was more of a friend than a lover. He couldn't be behind this. Mentally, she scratched him off the list of suspects.

Ellie hadn't dated that many men in the last five years. Hell, she could count them on one hand. Three had dumped her. That left Hilton—who she really hadn't dated—and Brian, but he was too by the book to do something as underhanded and passive aggressive as this.

She chanced another sip of her coffee, and the strong chicory perked up her brain. As much as she didn't want to run back to Vic, she had hired him to find this person. If Vic could trace the email to a specific computer and then to the perpetrator, she could be out of his life again sooner rather than later.

Ellie fished out Vic's card and called him. As the phone rang, her pulse turned erratic. Stupid body. It must be the altitude.

"El? What's wrong?"

She stilled. Vic must have put her cell number in his phone already. "I got another email." She appreciated his urgency, but it scared her at the same time. "I'm at The Happy Carrot Restaurant. Can you come over?"

"Sure." Vic disconnected.

She leaned back in her seat, picked up her cup again, and held it for support. Seconds later, Vic materialized in front of her. "How did you get here so fast?" she asked.

He smiled. "Been sitting on the other side of the restaurant for about five minutes. You need to be more aware of your surroundings, El."

She glanced around and spotted a table with a steaming cup of coffee on it. "You eat here?" Or had he followed her?

"Yup. Ever since my cholesterol turned dangerously high. It sucks getting old."

He'd just turned fifty a month ago. She'd warned him about his bad eating habits until she'd grown tired, but he never listened back then. "You okay, now?"

"Worried about me?" He cocked a brow and one side of his mouth lifted.

Grr. Why did he have to turn everything into something

personal? Just because they were married for nineteen years didn't give him the right to pretend the last five years hadn't happened.

"I worry about everyone." That seemed to be a safe answer.

He nodded at her phone. "May I see the email?"

She found the message, and then handed it to him. He sat across from her. "Who did you tell you were coming here?"

"Hilton, of course. And Wendy. She's teaching my class at the gallery while I'm gone."

"Wendy Jackson?"

She'd forgotten that he'd known her from when they were married. "Yes."

"Who else?"

Ellie bit down on her lip, running through her last two days in Virginia. "I asked my neighbor, Mrs. Albright, to report any suspicious behavior at my place while I'm gone. She's seventy-four. While she has cataracts and is a bit hard of hearing, she spends her days sitting in front of her window watching who comes and goes. I know for a fact she doesn't own a cell phone or a computer."

"I take it you asked her whether she saw anyone deliver flowers to your place?"

"I did, but she said she'd been napping at that time."

The waitress brought Vic's coffee over to their table. "You ordering lunch, Vic?"

"I'll have my usual."

The girl smiled. "You got it."

Who was this man? "You really eat here a lot?"

"I've changed quite a few things in my life, but right now, we need to find your stalker."

"Thank you." She was pleased he was interested in locating this man. "Short of flying to Virginia, how are you going to do that?"

"First, I'll forward this message to my phone. Mind?"

"No."

He tapped a few keys. "Next, I'll check the IP address it was sent from and see if I can get the video feeds from the source. The message is time stamped, so that will help. I have a friend in Washington on retainer. She should be able to narrow it down to the specific computer used."

She? The unexpected shot of jealousy stunned her and was totally uncalled for. Having someone on retainer meant he paid her not slept with her. "How long should that take?"

"Amy's good. I bet she'll know something by tonight."

Damn him. After the divorce, he'd dated an Amy Sanchez, but Ellie wouldn't ask if she was the same woman. As long as this person was competent, that was all that mattered.

Their food arrived quickly. Crap. Now she'd have to wait until he finished eating his large meal. Vic leaned back in his seat and ran his gaze up and down her body.

"Other than the dark circles under your eyes, which I suspect are most likely attributed to these recent events, you look good, El. The life of a gallery owner must agree with you."

Heat flushed her face. She didn't need his compliments, which in the past had been few and far between. He'd always told her that if he let his sentiments show, it would make his job more difficult because the thought of her would distract him.

"It does." This wasn't a date, though she had to admit she was curious about him. Not to mention, she wanted to get the attention off her. "Did it hurt?"

His hand raced to his neck. "This?"

"Yes."

"Like a bitch, though I was lucky. The terrorists beat me senseless first, so I was passed out when the burning board landed on me."

She hissed at the horror. "I'm sorry."

He lifted one shoulder. "Part of the job."

That was his standard refrain. She leaned forward. "Didn't it bother you? You act as if the burn was nothing more than a speed bump in your life. Weren't you ever scared that these men would come back and kill you?" Her voice had escalated and a few of the patrons glanced her way. Stupid man. She wanted to shake him.

There been a time when Vic Hart was loving and sensitive. Then the war happened, followed by his stint in the FBI. When he turned cold inside, she'd spent years trying to warm him up. She failed.

"I can handle myself."

Sure he could. Just like he'd handled his daughter rejecting him. "How did you get Charlotte to change her mind about you?"

"Aren't we inquisitive today? I thought I was just a hired hand." He inhaled. "Sorry, that was uncalled for. I played the *poor me* card with her. Told her the FBI didn't have a use for me anymore and that I was sorry I treated her poorly."

Vic would never do that. "Liar."

He leaned back and grinned. "Caught me. I'm pleased you don't think I've slept with the devil. I do have feelings. I just hide them. However, the part about apologizing to Charlotte was true. She deserved a good dad and I was never there for her. I honestly didn't expect her to ever speak to me again. She's a good kid."

"That she is."

"I give you all the credit."

This conversation was not where she wanted to tread. Besides, Vic needed to contact Amy, not rehash old times. Ellie hurried to finish her salad. When she was done, she waved to the waitress for the check.

"I got this," Vic said drawing a wallet out of his back pocket.

"Oh, no you don't. I'm in charge here. You work for me."

He laughed. "You're in charge? You do have a faulty memory. You loved it when I would arrest you for indecent exposure and then show you the errors of your ways." He winked.

A flood of images bombarded her. Naked ones. Bound. Seduced. Ravished. If she thought her face flushed before, this time flames licked her cheeks, as well as a few other body parts. "That was the past. I've changed."

"If you say so."

Smartass. Ellie wiped her mouth with her napkin then pushed back her chair and stood. "Let me know what you find out." She nabbed her jacket from the back of the chair and rushed out, not daring to look back.

Coming here had been a big mistake.

Chapter Three

E LLIE HAD REALLY botched that encounter. Why had she mentioned Charlotte? It was the one link she and Vic shared, but she didn't want him to use that to get back with her. While he had left Ellie alone after he'd called a few months back, she could see it in his eyes that he still cared. Truthfully, she thought he'd be put off by her larger size. Fifty extra pounds wasn't something she could hide, yet Vic seemed blind to her faults.

Damn him. If he'd made fun of her, she'd have been able to handle him better. As she strode toward her car, she spotted a sign for the Rock Hard Art museum. Since it would take Amy time to find the information—assuming she could get the owner to hand over the surveillance tapes—Ellie wanted to keep busy. And that meant doing something she loved instead of dwelling on Vic Hart.

So, for the next few hours she wandered first through the art museum, and then took in the Natural History Museum. On her way back to the hotel, she found a local gallery that looked interesting. The paintings of wild animals in the display window spoke to her. They were truly amazing. Ellie stepped inside and studied the brush strokes and the tonal quality of the composition.

"It's quite superb, is it not?" said a voice behind Ellie.

She spun around to find an older woman with wild blonde-gray hair, wearing a long skirt, scuffed boots, and what looked like a homemade shawl. She would have fit in well at the Davies-Hart Gallery.

"Yes. It's exceptional. Is the artist local?" Ellie would love to show some of his work in Virginia.

"He is. His name is Wolf Cunningham. I have his card at my desk. If you'll give me a moment, I'll find it for you."

Wolf? "I've never met a Wolf."

The proprietor laughed. "I've always assumed it was a nickname."

While the woman went in search of the information, Ellie looked around. The combination of artwork complemented each other very well. In fact, this gallery seemed to have many similar features to her own. Tears welled. She wanted to finish her vacation with her daughter, and then go home—back where she belonged.

"Here you are. Wolf is on vacation, but he should return in a few weeks."

Ellie checked to make sure his email was on the card. "Thanks."

By the time she returned to the hotel, she decided to spend some time reflecting on the many aspects of her life. It was time for her to figure out her next move—with Charlotte, with Hilton, and with Vic.

❖   ❖   ❖

BY THE TIME she awoke from her unintentional nap, it was around seven p.m., and she was starving. Not wanting to go out in the cold, she went down to the bar to grab a bite and to have a drink. God, did she need a drink after being with Vic today, or what? During the last five years, she'd maintained a high anger level toward him. He'd not been there for Charlotte so many times that she blamed anything that pissed her off on Vic. Unfair, for sure, but she had to take it out on someone.

It didn't help her mood that this stalker seemed to be every-where—both in Virginia as well as in Montana. Ellie had to conclude that Wendy must have mentioned where she was going. Or would Hilton have said something? He knew she was visiting Charlotte, while Brian did not, and Wendy knew all too well not to spill the beans to him.

Crap. Had her friend said something to Cal during one of their classes? There was only one way to find out: call Wendy and ask her.

Ellie slipped onto one of the barstools and grabbed a menu. Fried this, fried that. Yuk.

"What can I get you?" the female bartender asked.

She had to eat. "I'll have the fried pickles and fried chicken tenders. And I'll have a vodka tonic."

"You got it."

Ellie located her phone and called Wendy. She wouldn't be teaching tonight.

"Hey, there," Wendy answered with a ton of enthusiasm. "How's Montana?"

She explained how freaked out Charlotte had been when Ellie explained about the odd events. "She insisted I hire Vic to find this person, so now I'm in Rock Hard."

Wendy whistled. "Wow. How's that going?"

"Let's just say I'm sitting at the hotel bar and I've ordered a vodka tonic."

"That bad, huh?"

"I think Vic might be interested in me, and I can't handle that. He was so nice, which means he has an ulterior motive."

"Hey. Don't be so cynical. Nice is good."

"I guess. The bad thing was that I got another email during lunch, and I kind of freaked."

The bartender placed her vodka tonic on the counter in front of her. Ellie probably should wait until after she had some food in her stomach, but she wanted to get a buzz, hoping it would erase the jitters.

"What did it say?" The worry in Wendy's voice brought her back to the present.

Ellie sipped her drink. Within seconds, the chilled alcohol hit her bloodstream. She told Wendy what the message said. "Vic has someone in D.C. who might be able to help, but you'll never guess who that someone is." Wendy had known Amy when Ellie was still married.

"Who?"

"Amy."

"Amy Sanchez?"

"I don't know for sure. Vic didn't tell me her last name."

"I know Amy is doing freelance work in computers."

Damn. "Then it's probably her." Ellie polished off half the drink in two large gulps.

"Tell me the truth. How does he look?"

Wendy always could spot a lie. "Good." Ellie finished her drink. "He's thinner, but the scars from the fire are kind of sexy in a weird sort of way. He has a bit of a tan that goes well with his dark hair and mocha eyes." She inwardly groaned.

"Mocha, huh?"

"Slip of the tongue."

"Sure. Does Vic have any theories about who might be after you?"

"No, which was why I called you. Did you mention to the class where I was?"

"Hell, no. I figured it might be one of them."

The bartender placed a second vodka tonic in front of her, along with her not-so-healthy dinner. Ellie gave her a thin smile and swiveled on the seat to place an elbow on the bar. "Darn. I thought perhaps Cal was trying to catch my attention."

"By slashing your tires?"

Ellie shook her head. Didn't matter Wendy couldn't see her. "I think that had nothing to do with anything. Just bad luck."

A bell sounded in the background. "Hey, someone just came in," Wendy said. "I gotta go. Keep in touch, sweetie."

"Will do."

For the few minutes she was speaking with her good friend, the world seemed a better place. Now Ellie was alone again. The rich aroma of the food finally pierced her brain, and Ellie popped a chicken tender in her mouth. Mmm. She was pleasantly surprised at the burst of flavor. She alternated between her drink and the fried food until she finished the whole plate. When she returned to Virginia, she'd have to hit the gym for sure.

"Buy you another drink?" said a deep male voice.

Ellie spun back around and blinked. A good looking man in his mid-thirties, wearing a charcoal gray suit, but no tie, slid onto the stool next to her. He waved to the bartender. "Michelob please, and whatever the lady is having."

Ellie was so taken aback that she failed to object. He splayed his left hand on the bar and the gleaming wedding band shone in the light. She relaxed. He wasn't hitting on her—or so she hoped. He was probably just looking for someone to talk to.

"I'm Tom. Tom Travers, from Seattle."

"Ellie Hart, from Virginia."

"Hi, Ellie from Virginia. What brings you here?"

She wasn't sure she should answer, but there didn't seem to be any harm. Another drink appeared in front of her. "I'm visiting my daughter. You?" While her daughter wasn't in Rock Hard, Ellie didn't need to give him too many details.

"I sell energy-efficient windows. This is part of my territory."

Ellie relaxed. He was a salesman. A safe person. "Do your travels take you away from home a lot?"

He tipped back his beer. "Too much, but I have three kids to put through college. I have to work hard."

"I hear ya. I run an art gallery and it's non-stop work."

His lips pressed together appearing impressed. "What does your husband do?"

She'd heard that line before, but Tom seemed on the up and up. "I'm divorced."

He smiled.

✦   ✦   ✦

AMY FINALLY CALLED around nine, and Vic picked up right away. "Got something for me?"

"Yes, but it doesn't make any sense."

"Tell me."

"I'm sending the video clip now."

Vic clicked on his mail tab. "Got it. Give me a sec to look." What he saw was a young woman approach a computer terminal, take out a piece of paper, and type something on the computer. The camera was too far away to see what she wrote. Then it cut off.

"Not what you expected, huh?" Amy asked.

"This makes no sense. Are you sure this is the terminal?"

"Positive."

"You get a name?" He wasn't sure how she could, but he had to ask.

"I'm good, but not that good." Amy laughed.

"Thanks. I owe you."

As soon as he disconnected the call, he wanted to tell El his findings. He dialed her number, but her cell went to voicemail. Damn. She'd want to know that her stalker might be a woman. Wendy perhaps? He hadn't seen El's best friend in years, but it was possible the person El most trusted was out to drive her crazy.

When Amy had called, he'd been about to head home. Since the Park Hotel was on his way, Vic jumped in his SUV, drove the two miles down the main thoroughfare, and parked a half block away from the hotel entrance.

Inside, the lobby was cozy, especially since they had the fireplace lit. Two high-backed chairs faced the fire, looking romantic. A band tightened around his chest. He missed El. Missed her laughter, her gentle fingers, and her loving mouth.

Stop it.

Why did he keep torturing himself? She'd made it clear she wanted nothing to do with him. It didn't seem to matter that he'd changed. The best he could do now was to find the man after her.

Vic stepped up to the woman at the counter. "Can you tell me what room Eleanor Hart is in?"

"I'm sorry, sir, but I can't give out that information. I can call her room and see if she will give me permission to tell you. May I have your name?"

"Vic Hart."

"Oh. Is she your wife?"

Vic didn't lie. "My ex-wife."

The woman's lips thinned. From the sadness emanating from her, she might be a divorcee herself. She held up a finger and dialed. After ten seconds, she hung up. "Ms. Hart isn't answering."

"Thanks."

"Would you like to leave a voice message?"

"Tell her to call me."

"I will."

Where could she be? Taking a shower? He immediately squashed the image of her naked and delved into the logical part of his brain. He doubted El would venture out at night.

As long as he was here, he might as well check the bar, in case she wanted a nightcap, though when they were married, El rarely drank. Right before he entered the dark bar area, her lilting laugh reached him. Damn. Vic strode in and had no problem spotting her despite the dimly lit room. What he was having a hard time with was that El was smiling at a man in a charcoal gray suit. Vic clenched his fists and stalked toward her. Yes, she had every right to talk with whomever she wanted, but she couldn't possibly know this person. What was she doing?

"El?"

The man in the suit faced him. He was a decent-looking guy who had to be at least ten years younger than El. Shit. This guy was suave, where Vic was not.

"Vic? What are you do-oing here?"

Holy shit. El was drunk, and he didn't like it one bit. "I have some news for you."

"Good news or bad news?" She giggled then directed her gaze to the man in the suit.

Vic gently placed a hand on her arm. "Come on. Let me walk you to your room."

The man stiffened. "Ellie? You don't have to go with him if you don't want to."

She waved a hand. "It's okay. I know him." When she slid off the stool, her knees buckled, but Vic was able to hold her up. Jesus. What had happened? Had she received another message?

He wrapped an arm around her waist. "What room are you

in?"

"Three twenty-two." She looked up at him. "I think."

God. Vic dropped a twenty on the bar, slung her purse over her shoulder, and led her out. Once he loaded her in the elevator and pushed the button, she stepped close and placed her cheek against his chest. His ex-wife never would have leaned against him unless she'd had too much to drink. He inhaled her flowery scent and his cock stiffened. Damn. She hadn't changed her perfume since they'd divorced. Every time he saw a gardenia, he thought of her. Her hand clutched his jacket.

"You smell good," she mumbled, her lips against his chest.

Stay strong.

"We're almost there. Put one foot in front of the other." El staggered and he tightened his hold. "Easy."

Vic slipped the purse from over her shoulder and located the keycard. Once he swiped it, and the light turned green, he led her in. The room had a queen-sized bed, a small table with two chairs, a dresser, and a small flat screen TV. He set her purse on the table and walked her to the bed.

El dropped down on the edge, her eyes glassy. "I think I might have had too much to drink."

That was an understatement. He wanted to ask her why she saw fit to get drunk, but that would only anger her. "Could be."

She kicked off her shoes, one at a time, like she used to do, and the second one went sailing and hit the chair leg. She giggled and fell back on the bed. Oh, boy. It was time to take over.

"Let me help you." Vic sat her up and slipped off her sweater.

"You trying to get me naked?" When she looked up at him and grinned, his heart nearly stopped.

Chapter Four

VIC LOOKED GOOD—STRONG, sexy, and so fucking exciting. If only Ellie could stay awake long enough, she might chance a quick taste. That would be good. He'd always been the best kisser.

She hiccupped. Well, that wasn't sexy. The alcohol was making her light-headed and was cutting through all of her filters.

Her inner self warred. Most likely she'd be back in Virginia in a week, so what harm could come if they had a quick romp? Vic always was good in bed. She debated for a few seconds about what she should do and couldn't come up with one good reason why she shouldn't attack his body.

"You have any pajamas?" He glanced around as if she'd have tossed them on the chair or something.

Test him. "Pajamas? I sleep naked." She quickly closed her eyes to prevent him from detecting the lie. Vic always said the eyes held the truth.

"Since when?"

Damn him. Ellie looked up and smiled. "Since tonight." She giggled then slapped a hand over her mouth.

"All right. We'll play it your way." He leaned over, unsnapped and unzipped her pants then slid them off. Then he lifted her pullover over her head, treating her like she was ten.

Ellie slapped his hands away. "I can do the rest." When she reached around to undo her bra, Vic turned his back. So much for seduction. After fumbling to get the damn thing undone, she gave up and just lifted it up and over her tits. Then she ripped it over her head and tossed her bra on the floor, hoping to get at least a smile out of him, but Vic could act stoic with the best of them. Ellie slipped under the covers. "It's safe to look now."

He turned around, picked up her bra, folded it, and placed it on top of the dresser. He said nothing as he sat in the chair opposite the bed. "Go to sleep."

Wha-at? This wasn't how she'd pictured it. And why was he so far away? Shouldn't he be trying to crawl into bed with her? "Why are you here anyway?"

"I learned a few things, but I'll tell you in the morning." He dragged over the other chair and propped his feet on it.

"What was that?" She recalled he'd asked Amy to do something, but she couldn't remember what it was.

"You won't remember if I tell you now. Things will be clearer in the morning."

He was probably right. She waited a beat, expecting him to leave, but he crossed his arms over his chest and closed his eyes. "You're staying?"

"Yes."

"Why?"

He opened his eyes and blew out a breath. "For starters, I don't trust the man at the bar not to come up here. Secondly, I don't trust you won't go down stairs and cause more trouble."

She narrowed her eyes. "I wouldn't do that." *Or would I?*

"Sleep."

"What if I'm not ready to sleep?"

Vic had been her husband. There was nothing wrong with having a bit of sex to make this trip worthwhile, right? Sure, she might have had too much to drink, and her brain was a bit fizzed—or was it fuzzed?—but having those hands on her body again would be so nice. They were two adults. Consensual sex was fine, just as long as he didn't expect anything the next day.

"Try," he answered sounding amused.

Well, fine. Be that way. There was more than one way to skin the proverbial cat. She sat up and let the cover drop to her waist. Vic stared at her nipples and they hardened under his glare. She waited for him to do something, but he didn't move. He wanted her, didn't he?

Fuck. Maybe he didn't. She was old and fat. "Vic?"

He stood and walked over to the bed, his gaze now on her face. Ellie's heart slammed hard against her ribs as he leaned over and turned off the light. "We'll talk in the morning."

Talk? She didn't want to talk. "Why are you doing this, Vic?"

From his heavy footsteps, he was returning to his chair. When he didn't answer, her heart hardened. Well, damn.

✧　✧　✧

VIC BARELY SLEPT all night. The image of El's perfect breasts had been burned into his brain, keeping his mind active. Sure, she'd drunk too much, but it shouldn't have been enough for her to lose all of her inhibitions. Or had it? When she'd left his office, and again at lunch, she acted as if she could barely stand him. Then all of a sudden, she has a few drinks, and she wants to have sex with him?

Something must have happened in those few hours to make her change her mind, but what? Perhaps she'd spoken with Charlotte, or maybe she'd called Wendy and her friend had convinced El to enjoy herself while she was in Montana. But why? If Wendy was the stalker, did she hope El could distract him into not working on the case? That made less sense than

El's actions. Shit, but he needed some strong coffee.

Hmm. Did her best friend have designs on the gallery? If El moved out to Montana, Wendy could slip in and run the place. That had potential. Then again, so did all the other suspects.

Christ. He needed to wake up. Vic had battled with himself all night about whether he should have taken her up on her offer, but he respected her too much to take advantage of her in an inebriated state.

Light had already eased around the edges of the curtain. Vic probably should leave, but he didn't want her to wake up alone. He was quite confident she'd feel like shit, and having someone near might help lessen the incessant pounding.

As soon as she remembered showing him her breasts, she'd be mortified, and he wanted to assure her she was safe with him. What he wouldn't tell her was that it would take every ounce of his military training to keep his distance.

El moaned, and Vic sat up. If he thought she'd sleep another few hours, he'd have gone in search of some aspirin and coffee. She groaned, rolled onto her back, and had the wherewithal to keep the covers up to her neck. She licked her lips and his body woke up.

Her eyes cracked open as she lifted onto her elbows. "What are you doing here?"

How much did she remember? "I wanted to make sure you'd be okay."

"Am I?"

He chuckled. "You're alive. That's a good thing." El never was a morning person. "How about you take a shower while I order us some breakfast?"

"What happened?" she said, her voice muffled.

"You might have had a bit too much to drink."

She looked around the bed, probably for her clothes. "I

vaguely remember some guy in a suit. Or did I imagine him? God, but I feel like shit."

"You were laughing and enjoying yourself with him at the bar last night."

"Did I really? Can you bring me something to put on?"

When they were first married, she liked when he'd pick out her clothes. God, but he'd fucked things up since those blissful days. At least he had Charlotte on his side again. His beautiful daughter had been quick to forgive. While she looked so much like El, the two were very different.

"Sure." He stepped over to the dresser and pulled open the top drawer.

Damn. Why was everything all lacy and pretty? The colors were soft—pinks, yellow, virginal white. He closed his eyes for a moment then plucked out a pair of pink panties and a white bra. He didn't want them to match. From the next drawer, he chose a pair of worn jeans, a T-shirt, and a sweater that seemed too big. That should do nicely.

He gathered them in his arms and walked over to the bed. "Get dressed and I'll head downstairs and find us some food. After you shower, I want to show you something."

"What?"

"You'll see."

Vic couldn't leave fast enough. If he didn't, he'd be tempted to slide in next to her, bite her bottom lip, and then lick her silly, but he'd have to relegate that joy to his dreams.

✧ ✧ ✧

WHEN THE DOOR shut, Ellie plastered her clothes to her chest, placed her feet on the floor, and rushed to the bathroom. The throbbing in her temple increased to the point where she feared her brain might bleed. She set the clothes on the counter and leaned over the sink, praying for some relief. *Dear Lord, what have I done?*

Her mouth tasted like dirt and gravel. She couldn't remember drinking this much. Ever. What had she been thinking? Clearly, she hadn't been.

When she'd first woken up, she couldn't believe Vic was in her room. Here she thought she'd actually dreamed him. Then the image of some guy in a suit talking to her at the bar entered her brain. Next thing she remembered was Vic tugging off her pants and shirt. The final memory was her sitting up in bed and showing him her tits. Could this get any worse? Now, he'd believe she wanted him.

Okay, she did in a way. Actually, what she'd wanted was a pleasant experience to dampen the nightmare, but in her drunken state, she hadn't realized that if she had given into her carnal desires that it would complicate matters too much. Charlotte had been hurt once, and Ellie didn't need to make things worse.

She turned on the water and stepped into the shower. Even though she washed her hair vigorously and scrubbed her body hard, no amount of heat or cleaning could take away the embarrassment of her practically propositioning Vic. Jeez, she was a mess.

Now what was she supposed to do? He had to realize that she found him attractive. She'd admit that when he was near, she felt safe, but that wouldn't be enough in the long run. Keeping her distance was the only option, mostly because she needed to give Vic space to focus on finding this guy. He didn't need her to upset the balance of his life.

The room door opened and feet shuffled. "Be right out," she called.

For a split second, she thought perhaps someone else might

have come into her room until she realized Vic would have stopped anyone from getting near.

"Food's ready," he called out.

She smiled—but sobered instantly when a sharp ache stabbed her eye. His comment implied she had to hurry. Vic hated when food wasn't piping hot, whereas she could take it any temperature. They had more differences than similarities, but those first years of marriage had been idyllic. Her hand went to her belly. When they'd found out she was pregnant, Vic had gone crazy with joy. He couldn't wait to feel the baby kick and even insisted on singing to Charlotte before she was born. When their daughter was three, he was deployed to Afghanistan. When he returned, he was never the same.

She stepped out of the shower, toweled off, and dressed. Thinking about the good old days wouldn't help her sanity one bit. She dressed as quickly as she could, not caring that her damp hair stuck out. She opened the door and the rich aroma of food almost made her gag. Her stomach was not ready to eat, but she knew she had to try.

"Found some aspirin." Vic stepped close and held out two pills and a glass of orange juice.

His presence made her pulse rise, which only caused the pounding to worsen. "Thanks, but do me a favor?"

"Sure."

"Don't let me drink again. Ever."

He chuckled. "I think you've learned your lesson. What made you do it?"

She shrugged. "Just all the shit coming down at once made for some bad decisions." She swallowed the pills, along with half the juice, and handed him back the glass.

"Come sit at the table and have a bite," he said.

She agreed mostly because she wanted to know what he'd

found out. Once seated, she placed a few bites of scrambled eggs on her plate, along with a slice of bacon and a half piece of whole-wheat toast. "May I have some coffee?" She nodded to the white carafe next to him.

He poured them both a cup. "Drink and I'll tell you what Amy found out."

From the way he was frowning, it wasn't good. Oh, shit. "Was it Hilton? Or Brian?"

"Neither."

She should be relieved, but that only left Cal. "Then it was Cal Forsythe. Damn. That little creep."

"Wasn't him either."

While she ate, Vic loaded up his iPad then turned it toward her. She watched as a woman with shoulder length brown hair sat at a computer. "Who is she?"

He cocked a brow. "I was hoping you could tell me. I thought it might be Wendy."

She shook her head, not happy he believed she could have been fooled like that. "Wendy cut her hair short and dyed it blonde a few months back." The video stopped. "You don't have one of her face?"

"No. She was careful to keep it averted. It was as if she knew the camera's location."

"You're sure she sent the message?"

"Yes."

Ellie finished a few bites then sipped her coffee, hoping the caffeine would help the headache. "Why would a woman send me creepy emails?"

"It's possible that Brian dumped her before dating you. Maybe she's worried you two are still a couple."

"I suppose, though it's not likely. She had a piece of paper in her hand. It's as if she's just following instructions."

Vic's eyes widened, seemingly impressed. She glanced away, not happy that he looked so young all of a sudden—so like he used to when she first met him.

"If you give me the rest of the names of the people in your class," he said, "I'll do a quick background check on them."

Vic was going above and beyond the call of duty. "Can do."

After she finished eating as much as she could, Ellie's head didn't ache as much and her stomach seemed to be settling. She wrote down the information he asked for. "That's all of them."

Vic slapped his thighs and stood. "Are you going to be okay by yourself?"

"Yes. If I go out, I'll be sure to stay on the main drag. Or, I'll download a book and stay in and read."

"Good. I'll let you know if I find anything." His tone had turned professional. That worked for her.

Vic nodded and left. Ellie had debated apologizing for her behavior last night, but she wasn't ready to talk about what she did. Knowing Vic, it would only lead them to a place she didn't want to go.

Chapter Five

NEVER HAVING MASTERED the art of sleeping comfortably in a chair, Vic rolled his shoulders to work out the kinks. As much as he'd like to stretch out on his office floor and take a nap, he had to keep working. If he didn't, his mind would wander back to El. Beautiful El. The last five years had made her a resilient woman, yet at the same time, a lost soul. He didn't dare speculate why.

With the list of suspects before him, he went to work researching each person, starting with Hilton Davies then moving on to Brian Lovett, before tackling El's best friend, Wendy Jackson. He refused to draw any conclusions until he knew what each of them ate for breakfast. One of them had to have a reason for targeting El.

Sharon had offered to do a lunch run for him and then, five hours later, ran out and picked up dinner. She'd earned a raise this week for sure.

She set the container of fish, steamed broccoli, and coleslaw on his desk. "You plan on working all night?" He could see from the way she was shifting her weight that she wanted to get home. It was Friday night, after all, and last week she'd met someone new.

He looked up at her. "You go ahead. I'm working my way

through the last of the suspects."

"You're the one who needs to go home. Your eyes are bloodshot. You'll be fresher in the morning. You always are."

He smiled, but it took an effort. "I'll eat and then decide my next move. Thanks for holding down the fort today." She'd fielded several phone calls, telling people Vic could not be disturbed. She acted more like his keeper than his secretary. "Go. Have a good weekend."

"You can rest assured I will. Got a date tonight." She grinned.

He was happy for her. After she headed out, Vic began with the members of El's class, starting with Cal Forsythe because he seemed to be the most interesting of the lot. Vic quickly learned that Cal's father had died when he was five. That might not have been so bad had his mother not been a drunk. Cal was eleven when she passed away from alcohol poisoning. After that, he was put in a foster home. His first foster parents were artists and taught him to appreciate art, but when they couldn't afford to keep him, he went back in the system. From some of the awards Cal had won, he had some artistic talent.

The man was forty-one, but the only picture Vic found of him was as a twenty-five year old. He had classic good looks despite being on the thin side. El claimed he had a crush on her. As someone who might be able to help Cal with his career, it made sense he'd gravitate toward her. The motive for him stalking her wasn't apparent, however. Damn.

Vic had to be missing something. He leaned back in his chair and stretched. It was almost nine. Sharon was right. Things might be clearer in the morning, so he packed up his files and laptop and headed out. Wow. He hadn't expected snow. The wind was quite still, making it pretty but cold.

His mind continued to swirl with scenarios as he headed out

of town toward his house. Vic wasn't ready to eliminate Hilton, but he seemed the least likely suspect. The man's wife had passed away seven years ago, and she left him quite a lot of money, much of which he'd invested in the Davies-Hart Gallery. Surely, he had to know that El was no longer seeing Brian, which might explain the flowers, but not the emails and texts. Unless, what El said was right—that they were dealing with more than one person. That would complicate things.

Halfway to his house, a pair of headlights came behind him—fast—and he flipped up the rearview mirror to prevent the glare from blinding him. With no streetlights this far out, he couldn't see much. Vic slowed then moved closer to the side of the road to let this ass pass. The lights drew near. Just as Vic was about to press hard on the accelerator to speed up, the guy rammed the back of Vic's SUV.

What the fuck?

He gripped the wheel tight and slammed on the brakes, but the large truck behind him had the momentum. One minute Vic was on the road and the next he was sliding down the snowy embankment, bouncing on two wheels and then flipping over. Upside down, the car slid on the roof, jarring Vic right and left, his head hitting the side window with force. Shit. The seatbelt yanked him back as his body tried to fly forward. Glass broke and Vic's face was sliced open. Blood trickled down his cheek. The car rammed into something solid, and then blackness engulfed him.

THE RINGING PHONE in Ellie's dream caused her to jerk in her sleep. She was in the middle of a recurring dream in which she was young, thin, and happy. She and Vic were holding hands, wading ankle-deep in the clear blue waters of the Caribbean.

They'd been married only a few years but were still talking about their exciting future—how he wanted to protect mankind while she wanted to make the world a better place, one brush stroke at a time. Then his cell rang, like it always did at this point. It was the call they knew was coming—the one that would signal the end. Vic was being deployed.

Every time she reached this part, Ellie had woken up—the rest of the vacation bitter, argumentative, and very painful. Then why was the phone still ringing if Vic's cell was at his ear and he was talking?

A rush of reality reached her. Her phone was ringing. She jerked awake, but it took a moment to recognize that she was not at home but rather in Montana. She reached across the bed to the hotel phone. "Hello?"

She glanced at the glowing clock. It was three in the morning. WTF?

"Ms. Hart?"

"Yes. Who is this?" Had her stalker finally decided to confront her?

"This is Dr. Randy Carstead. I work at the Emergency Room of the Lucy Ambrose Center For Excellence Hospital."

Was this a joke? No hospital had that many names. "Okay."

"I'm calling to let you know your husband was in a car accident this evening."

"What?" Her heart pounded, and suddenly the cobwebs that had a strong hold on her mind disintegrated.

"He's fine even though someone ran him off the road. The paramedics on the scene said he was lucky to be alive."

Ellie's heart sputtered and then froze for a moment. She wanted to tell the doctor that Vic wasn't her husband, but no words would form. Fine could mean a lot of different things. "How is he? Really."

"We're still assessing him now, ma'am. He's conscious and seems—"

Just conscious? How is that fine? "Can I see him?"

"Yes, ma'am." Dr. Carstead gave her directions. "Be prepared for a belligerent patient, though. I've given him a pain pill that should kick in soon."

This almost made her smile. Vic's feistiness implied he'd be okay. "Thank you for letting me know."

When she hung up, she needed a moment to process what happened. This was all her fault. She never should have come to Montana and chance drawing this mad man out here. Whoever she'd pissed off, wanted to harm the people she cared for. Damn him.

As fast as she could, she dressed. Her head pounded anew with another headache. Poor Vic. As soon as she knew the extent of his injuries, she'd call Charlotte to let her know.

Ellie rushed out, got halfway to the elevator then had to return because she'd forgotten her phone. Christ. Where was her head? On her second attempt to leave the hotel, she'd made it as far as the front door before she realized she'd forgotten her car keys. Double shit. Back upstairs she went for hopefully her last trip. Finally, she made outside. *Really?*

Snow was falling heavily. Finding her way to the hospital would be hard enough in the middle of the night. She didn't need the roads to be slippery. Ugh. Ellie inhaled to help gather her thoughts, but all that did was freeze her nose hairs. Being careful not to slip, she reached her car and jumped in. The engine turned over but she let it run thirty seconds for the inside to warm.

She took off, still not believing Vic was in the hospital. Driving under the speed limit, she headed east on Second Avenue then north on Arbor Way. The last thing either of them needed was for her to wreck. While it was probably less than two miles, it seemed like twenty. The hospital lot was almost deserted, which allowed her to park close to the Emergency Room entrance.

Pulling her coat tightly across her chest and keeping her head down, Ellie rushed inside. At the nurse's station, she asked for information about Vic. As the nurse typed his name into her computer, an angry voice sounded at the end of the hall, and the tension in her body released. It was Vic, issuing orders like he used to.

"He's in room seven," the nurse said nodding to her left.

"Thank you." Ellie straightened her shoulders and hurried toward the room.

Just as she placed her hand on the curtain to pull it back, a tall, broad shouldered doctor stepped out.

"Oh. Are you Mrs. Hart?"

She didn't want to mislead him. "I'm Ellie Hart, Vic's ex-wife."

"I'm glad you're here." He didn't address the *ex* part.

"How is he?"

"He'll make a full recovery. Vic does have a concussion, a small cut on his forehead, a gash on his back, and a dislocated shoulder. As you can imagine, he's chomping at the bit to go home, but I was hoping you could watch him for a day or two. Concussions can be tricky and Vic is a stubborn SOB."

She smiled. "You know him well."

"We've met a few times. Friend of a friend and all. I'm about to write up the release papers and I'll note the aftercare instructions. You can go in, but don't let him leave until after I release him."

Even if she didn't owe Vic for bringing this tragedy on him, she'd have stayed. She drew back the curtain and winced. Vic was sitting up, holding the arm in a sling. Blood and dirt caked the front and side of his blue shirt, and he sported a fresh bandage on his forehead.

He glanced up, smiled, and then winced. "I told Randy not to wake you. I'm sorry."

"Vic. It's okay. How are you feeling?"

"I'm fine."

No, he wasn't, but she'd learned long ago not to argue with him when he was in soldier mode. She sat in the chair that was against the wall. "Tell me what happened."

He inhaled then started with the bright lights in the rearview mirror. "Next thing I knew, I was rolling down the hill. Couldn't do anything to stop it." The corner of one lip lifted. "The tree did the job, though."

How could he act so casual about almost dying? "Could you tell what kind of car it was that rammed you or who was driving?"

"Except that it was a truck, no. By the time I suspected this ass was trying to run me off the road, it was too late."

She stood and stepped next to the bed. If the hand closest to her hadn't been in a sling, she would have held it. "I'm so sorry. If I hadn't come here, this wouldn't have happened."

His brows pinched. "The accident had nothing to do with you."

"You can't know that."

"You really think someone like Brian or Cal would fly out here and harm me? Or hire someone to do it?"

Their game would be more cerebral than physical. "Not really."

Vic rubbed the back of his neck. "I'll be good as new in a few days, and I'll find the culprit."

"You trying to convince yourself? Or me?"

"Both?"

About an hour later, Dr. Carstead came in pushing a wheelchair. Vic was already beginning to fade—his eyes kept closing and his chin dropping.

"Sorry, I took so long," the doctor said. "Here are the instructions. If he vomits or the pain worsens, call 911."

That sounded ominous. "Thank you."

They tried to help Vic into the wheelchair, but he kept batting away their hands. He probably would have insisted he walk out on his own, except he must have known the hospital rules.

When he finally sat down, she wheeled Vic to the entrance. "I'm parked just outside the door. Let me help you up."

Because he only had one good arm, she was able to keep to his injured side and help him.

"I can walk."

"I'm sure you can." She wasn't his wife anymore. If he ached or threw up, it would be his own stubborn fault.

Once they were in the car, she debated the pros and cons of taking him to the hotel versus going to his house. If she took him home, he'd just tell her to leave, so the hotel it was. Plus, it was closer. While the snow had stopped, the roads still looked slick.

Once in town, she pulled into the side lot and parked. "Come on. Let's get you to bed."

He smiled. "If my head wasn't pounding, I'd take you up on your offer."

"It was not an offer." *Grr.* She would never live down her stupid mistake of showing him her breasts.

Though, how she was going to take care of him without remembering the past was anyone's guess.

Chapter Six

V IC DIDN'T NEED a babysitter, but if it made El feel better to help, he'd spend the night. He totally got that she had no desire to rekindle their relationship, but a man could dream. Her showing him her tits had been some kind of drunken challenge, which he fortunately hadn't acted on.

"Sit on the bed and let me take off your shoes," she said in the same tone of voice she'd used on Charlotte when she was little.

"You can take off more than that if you want." Christ. Why did he say that? Hadn't he just recognized that they could never turn back the hands of time?

El rolled her eyes. "Be good or I'll make you sleep in the chair."

No she wouldn't. He wanted to continue bantering with her, but he was having a hard time staying awake. Those stupid pills Randy made him take were kicking his butt. If El did slip into bed, it would have been nice to absorb her heat and at least imagine having her place her head on his shoulder like she used to. Most likely, he'd remember nothing until morning.

With some effort, he unhooked and unzipped his jeans while she removed his boots and socks. He then placed his feet on the floor and stood. Whoa. His head spun, forcing him to sit back down.

El pressed on his good shoulder. "Lie back down and I'll take your pants off."

Even if she had been willing to make love with him, he was too messed up to do anything about it. Once prone, he lifted his hips to make it easier for her to pull off his jeans. With his good hand, he held onto his briefs. He didn't need a reveal just yet. Imagining the possibilities of the night to come, his cock stiffened half way. Thankfully, the drugs helped prevent a full erection.

"Now sit up so I can take off that nasty shirt. I don't need blood on the sheets," she said.

"Yes, ma'am. You'll have to take the sling off first, but be careful."

With care, she undid the snap at the neck, slipped off the sling, and then unbuttoned his shirt. Damn but she smelled good. She was so lovely, especially with no makeup. He always loved when she went all natural. With efficiency, she undid his shirt and peeled down the sleeve on his good arm.

"I'll handle this side," he said. Vic managed to get it off with little pain.

She took the bloody mess from him. "I'll see if I can get out some of the blood."

Before he could tell her not to bother, she disappeared into the bathroom. The water ran and he slipped under the covers and closed his eyes.

✧ ✧ ✧

"BREAKFAST."

Vic had been in and out of wakefulness for about an hour, but he hadn't wanted to move. His head hurt, as did his shoulder, but the rest of him seemed better. Unfortunately, when he sat up, a fierce ache stabbed his shoulder. "Son of bitch."

El rushed over. "Can I help?"

As much as he'd liked another pain pill, he needed to get home. "I'm good. I just need to eat and then shower."

"Let me help." She pulled back the sheets then averted her gaze. "Oh, my."

He chuckled. "I didn't think I had to warn you." His cock was rock hard from sleep. The meds had definitely worn off.

El turned back toward him. "I wasn't thinking."

She stepped away and let him ease to a stand. When he glanced at her, she was staring at the burns on his shoulder. "Pretty, ain't it?"

"Oh, Vic. You've suffered so much."

None more than when she'd left him. "It was for a good cause. We got the bastard who wanted to terrorize a bunch of innocent people for his cause."

She pressed her lips together in understanding. "Food's hot."

It did smell good. This was one of the pluses to being at a hotel. Wearing only his briefs, he edged his way to the table and slid down onto the seat. Thankfully, his left shoulder was the one damaged instead of his right. She'd already poured his coffee so he brought the cup to his lips.

"Do you believe it was my stalker who tried to run you off the road or someone from your past wanting to harm you?" she asked as calm as could be.

"Remember, I'm a private investigator. I piss off people daily. My suspect list is long, but it was my fault. I should have been paying better attention."

"How exactly could you have prevented him from ramming you? Does your car have rockets out its ass that you can shoot at people?"

He laughed, but quickly sobered. The movement hurt his head and his shoulder. "I wish. I should have sped up, but I was distracted."

She shook her head. "We're you trying to figure out who my stalker was?"

His mind never rested until he'd solve a case. "Yes."

"See? It was my fault."

He didn't want to get into a blaming game. Right now, he needed to heal so he could get back on the job. They both dug into their meal. After he ate, he felt significantly better.

El cleared the plastic containers and faced him. "I need to change the bandage on your back. Dr. Carstead gave me extra pads and some ointment."

"Can it wait until after I shower?"

"Sure. Your shirt should be dry. It's hanging up over the shower rod."

For a split second, it was like the good ole days. "Thanks."

He stood and dizziness assaulted him, and then the waves of unsteadiness passed.

"Are you okay? Do you need help?"

With getting naked and washing his body or guiding him to the bathroom? *Don't go there.* He inhaled and straightened. Surprisingly, his shoulder didn't hurt nearly as much as it had yesterday. "If I need anything, I'll holler." He couldn't help but smile.

She chuckled. "Nice try, but I'm not washing you or helping you dress. You get naked and you're on your own."

A thousand improper responses floated to his brain, but he exercised willpower. "Roger that."

Once in the bathroom, he closed the door and inhaled. El might deny there was an attraction, but he could see she wished she could go back to those days, too. He'd changed a lot since then. What he wouldn't give to show her the person he'd become.

Vic wasn't kidding when he said he needed to shower. He stunk and had patches of dried blood on him. He ditched his briefs. Keeping his arm by his side, he turned on the water. When it warmed, he stepped in. The heated blast cut the ache in his head by half. Using his good arm, he shampooed his hair.

Damn. He couldn't reach his back—the one part of his body that was probably smeared in dried blood. Guess rinsing would have to do.

El knocked on the bathroom door. "You okay in there?"

Why wouldn't he be? Had he taken too long? He held up his hand. Crap. His fingers had pruned. "Be right out."

He shut off the hot water, stepped out, and then worked to towel dry. He was able to replace the bandage on his forehead, but not the one on his back. After donning his briefs, he left the bathroom, carrying his rather clean shirt. "I'm ready, doctor, for you to change the bandage on my back."

"Sit on the bed. While you were in there, I called Charlotte. Be prepared for a call. She kind of freaked."

He sat down and sagged. "I wished you hadn't done that. I don't want her to worry."

El glanced to the ceiling, acting as if it took effort not to yell at him. "She's your daughter. For some unknown reason, you're important to her. She should know if you've been injured, you lug."

He held up a hand. "I get it. You're right. It's not just about me."

"Thank you. Now twist around, so I can reach your back and see how tiny the cut is."

They'd put in about ten stitches, so he prayed his injury didn't make her squeamish. First she removed the old bandage, and because it was wet, it came off easily. When she stepped passed him toward the bathroom, he spotted the blood on the pad. Now, she'd fuss over him even more. Thank goodness they hadn't been married when he'd been burned. If she'd seen him then, she'd have struggled to recover.

El returned with a wet towel. "You suck at washing."

"Would you have come in and taken care of me if I'd asked?" He hadn't flirted in a long time, and it felt good.

He expected an instant, no. Instead, she inhaled audibly. "Probably not."

"I'll remember that the next time."

She sat on the bed next to him, and with a soft touch, she cleaned his back and reapplied the bandage. "There."

Vic twisted around and there she was, her gaze on his face, looking hungry. "Thank you."

He expected her to cast her gaze to the side and move away, but she didn't. Instead she tugged on her bottom lip then let her gaze travel between his legs. His cock twitched at her perusal. He knew that look. It had *take me* written all over it. Vic leaned forward and let his lips part.

Kiss me. Being together like this had stirred deep memories while at the same time formed new ones. He hadn't let a day pass without thinking about her—what was she doing, if she was happy, and did she wonder about him? So what if she'd turned down a date a few months ago. That was before she needed him.

"Vic?" The whisper signaled her desire.

When El placed her hand on his, adrenaline and hormones slammed through him, robbing him of rational thought. With his good hand, he cupped the back of her head and drew her close, giving her every opportunity to tell him no. When her lids slightly lowered, he made his move. Christ, it was like he was fifteen again.

The second their lips touched, chaos washed over him. Hungry for her, he scooted closer and nipped at her bottom lip, praying she wouldn't move away. Was this wise? Fuck no, but he couldn't stop himself. He had to taste her, even if it was only one more time.

"We shouldn't," she panted between tastes.

"No, but I want you too much to stop." He held his breath. El wasn't drunk now. If she let him touch her, just a little, he'd be a happy man.

"You're injured."

He lifted his left arm enough to clasp her elbow. His shoulder was stiff but the pain was worth it. "Kiss me and I'll show you how healthy I am."

He teased open her lips, loving the mix of flavors from coffee to bacon. El groaned and he dove in. Sweetness surrounded him as he explored her familiar mouth. When she returned with a thrust of her own, his cock strained for release. He then lowered his right hand, clasped hers, and placed it on his cock. "I want you."

She tightened her grip and he thought he'd burst right there. "We shouldn't," she whispered.

"You said that before and yet here we are." If they discussed the pros of cons of what they were doing, she'd convince herself this wasn't wise. Sometimes a man just needed to take control. "Take off your clothes and let me love you."

She hesitated and his heart hitched. Vic stood to show her how amazing it could be between them. Without any sudden moves, he lowered his briefs with one hand. "My body is burned and scarred. I wish it were different, but it's not."

As soon as he stepped out of his shorts, she zeroed in on his fully-erect cock. When she licked her lips, he wanted to slam her against the wall and take her, but with El, he needed to be patient.

She ran a finger down his abs. "You look amazing. I'm the one who's gotten fat."

He'd lost weight but not much muscle. "You look better now. Sexier. More feminine."

Her smile trembled. "You're just saying that."

He grabbed his cock with his right hand. "Does it look like I'm not attracted to you?"

"No."

He nodded to her. "You need help getting naked?"

"Uh-huh."

While he had a condom—an old one—in his wallet, he loved to go bareback. "I've been tested. I'm good if you are."

Now she smiled. "You just hate to wear protection. If I recall that was how Charlotte was conceived."

"Guilty." Lying would serve no purpose. El's fingers moved to the bottom of her shirt. She hesitated and he closed his eyes to garner some control. "Are you torturing me on purpose?"

"I'm scared."

He opened his eyes. "Of me? That I'll hurt you?"

She lowered her hands and leaned closer. "Of course not. Of disappointing you."

His heart nearly cracked. "You could never disappoint me." He crossed his heart, and then helped her with her shirt.

She swatted his hands away. "I have this." El removed her top and let it drop to the ground.

He licked his lips. "Keep going, darling, but hurry. I'm not sure how long I can stand here and just watch."

Reaching behind her, she unhooked her bra then slowly lowered the straps. Time stood still. Her heavy breasts sagged, but they were so divine. "Christ, but you're a sight for sore eyes."

She smiled. "You don't have to say something nice. I know what I look like."

"No, you don't."

He didn't need to hear one more negative word coming from her mouth. He wanted her naked. "Take off your shoes."

Her fingers trembled as she unlaced her boots. Seeing her breasts sway made him grab his cock and pump once. She glanced up. "What are you doing?"

"Waiting patiently."

She lowered her head again, but not before he caught her smile. After she kicked off her boots and removed her socks, she stood, lowered her jeans then stepped out of them. His mouth turned dry. She ran a finger across the top of her panties. "Do you want to do the honors?"

He couldn't respond if he wanted to. He moved within inches of her then dropped to his knees on the floor. As much as he needed to impale her right there for his own satisfaction, he wanted to bring her pleasure more. Vic carefully eased her panties to her thighs and inhaled her scent. Home, happiness, and contentment assaulted him—all three helping to erase every ache and pain he'd ever endured.

His eyes must have glazed over or something because El stepped back and finished taking off her panties. "Lick me," she demanded.

He glanced up. "You aren't in control anymore. I say when I lick you." Which was right now. Vic reached out and drew her closer.

"You always were such a control freak." She smiled.

"Don't deny it. You loved it."

Wanting to drive her crazy, he cupped her pussy and slipped

a finger into her dampness. She moaned, and as her fingers dug into his scalp, she tried to close her thighs.

"None of that. Spread your legs wide and let me take you to heaven and back."

"Oh, yeah."

Chapter Seven

E LLIE SHOULD JUST get dressed and insist Vic crawl into bed, but damn it if he wasn't turning her inside out. Tomorrow, she'd put distance between them but right now, she wanted to forget. Forget someone was after her, forget all the disappointment she'd gone through with this frustrating man, but most of all forget how happy she had been all those years ago. They were different people now, and she didn't need any more temptation.

Then why did his breath on her inner thighs still ramp up her desire like nothing else? She needed to just let go for once and enjoy.

For the sake of her sanity, she would—this one time. The tension and pressure from these last months had made her desperate for some inner peace. Needing this release, she bent her knees, hoping he'd explore higher, but damn him, he didn't. She understood his game. He wanted her to beg—but she wouldn't. That would give him too much power.

Vic looked up. "Do you still like to have your sweet little clit played with?"

"Bastard."

"I'll take that to be a yes." He grinned, leaned forward, and swiped his tongue around the outside of her clit, never touching the sensitive nub.

Knowing that one lick could send her toward her climax, she snarled. "I can hurt you, you know."

He laughed. "Even with one good arm, I could take you. Wanna try?"

No. She didn't want to chance injuring him further. "How about I suck on your cock since you don't seem interested in taking care of me?" They always used to banter and challenge each other. It was their unique form of foreplay.

He shook his head and pried open her lower lips with his thumb and forefinger. Ripples of lust tripped up her spine as his tongue gently massaged her sensitive flesh. "Yes, oh, yes."

She clenched her hands and dropped back her head. She wanted it harder.

Vic chuckled. Damn him. He always could bring her to her knees. Too bad the man had the willpower of ten men. At least he did when they were together. Since his extended stay in the hospital last year due to his burns, had he even had sex? Would he be weaker when she clamped down hard on his dick? She hoped so.

Vic stood, his body touching hers. "I want to taste every inch of you."

His lips captured hers before she could respond. His right palm splayed across her back, his fingers curling against her spine. All thoughts of teasing him flew out of her head. Their tongues dueled, and with each thrust, her need grew. His cock pressed against her belly, making her wish he were inside her.

She broke the kiss. "Take me. It's now or never."

Throwing down the gauntlet was more artful foreplay, but Vic was different now. Did he still like it when their wills battled? Keeping his gaze on her, he backed her up until she was pressed against the outside door. The way he moved was feral and primitive.

"Wrap your legs around me," he commanded.

She loved when he took control. Ellie looped her arms around his neck and hooked her right leg at his waist. The added weight would make it hard to jump up. "A little help, please?"

He smiled and cupped her ass. "My pleasure."

With her back pressed against the wall he boosted her up with his knee and right hand. God, but he was strong. As much as it was wrong to think back to any of her lovers at this moment, she was positive none of them had been powerful enough to lift her like that.

Vic spun around and placed his back against the wall. She leaned back, hoping he'd be enticed by her breasts. Vic used to dote on them.

"God, but you are a vision." He leaned over, and when he nabbed her nipple between his teeth, streaks of pleasure shot every which way. An unintentional moan escaped. It wasn't that her sex life sucked, it was that Vic had spoiled her all those years ago.

Biting gently, he swirled his tongue in circles, and anticipation soared through her. Ellie pressed her feet against his thighs, lifted up, and then leaned back a few more inches to align her pussy to the tip of his cock. The pressure on her wet opening made her desperate for him.

Vic shifted his attention to her other breast. This time she leaned closer, pressing her breast hard against his mouth. He moaned then twisted and twirled the tip until she couldn't take the waiting any longer.

"I need your cock."

He let go of the tip. "You begging me to fuck you?"

She swore she'd never beg, but the overwhelming urge to have him consumed her. "Yes."

"You sure you can handle it?"

Why was he drawing this out? She'd made love with Vic for years. "You'll have to try me out and see."

Desiring to help, she reached between her legs, grabbed his dick, and placed her pussy over the head. Before he could move, she plunged down.

Holy shit. Even his eyes opened in surprise. She'd forgotten how thick he was. Her eyes watered and her pussy pulsed. And that was from his cock being inside her only half way.

"Fuck, you feel good." Vic withdrew an inch then edged his way in again. "I don't want to hurt you."

Emotionally or physically? What she wouldn't have given if he'd held those beliefs before he went undercover with the FBI. "You won't." Only because she was slicker than rain on glass.

He slid his hand up her back and drew her closer as he glided into her wet channel. Her inner walls stretched, but with it brought a myriad of emotions and erotic sensations that electrified every inch of her body. Ellie shut down the analytical part of her brain and thrilled to the joy beating around her heart. She took the lead, and when she engulfed as much of him as she could, her pussy throbbed.

"Kiss me," he said. He closed his eyes and parted his lips.

She'd never seen Vic this vulnerable before, but she liked this new side to him. Like a tide's response to the nearing moon, she was drawn to him. She darted her tongue in his mouth, loving each lick and twist. It was as if he was her air and she had to have him to live.

He cupped one cheek and pounded into her. When his cock reached the end, she had to break the kiss. Ellie gulped in a breath as her arousal coiled, ready to explode.

Wanting to make this last as long as possible, she leaned back once more and offered him her breasts.

"You know my weakness." Vic pounced again, licking and

sucking until her whole body caught fire.

She was close to the edge. Just as she was about to lift up again, Vic lowered her to the ground.

"I didn't come." She sounded childish, but the depravation alarmed her. He didn't dare stop now.

He switched places with her. "Turn around and plant your hands on the wall. That way my cock can enjoy your creamy pussy, and my fingers can love your luscious tits."

When had he turned so sentimental? She wouldn't complain. His cock always went in deeper when she bent over. She assumed the position and spread her legs wide. When Vic's muscled chest pressed against her back, she absorbed his heat.

Instead of taking her right away, he cupped both breasts with one hand and pushed them together.

"I love their fullness." Vic rubbed his palm across each nipple, sending spikes of pleasure straight down to her clit.

"Don't I get your cock?"

He laughed. "You always were the impatient one."

That was true, but she bet he was trying to calm down from before and was biding his time so he didn't embarrass himself by coming too soon. "Which is why you better put that cock in my pussy before I take her away from you."

He laughed. "I don't believe you could walk away, but just in case, I'll grant your wish."

"Smart ass."

He chuckled. A second later, the tip of his cock nestled just inside her opening. Not willing to wait, she pressed her hips back. Vic squeezed her tits and plunged in.

"Jesus, El. You feel fucking amazing."

When he pulled out and drove back in again, flames licked her insides. She lowered her head to draw in more air. As if a start gun had fired, the two of them thrust and pushed, her need out of control. With each foray down her pussy walls, bolts of electricity pricked every cell. Her climax teetered on the edge, but she wanted to wait until Vic was ready. If this was the last time they were together, she wanted it to be incredibly memorable.

His tongue licked her shoulder, and then his lips left a trail of kisses up to her ear. When he nabbed the bottom of her ear and tugged, she spiraled out of control.

"Oh, oh, yes!" she panted.

Squeezing her eyes to maximize the pleasure, she let him transport her far away. He drove in once more and then wrapped his arm around her waist, acting as if she was his cherished possession. As his cock expanded and pulsed to the beat of his heart, hot cum seared her insides. Stars burst behind her lids and she screamed his name.

As he held her tight, Vic said nothing, but his moans of delight were enough to tell her he'd been transported far away, too. For that one slice of time, they'd become one.

✧　✧　✧

CHARLOTTE DIDN'T BELIEVE her mother when she said Dad was totally fine. If he'd been that good, he wouldn't have gone to the hospital in the first place, and the ER doctor wouldn't have asked Mom to watch Dad for signs of a concussion. Not trusting either of them to tell her the whole truth, she only had one option—drive to Rock Hard. While it would only take two hours, she had to make sure she could get away for a week or two. No telling how much care her father needed. With the way Mom acted toward him, she might not be much help at all.

It had taken Charlotte an hour to get hold of her boss to tell her that she had to leave for a few days. Fortunately, they were finishing up with a client, and Patty said she could handle anything that came their way. Charlotte was lucky to work for such an awesome lady.

She'd been to her father's place only twice, but on the last visit, he'd insisted she have a key to his house. He said there might come a time when she just needed to get away. She debated calling him to let him know of her impending arrival, but knowing him, he'd tell her not to come. Dad could be stubborn. Men like him never liked to admit they needed someone.

After waiting for her boss to give her the okay, packing, stopping for a snack, and driving carefully in the inclement weather, it was a little after one before she pulled into his drive. No car was there. Mom had texted earlier and said they'd be home sometime today, but she didn't know exactly when. She'd taken care of him at her hotel room last night.

Charlotte parked, grabbed one of her two suitcases from the trunk, and headed up the front porch. The wind gusted and blew her long hair wildly, forcing her to rush to let herself in. "Hello? Anyone here?" She didn't know why she called out. She didn't really expect a response.

Dad's ranch style home had three bedrooms. He'd already specified which one was hers, so she dragged her case to the room then returned to the car for her other suitcase, which she'd set on the floor on the passenger's side. Head down to block the wind, she opened the door and attempted to lift her second case. *Crimeny.* It was a lot heavier than she'd remembered, and as she tried to tug on it, she lost her balance and stumbled backward.

Just as she almost righted herself, the car window shattered next to her head. Adrenaline swamped her. What the fuck was that?

A gunshot. Holy shit. All she could think of was to run as

fast as she could to get the hell to safety. Zigzagging to the porch, she hoped whoever had tried to kill her was a bad shot. Her knees trembled and bile rushed up her throat. Oh, my God. This couldn't be happening.

Charlotte yanked open the door and had the wherewithal to lock it. Without taking the time to check out the window to see if she could spot her assailant, she charged down the hall to her bedroom. After locking that door, she grabbed her purse off the bed.

The phone wasn't in its usual spot. *Where the hell are you? Come on. Come on.*

Her fingers finally connected with her cell. Sweat beaded on her forehead as she fumbled to get it out of the side pocket. Once free, she pressed 911.

She paced as it rang and rang, her heart jammed in her throat the entire time.

"911. What is the nature of the emergency?"

"Someone just shot at me."

"Are you injured?" The operator was almost too calm.

"No."

"Are you in a safe place now?"

"Yes. I'm at 13406 SR 25 in Rock Hard." She rushed to the bedroom's side window, hoping to catch a glance at him, but this bedroom was in the back of the house. Damn. She couldn't even see the drive.

"Officers are on the way. Remain in a safe place."

Safe place? She looked around to find one. If she hid in the closet, and if this person broke in, he'd find her for sure. Damn. There wasn't a safe place, but keeping out of sight would be smart.

"Is the front door locked?" the operator asked.

She had to think for a moment. "Yes."

Charlotte ducked into the hall bathroom and kept the lights off. While it probably wouldn't make any difference, she hid in the shower with the curtains closed.

Then her body began to shake.

Chapter Eight

WHEN SIRENS SOUNDED, Charlotte almost collapsed with relief. She stepped over the edge of the tub then pushed open the bathroom door to listen for footsteps. If the man with the gun had stayed around to see if she would come out to investigate, the arrival of the police would have him running.

The wails grew louder, easing her fears. Charlotte rushed to the front of the house and looked out. Two police cruisers and a red Jeep pulled into the drive. She unlocked and opened the front door, the wind momentarily refreshing her heated body. Men in uniform piled out of the cruisers, while a man in blue jeans and a brown leather bomber jacket stepped from the Jeep. He motioned them to check out the area then took the front porch steps two at a time.

Whoa. He stood a few inches above six feet, had light brown hair, cut short on the side and longer on top, and kind of looked like her dad in the muscle department. His face, however, was in a whole different league. Straight nose, classic cheekbones, and deep-set eyes the color of green glass. She shouldn't have noticed his stellar appearance given the severity of what just happened, but it helped calm her to focus on something that pleasant.

He displayed a police badge in one hand while he offered a

shake with his right. "I'm detective Trent Lawson. Are you Charlotte Hart?"

"Yes." She liked his firm handshake. His palms were warm and slightly calloused.

"Any relation to Vic Hart?"

If he knew her dad, he probably knew this was his house. "He's my father."

"May I come in and take your statement? It's a might cold out here."

"Yes." She showed him in. "I just arrived myself." She slipped off her jacket and tossed it on the back of the sofa. "I'd get you something to drink, but I don't know where anything is."

He smiled and his face lit up. He was so hot. "I appreciate the offer, but I'm okay. May we sit at the table?"

"Sure."

"Can you tell me what happened?"

If her father were here, he'd have asked the same thing. Oh, shit. When Dad found out that someone had taken a shot at her, he'd go ballistic. His reaction would occur no matter what she said or did. Charlotte inhaled and told Detective Lawson all she knew. "As soon as I realized the sound had been a gunshot, I ran."

"You didn't look around?"

"And give him another chance at me? Hell no. I zigzagged my way up the steps, ran in, and locked the door. Then I called you guys and hid."

"Smart." He jotted his notes on his iPad. "Have you called your father?"

"Not yet."

The detective pulled out his phone and punched in a few numbers. Did he have her dad's number in his contact list? It made sense. Dad was a PI. "Wait. Don't call him yet."

He pressed the off button. "Why?"

"Because Dad was in a car wreck last night. Someone rammed him from behind and drove him down an embankment. I don't want him upset any more than necessary. That's why I'm here. To take care of him."

The detective stilled. "Is Vic still in the hospital?"

This was getting complicated. "No. My mom's staying with him at her hotel. But they're divorced. She's only here because she has a stalker and had hired my dad to find out his identity." While he kept a lot of emotion off his face, she could tell he was struggling to put all of the pieces together. Then reality slammed into her. "Oh, shit. Do you think someone is targeting our whole family?" Until she'd listed the offenses, she hadn't considered that fact.

"Anything's possible. In light of your mother's stalker and your father's recent attack, we should consider putting you in protective custody."

She didn't want that. "After I see Dad's okay, I'll just drive home to Kalispell."

He shook his head. "Not good enough."

"What do you mean?"

He pushed back his chair. "Excuse me. I'll be right back."

Was he kidding? He dropped the bomb about protective custody, and then just walked out? Charlotte rushed to the window. Trent Lawson was speaking with two different policemen. Was it to begin the investigation? The cops would want to retrieve the bullet to figure out the type of gun used. Given about an inch of snow lay on the ground, there might be footprints or tire tracks that could be traced, too. While she and her dad hadn't spoken for many years, she'd learned a lot from him about forensics when he had been home.

Detective Lawson, who didn't look much older than she

was, then called someone. Whether it was her dad or his supervisor, she didn't know. Damn, but this was one big clusterfuck. She'd come here to make sure her father was taken care of, and what happened? She'd dodged a bullet. Christ.

Wait a minute. She thought of something else. Donning her jacket, she rushed outside. Trent looked up at her and jogged toward her.

"You remember something?" He looked hopeful.

"In a way. After I put the first suitcase in the room, I went outside to retrieve my second case. This time I pulled my hood over my head because the wind was intense. I also was looking at the ground to make sure I didn't slip."

"And you think your shooter mistook you for someone else? Your mother perhaps?"

Damn, but he was good. "Yes." She straightened her shoulders.

"I'll make a note of it. Regardless of whether this person was out to harm you or your mom, it's not safe to be here alone."

"If I can't go back home and I can't stay here, what do you suggest?"

"You can stay with me."

VIC'S CELL RANG and when he saw it was Trent, tension knots bunched his shoulders. While Trent, as well as Max Gruden, had been instrumental in bringing down Ed Hanson and his group of terrorists, Vic usually only spoke with Trent when he needed the RHPD's help or they needed his expertise.

"Trent?" Perhaps he'd found the identity of the man who'd run him off the road. That would be great.

"Vic, I'm afraid there's been an incident at your house."

"What, someone spray paint graffiti on the walls? Is it if-at-first-you-don't-succeed-try-try-again-kind-of-thing?" That was what happened at his crime scene. He almost chuckled. If it wasn't one thing, it was another. *Fuck me.*

"I'm afraid not. This is serious. Your daughter came to your house to nurse you back to health. Someone took a shot at her but missed."

All cheer disappeared as Vic's blood ran cold. He edged over to the hotel bed and sat down. El looked up at him with pinched brows. He held up a finger. "She okay?"

"She's a bit shaken, but she's holding it together." Trent detailed how she was taking her suitcase from her car, when someone fired into the car window. "She was smart enough to run into the house, lock the doors, and call us."

"I trust she didn't see who it was?"

"'Fraid not. Charlotte has a theory that because her head was down, and she was wearing a hoodie, the person might have confused her with her mom."

Fuck. "Where's Charlotte now?"

"We're all at your house."

"We'll be right there." He disconnected the call and looked up at his ex-wife. "Charlotte's unharmed." He wanted to start with the good news. He then relayed what Trent had told him.

El slumped back against her chair. "Why? Why would some-one want to harm her?"

Vic stood. "That is the sixty-four thousand dollar question. If we want answers, we need to head on over there."

"Should we pack our bags?"

He wasn't sure where it would be safest to stay. "I want to hear what Trent has to say first. Then we can decide."

El stood and grabbed her coat. "My poor baby. Charlotte must be beside herself."

"I would be if someone took a pot shot at me."

His pain ran deep. While Vic didn't have proof, it was look-ing more and more likely that the perpetrator was after him. El and Charlotte might have been distractions to keep Vic off balance. The biggest chink to his theory was that El had been targeted in Virginia before anything happened to him. Then again, Vic had worked out of the Washington, D.C. office for years. He'd just have to figure out who he'd pissed off enough to do this, and why target his ex-wife? Why wait so long for retaliation? He'd been gone from the area close to a year.

He could only hope his former FBI boss, Ted Knowlton, might be able to provide some answers, but first, he wanted details from Trent. Neither said much on the drive to his house, other than him providing El directions.

She slapped the wheel. "I told Charlotte not to come. If she'd listened, she'd be safe now." El glanced over at Vic. "She takes after you, you know."

He nodded. "She believes in justice."

Flashing lights greeted them at his house. A set of techs were taking photos of either tire tracks or footprints, while another group seemed to be looking for the bullet. Charlotte's car door stood open, her side window shattered, and her suitcase lay on its side by the car. Damn it. His baby didn't deserve to be tainted by his world.

As soon as El put the car in gear, he eased out and came over to her side. Since he recognized a few of the men, he nodded to them then helped her out of the car. Her hand was actually shaking.

"Charlotte's fine," he said.

She swallowed hard then sniffled. "For how long? And when will you have another accident?"

He wanted to ease the strain on her face. "You worried about me?"

"No."

He chuckled. "Could have fooled me."

She punched him in his good arm. With his hand on her back, he led her up the porch steps. Inside, Trent, Charlotte, and an officer he didn't recognize were seated at the dining room table. Their daughter looked pale.

She jumped up and ran to him. "Oh, Daddy."

She wrapped her arms around him. While his left shoulder throbbed, he'd take the ache any day to be able to hold her. "How are you doing, honey?"

She looked up at him. "Physically, I'm fine. Mentally, I'm a mess. Detective Lawson won't let me go home. He said I have stay with him." She groaned, her jaw clamped tight.

Vic stepped out of her hug and El swooped in. While El mothered Charlotte, he walked over to Trent and sat across from him. "What did Charlotte mean when she said she was staying with you?" Vic couldn't keep the protectiveness out of his voice.

"I know you'll say you can take care of both women, but I'm not sure that would be wise."

Trent had worked tirelessly to take down Hanson and his gang. Hell, he even took a bullet for his efforts. "Why?" Vic asked.

"What if the three of you are together? It makes for an easier target. Perhaps that was the perpetrator's plan."

He had a point. "You're suggesting my twenty-three year old, single daughter stay with you?"

Trent held up his hand. "I resent the implication. I promise I will do my duty and protect her. That's all."

He remembered promising El's dad that they'd wait until after they were married before engaging in sex. That promise was broken within a week. "Whose idea was it?"

"Dan Hartwick's."

The lead detective and Trent's boss. Vic recalled when Ed Hanson's gang went after Jamie Henderson, thanks to Vic's stupid move of planting evidence on her, the department didn't have the funds to protect her. Max Gruden, the arson investigator on his case, had volunteered to take care of her. Now they were married. But what choice did Vic have?

"How can you protect Charlotte when you have to go work?"

"I have vacation time coming and Dan suggested I take it."

That was going above and beyond the call of duty, but that was the kind of man Trent was. "Thank you."

"I promise I will protect her with my life."

Vic hoped he could do the same for El.

Chapter Nine

"**S**HE'LL BE OKAY." Vic placed a hand on Ellie's elbow and turned her toward him. "Trent's the best. He helped catch the guy who did this to me." He placed his other hand on his burns.

Despite being relieved that Charlotte would be safer with Trent than if she'd remained with them, Ellie wasn't ready to discuss her baby girl going off with a stranger. It didn't matter if he was a cop. He was a good looking man, too.

Ellie glanced once more at the retreating car then stepped away from the window. Crying wouldn't be pretty, so she drew on whatever reserve she had left and sucked it in. "You should put your sling back on. The doctor said to keep it immobilized for a week."

"I have other things to worry about than a bit of pain." His gaze never left her face.

She shook her head. He was a grown man, and she was no longer his wife. "Got any coffee?" She was too tired to argue with him.

"Sure. But I'll need help."

"You're playing the injured card now?" He had changed.

He shrugged. "I like doing things together."

"You do?"

He slid his hand to the small of her back. "Yes. Ever since you walked into my office, I realized how much I missed being with you."

His words had her heart sputtering, but she couldn't think about her needs right now. Making sure her daughter was out of harm's way was all that mattered.

Admit it.

She'd be devastated if anything happened to Vic. He was up to something, though, but she couldn't figure out what it was. At the beginning of their marriage, Vic had shown spurts of sentimentality, but he hadn't toward the end.

"Right before we divorced, you said you feared the dangers of your job might end up causing me harm, and that was the reason you had to put distance between us. Why aren't you stepping back now? Does that mean you don't think these episodes have anything to do with your job?"

Vic led her into the kitchen but didn't answer. Damn him. He scooped the coffee into the machine, and then poured the water into the coffee maker. Clearly, he didn't need help.

"Truthfully? I'm scared shitless. You're right about my job getting between us. I saw the bad side of life, and I never wanted you to know what it was like." He stabbed a hand over his head. "But now, I don't have as many rules to follow. I don't have to immerse myself in their world. Knowing what I know now, I never should have married. I was told of the dangers, but when you came along, I fell in love. I didn't want to be without you." He stepped close. "I'm sorry I put you through hell all those years."

She wished he'd said those words five years ago. "You were a great husband for a while."

He retrieved two cups from the cupboard and set them on the counter. "Perhaps, in the beginning. I have many regrets in my life, but marrying you isn't one of them. Becoming an FBI agent while being married and having a daughter might not have been the best choice in my life."

"At the time, neither of us understood how your work would affect you. But that's water under the bridge, as they say."

"True."

The coffee finished perking and he poured two cups. "Let's sit in the living room and decide how to move forward."

He was going to let her provide some input? That was a first. Vic balanced his cup on his bad arm as he ambled past the dining room table. They both set their drinks down, and then sat next to each other on the sofa.

He twisted toward her. "Given what happened here today, do you have any theories?"

"Me? That's why I came to you for help."

"I know, but we can either assume this person is trying to harm me to give you as much pain as possible or it's the other way around. Given you've probably not painted me in a very good light, I can't see anyone trying to harm me to hurt you."

Vic was perceptive. She might have said a few disparaging things about Vic over the years, especially to Charlotte. She regretted that now. "Brian did ask about you a few times, and I will admit I was never very complimentary." She wouldn't tell Vic that she once said he could rot in hell for all she cared.

"Would Hilton, Brian, or Cal be related to someone I targeted? Do you remember any of them discussing relatives who were on the wrong side of the law?"

"No. Then again, Cal and I never discussed anything personal. He knew I had a daughter, but that was all."

Vic pulled his cell from his pocket. "I want to speak with my former boss, Ted Knowlton. I'll ask him to pull all of the files I worked on to see if any of them are related to one of our three suspects."

She leaned her head back against the seat. "I never should have come here."

Vic clasped her hand. "Why? If you hadn't, your stalker would have kept targeting you. I would still have been in that accident and Charlotte would have raced to help me. She and I might have been together when the man took the shot."

Why did he always have to be the voice of reason? "You act as if the two aren't related."

"I don't know what to think anymore, but I intend to find out."

ON THE DRIVE back to town, they discussed their next step. Staying at the hotel was not only expensive; the lack of space would drive both of them crazy.

"If we stay at my house," Vic said, "you'd have to come to work with me. I won't leave you there alone."

She wouldn't feel safe if he did. She didn't remember a spare room in Vic's office, but if he had one, she might be able to purchase a canvas and some Acrylics and work on some calming art. She liked that idea until she pictured the creep coming into the office while Vic was off doing his thing.

"Are you going to arm Sharon and me, in case he starts firing at the office window?"

"I'll ask Sharon to bring her arsenal to work. She hunts, you know."

"Really? She doesn't look the type. Maybe it's the blue hair that threw me off."

"That's a fad. Last week, she was a mousy brown. So you know, Sharon is quite the marksman. If you look at the wall behind her desk, you'll see some awards she's won."

"Good to know."

Vic's smile was brief, but it was there. "We'll eat healthier if we stay at my place."

"You cook?"

"Had to learn."

"I say we've decided. We'll need to pack up and check out." She clasped his wrist. "How are you going to get around without a car? Not to mention you aren't cleared to drive yet."

He shrugged his good shoulder. "I figure I could use your rental if I have to or you can chauffeur me." He smiled.

"So that's all I'm good for? Transportation?"

His brows rose. "What else did you have in mind?"

She glanced over at him. "Do you always have sex on the brain?"

"Who said anything about sex?" He held up a finger. "If you must know, no. Only after you showed up."

"When did you learn to flirt?" In the last few years of their marriage, he'd grown serious.

"Got lots of practice after the divorce."

That stung but only for a moment. He was lying. "Will insurance replace your car?"

"I haven't filed the paperwork."

She groaned as she pulled into the lot next to the hotel. "Ready?"

"Yup. Oh, one more thing to keep us safe. We shouldn't remain in one place for too long. It will be harder to target us that way."

She shivered, not wanting to think about something more happening to any of them. "Meaning what? You want to leave town?"

"No. I was thinking that instead of sitting in front of the tube all night, we could go to the movies, eat out a few times, and maybe even do some outdoor stuff—like horseback riding or something. We won't keep a schedule."

Ellie couldn't decide if he was trying to ask her out on a date or wanted to play bodyguard. *Let it go.* "Sounds good."

When they informed the front desk that Ellie would be checking out early, Vic requested they text him if anyone asked about her. "Please don't tell anyone she's not here. We have reason to believe someone is trying to harm my family."

The young man's cheeks sagged. "Of course, Mr. Hart. I'll make a note in the computer to let the other reservationists know."

"Appreciate it."

As they made their way to the elevator, Vic glanced around. That made her more nervous. "You think this person is lying in wait?" she asked.

"I didn't live this long by being careless." He looked behind them once more. "Though the car crash never should have happened. Fuck. I was too distracted."

She placed a hand on his arm and stopped him. "First off, you couldn't have prevented it. Secondly, stop pretending you're some impenetrable soldier. I like it better when you admit you're afraid or that you're actually human."

He held her gaze for a moment. "See why I need you?"

Don't go there. "Standing here makes me more vulnerable, right? Let's get to the room." She pressed the elevator button.

Now he smiled. "I hear ya."

Ellie hoped she was doing the right thing, but Vic needed the time to find this madman. He'd worry less if she stayed at his place.

Once in the room, she set her suitcase on the table and opened it up. Vic moved behind her and wrapped his arms around her waist. "It's so good to have you back."

She twisted around in his arms. "Vic, I'm not back." He leaned closer and her pulse raced.

"I know, but until I find this person, we might as well make the most of the situation, and enjoy life while we have the chance. That's all I'm asking." He stroked her cheek with a knuckle, and memories rushed back as waves of familiarity washed over her.

They were both consenting adults. For a moment, it was as if twenty years had disappeared. "I don't know if it's smart to get involved." She didn't want to admit they already were involved.

"You afraid you won't be able to walk away? From this?" He placed her hand on his rigid cock.

The man was a master at making love. No one else could take her higher or faster. "Yes, I can."

"Then what's the problem?"

Damn. She had no answer. He squeezed her hand on top of his dick and a spray of lust hit her. The bed was rumpled from last night. The release might help push what happened to Charlotte out of her mind for a few minutes and provide some peace. God, she was so full of rationalization it was pathetic.

Should she or shouldn't she? Where was that daisy when she needed it?

Chapter Ten

"I F I HAD my cuffs, I'd arrest you, and demand you do as I wish." Vic stepped back and pawed through Ellie's suitcase.

She chuckled. Vic was his old crazy self today—the self that existed only during their first years of marriage. "What are you looking for?"

"Something to tie you up with." He whipped around and faced her. "You don't have a flogger in there, do you? I think someone needs to be punished."

She suspected he was trying to lighten the mood. "You are a piece of work. I don't need any of that stuff anymore."

"You like it the old-fashioned, boring way?" He moved closer.

She opened her mouth. "Did you think what we did was *boring*? We didn't use anything."

"True, but I was thinking more about you just now. You always appreciated a bit of spice."

Damn him for baiting her. She hadn't decided if it would be wise to engage in sex with him again, but Vic knew what he was doing. The downside was that the more intimate they became, the harder it would be to leave—but leave she would. Ellie had her gallery to run.

In the old days, she had liked to change thing up in the bedroom. "That was the old me."

He tugged her close. "Good to know. So, if you want me to crawl on top of you and do it missionary style, I can oblige. As long as I get to suck on your bountiful breasts and fuck your sweet pussy, I'll be in heaven."

Now she actually laughed. "You have a dirty mouth."

"Oh, yeah? How about you help me wash up first then?"

She wasn't talking about physical dirt, but showering after rushing to make sure Charlotte was okay had caused her to perspire—and not in a good way. "Sure."

He grinned. "Since I'm so incapacitated, can you help me with my shirt?"

"You mean your bloodstained shirt? Sure. You should have picked up a clean one when you were home."

"I was a bit preoccupied."

As was she. Once she removed his shirt, she pressed on his abs and directed him back to the bed. Being in control was a heady experience. "Boots are next."

She dropped to her knees and tugged them off.

"You look good down there," he said.

Ellie gave him the finger. "Watch it."

He laughed. "If I recall, you used to like getting on your knees and sucking on my cock."

That was true. "I was young and stupid back then." Giving him a bigger head wouldn't help either of them.

"Guess, you aren't interested in a lick then."

She hadn't meant that, but she wisely kept quiet as she took off his socks. She stood then leaned over to undo the button on his jeans. A moment later, she was on her back on the bed with Vic on top of her.

"Your arm. Don't hurt it." He was leaning on his elbow.

"It's fine." He dipped his head and placed feathery kisses on her lips.

The soft touch surprised and delighted her, making her want more. Ellie cupped the back of his head and begged for entrance. He obliged. Boy, did he. With a passion she hadn't experienced in a while, Vic plundered and demanded her submission, and Ellie gave herself willingly.

As much as she wanted to get naked and make love with him, she needed the shower. "I thought I was going to wash you."

"Hmm. We do have all day to spend in bed, I guess."

No, they had a potential killer to catch, but she wouldn't argue semantics. Her pussy was in too much need.

Vic pushed up off the bed and held out his hand. "I'm ready."

So was she. "Get the water warm, while I undress."

"Let me help you," Vic said. "It'll be faster."

If he couldn't manage to take off his own clothes, how could he take off hers? Sometimes, she suspected Vic acted contrary just to make her feistier. "Fine."

She sat on the bed and held her legs out straight. After two quick tugs, her boots landed on the floor. He slipped off her socks then pulled her to her feet using his uninjured arm.

"Now for the good part." He grinned. "Don't move."

Oh God. She remembered all too well when he used to ask her to remain like a statue. The less she was able to move, the more she wanted to. "Just wait until it's your turn."

The image of her sucking on his cock in the shower came to mind. He'd fold quicker than Kenny Rogers with a busted hand. This ought to be fun.

Vic remained silent as he slipped off her shirt. Instead of letting it fall to the floor, the neat freak folded it and placed it on top of her suitcase. Why he left the shoes in the middle of the room was anyone's guess.

"I love your choice of lingerie." He licked his lips and her damned nipples puckered.

"No tasting until after I've washed."

"Did I say I was going to pounce on them or tug and tease them until your pussy dripped?"

She glanced at the ceiling. "You are so going down."

"I can't wait." He slipped off her bra, set it on the bed, and then undid her jeans. "You can help me with the right side."

Together they lowered her pants. She stepped out of them, and as expected, he folded them, and then placed the bra and jeans with the shirt.

"The panty removal is my favorite," Vic said, his forefinger tracing a line across the top of the waistband. "I love to see what's hidden underneath, even if I've just tasted it."

"Better hurry. The offer to wash you expires in three minutes."

"That so?"

He stepped behind her, slipped his palm down her belly, and dipped two fingers into her very wet pussy. The man could make her come with a look. "You're not being fair. You have your jeans on."

Which meant she couldn't grab his cock. She didn't care about his rule not to move and turned around to face him.

"Fine." By twisting his hips, he was able to get out of both his jeans and briefs using one hand.

"You know, despite your advanced age, you still look good." A hell of a lot better than she did.

"Advanced age, huh? You'll pay for that. Panties. Drop 'em."

He wanted her to do it? Fine. She turned her back, hooked her fingers in the waistband, and slowly lowered them. While she wasn't proud of her rear, Brian always claimed it was her best feature. One more reason why she'd been smart to drop him. Once she stepped out of the bikini bottoms, she faced him again.

Vic sucked in his bottom lip. "We need to shower fast because I'm not sure I can wait much longer."

He sure was good for her ego. Ellie held out her hand. "Then let me escort you to the cleansing chamber."

While the water warmed, he removed the bandage from his forehead while she pulled off the pad from his back. The area wasn't as red as before and looked like it was healing nicely.

They stepped into the tub, and while it was too small for sex, it would do for washing.

"I can't help with washing your hair, but I can do your pussy," he offered.

She cracked up. "It's too tight in here to be doing stuff like that. Let me wash you first then you can do me."

"I like the sound of that."

They slipped by each other until Vic was under the showerhead. He dipped his head to wet it then poured some shampoo on his hair. He'd kept it short, so lathering it with his good hand wasn't difficult. Once his hair foamed, he rinsed quickly.

"You want to do my back?" he asked over his shoulder.

"Yes."

She lathered her palms and washed his shoulders, remembering very well that they used to do this every night. Vic's muscles were more pronounced now. He was leaner and fitter. When her fingers edged close to his burn, she hesitated. "Will it hurt if I touch it?"

"Can't feel a thing."

She didn't want him to be self-conscious, so she scrubbed that area the same as the other shoulder. When she cleaned his back, his muscles flexed. Oh my, how she loved his powerful body.

His ass was next, and what a fine ass it was—two perfect round orbs that were hard as steel when he tightened his cheeks. She dragged the bar from hip to hip then dipped the bar in between his butt cheeks.

"Tickles."

She did it to see him clench. "You are such a girl."

He whipped around. "Your turn and we'll see who's a girl."

"I haven't done your chest yet." *Or your cock.*

He let out an exasperated huff, but she could tell he was putting on a show. "Be quick."

She dragged her hands down his pecs and stopped to cop a squeeze. His body was pure heaven. She lowered her gaze to his rippled abs—abs that belonged in a magazine. "Don't you eat bad stuff?"

"Occasionally."

Ellie continued washing his body, moving closer to his cock.

"That's far enough." He stepped around her and moved her under the spray.

She hadn't planned to wash her hair, but it was too late now. As she lowered her head, Vic moved close behind her, slid his palm down her belly, and dipped a finger into her pussy.

"Ooh." She hadn't expected that. One finger shouldn't excite her so much, but it did. Trying to ignore the pulses skipping up and down her body, she dumped some shampoo onto her head and lathered quickly.

"I'm turning around now, so I can rinse." He needed to move out of the way.

"Go ahead. That way I can play with your tits."

He was incorrigible. Had he always been this playful? Somehow, all she remembered were the last few years that hadn't been good between them. Vic was never home, and going undercover meant he couldn't be with his family. At the time, she thought that was his way of saying he didn't want to be married anymore. Now, she believed he truly wanted to serve his country, and she was merely a casualty of war.

Ellie dipped back her head to rinse out the soap when Vic's mouth captured a breast. "Yikes. You'll get soap in your mouth."

As if he cared, Vic licked her other tit. She reached out and grabbed the bar. "How can I wash if your mouth is latched on to me?"

He leaned back and held out his hand. "I'll clean you then." All kidding seemed to disappear.

Now that he'd detached himself, she could do it, but Ellie handed him the soap anyway. Vic rubbed the edge from one nipple to the other. His actions implied this shower wasn't about getting clean, which suited her fine. Vic wanted to make love to her the way he used to when they were happy, and that was all that mattered.

He lathered his hands, set down the soap, and then massaged her breasts. She loved his gentle touch. Needing to do the same for him, she soaped up her palms then grabbed his already hard cock. "I forgot to wash it."

"No matter. It's only been in your pussy."

"Uh-huh." She stroked his hard shaft up and down while leaning into him, loving the pressure on her breasts. "I have more skin than on my breasts."

"You do. I'll make sure all of you is clean."

He washed her arms and belly quickly, then dropped to one knee. With his good hand, he started with her foot and lathered her right leg. The closer he came to her pussy, the slower he went.

"She's very dirty, you know," she said.

He looked up. "I'll be sure to be extra thorough."

Just as he reached the top of her right thigh, he began anew with her left leg. Anticipation built and Ellie bent her knees. "You missed a spot."

"I did?" Vic smiled then swiped the soap across her opening.

That small amount of pressure helped relieve a bit of need. "You're going slow on purpose, trying to drive me mad."

"Remember, I'm the master at being patient."

"Ha. We'll see when I get a hold of your cock."

"Promises, promises." Vic stood, rubbed his palm across her pussy a few times, and then rinsed her.

Whether every inch of her body was clean or not didn't matter. She wanted Vic on top of her, and then in her.

She shut off the water. "I want to dry you." Vic had a tendency to leave spots of his body wet when he climbed into bed.

He stepped out and held out his arms. "I'm all yours."

With the tip of the towel, she swiped his chest then made sure to dry his cock and balls.

He growled. "You're asking for it."

She could go on for a while, but she wanted him plastered against her more. Because she was wet, she quickly dried. Without a word, she flung the towel at him and raced into the bedroom. She dropped onto her back on the bed and folded her arms behind her head.

Vic strolled in a minute later. "Don't you look comfy and inviting? Mind if I join you?"

She tapped her chin. "That depends. Know anyone who's a good lover?"

Chapter Eleven

V IC WAS SCARED he'd mess this up. El was in a spunky mood, and he didn't want to disappoint her by turning serious. Sex had always been great between them—at least it had been when he managed to get home. He wanted to show her that he would put her first from now on, but if he pressured her too much, she might withdraw. Keeping it light seemed the best option.

"I'd like to apply," he said as he crawled onto the bed, careful not to put too much weight on his arm.

"What can you do for me, mister?"

He loved she was giving him an open invitation. "How about if I just show you?"

Vic slipped between her legs and wished he could tie her ankles to the bedposts. He fondly recalled how every time she groaned then wiggled, trying to close her thighs, his cock went wild.

Not wanting to delay her satisfaction any longer, he swiped his tongue across her slit, and sweetness assaulted him. No other woman tasted better.

"Yes, that's it." Her back arched.

He smiled and returned to pleasuring her. With his right hand, he reached up and cupped a breast. Her tits were so full and round, and the nipples perfect for plucking. The smooth skin electrified his palm. As much as he wanted to suck on them, he needed to bring her to a climax first.

He lowered his arm and slipped two fingers into her pussy. She bucked, and his fingers went to work, curling inside her to find that perfect spot that made her writhe and moan.

"Holy fuck, Vic. You hit it. Yes."

When El was in the zone, she was easy. Then again, so was he.

She clasped his head. "I want you."

He loved when she teetered on the edge. "How?"

She pushed up on her elbows. "I want to ride you like a good cowgirl should."

He laughed. Raised in Virginia, she might have ridden in an arena, but not in the open field, but he'd take her any way he could get her—real cowgirl or not.

Vic pushed up and managed to get on his back, keeping his arms to his side. Because he expected this to be quite a ride, he hoped the stitches in his back held. "Saddle up, girl."

She grinned, just as he'd hoped. When El straddled him, he thought he'd died and gone to heaven. He still couldn't believe she was in his bed. So many nights, he'd fantasized about what he'd do to her. In those dreams, he could go all night, fucking her long and hard. Now, he could see he'd been delusional. Vic would be lucky to last a few minutes once her pussy wrapped around his cock. He was glad he'd fought through the haze of pain from his burns. Surviving had been worth it to love her once more.

She opened her pussy lips, but instead of lifting his cock and sitting on him, she delved her own finger inside. He grit his teeth and gave her his meanest look. "Lady, you are a cruel one. That should be my cock inside you."

"Just wanted to make sure I'm ready."

Was she trying to insult him? "You get your sweet pussy on top of my cock or else." He lifted his dick waiting for her divine warmth to encase him.

She smiled, placed her pussy on the tip, and slid down an inch. Then she leaned over and kissed him. *Tease.* As he opened his mouth to receive her, he clamped down on her hips and drove up into her slickness. Glory be.

"Bad Vic. It's my job to ride you."

"Kiss me, girl."

She smiled and did just that. As soon as their tongues collided, he lost all sense of time. It was as if he was crawling in the desert and she was the only water in sight. He plunged into her tight pussy, the friction sending him higher and higher. Her moans, along with the way she grabbed his ears for dear life, made him lose his mind. His balls drew up tight as he plowed into her again and again.

When she clamped down on his cock with her inner muscles, he groaned. "Don't do that. I'm about to burst."

She closed her eyes and sat back up, breaking the kiss. "I'm almost...there, too."

When he reached across to rub her clit, she lowered her head and gulped in air. As her climax arrived, she once more tightened her pussy, and he gave up the battle. His cock expanded and his seed shot out hard and fast.

Every good memory he'd ever had swam in his brain. Dear God, what he'd give to stay right here—inside her—forever.

CHARLOTTE COULDN'T BELIEVE she'd be staying with Trent Lawson, the hunky cop. Too bad, reality sunk in when the detective barely looked her way during their ride to his place.

Turns out, he really was just her bodyguard. Bummer.

"How far away is this place?" She swore they'd been driving an hour.

"Not too far from here. The cabin's in the mountains. Actually, this was my dad's home away from home. We'll be safe there. I can see anyone coming up the drive."

She could picture him sitting at the window, waiting, while she sat there twiddling her thumbs. "Do you have satellite?"

"We have a dish for the Internet, but Dad never bought a TV."

Really? "What do you do to entertain yourself when you come here?" The image of Trent with a woman's long legs entwined around him shot to the forefront of her brain, but she pushed it away. That woman had long, black hair—not blonde like hers.

He chuckled. "I don't come here often, but when I do, I read. If I bring some buddies along we play cards or board games."

Was this man for real? "You hunt?"

"When I get the chance, which isn't all that often. You'll be able to tell, because the place needs some serious airing out. It's been a while since I've gotten away."

Then games it would be. At least, she was pretty good at checkers and chess. And there was always poker—strip poker if she had her way. "Do you have indoor plumbing?"

While Charlotte didn't really consider herself a princess, she had her limits, especially in the winter.

He glanced her way. "Yes. We even have hot running water for showers, as well as a decent-sized refrigerator and a stove top."

That was some consolation. "Has my dad ever been there?"

"No, which was one reason why I came up here."

Charlotte needed to think about that reasoning. "You think someone will try to torture my location out of him?"

"If they try, they won't succeed. Vic doesn't know the town's name let alone the street the cabin's on, so he can't leak the location even if he wanted to."

That made sense.

They turned off a long, boring road then headed through a town of sorts. There was a gas station, grocery store, sporting goods store, a clothing store, and an assortment of other places. The town itself was maybe three blocks long.

Trent pulled in front of the food store. "We need some supplies if we're going to eat. You cook?"

"I make do, but I'm no gourmet."

"Neither am I."

Well, wasn't this going to be fun? Trent got out of his side, rushed over, and opened her door. She liked that. As she stepped out, his gaze was on the surroundings.

"You're kind of scaring me, Detective. You can't possibly think this crazy dude followed us here, do you?"

"I hope not, but I can't be too careful."

Now he sounded like her dad. "True."

"By the way, call me Trent. It will look less suspicious. While I don't come here often, a few people know me. I'll say you're my girlfriend, which will cause less gossip."

Did he bring many women here? Is that why it wouldn't look odd? Whatever. She bet he wouldn't like it if she acted like a real girlfriend, hugging him close then planting a kiss on his cheek when he did something thoughtful or sweet. Stupid idea, but she needed something to distract her from freaking out about the crazed lunatic taking another pot shot at her.

They entered the small, country store. "What do you like to eat?" he asked.

"I'm easy. I make a mean chicken, rice, and stewed tomato casserole."

He smiled, and she thought she just might have to thank that shooter for forcing her into confinement. "Sounds great. Hamburgers or spaghetti?" he asked.

"Spaghetti." She liked this game. "For breakfast, are you more of a scrambled eggs and bacon guy or pancakes with a ton of syrup man?" Given his flat abs, she bet he only ate organic eggs.

"Eggs."

Figures. As they went down each aisle, he gave her choices. At first, she'd thought Trent was rigid like her dad, but now he presented a more fun and friendlier side than he'd shown at first.

He paid, and they hauled the groceries to his car, but not before he checked out the lot. Charlotte had never had anyone watch over her so carefully. It was a not-so-bad experience.

The drive to his dad's house only took ten more minutes. To her delight, the one-story brick home looked well kept, and she loved the large wooden porch in front. Even though covered chairs were shoved to one end, she bet in the summer, this would be a great place to sit and have a drink.

Once inside, Trent pointed out where things should go, and they put the groceries away.

"Do you think you can handle making the hot chocolate while I light the fire?" he asked. "I'll leave the door open for a few more minutes to air the house out."

"Sounds good."

This whole playing house thing was strange, but cool in an odd sort of way. Charlotte had dated her fair share of guys, but she'd never lived with anyone, if she could say that was what they would be doing for a few days. Wanting to show him she could be useful, she set about heating the milk for the hot chocolate then located the mugs.

By the time she brought out the drinks, Trent had the door closed and a fire going. She loved the smell of the burning oak. He was on the sofa with his laptop booted up.

He glanced up, took the proffered mug, and inhaled. "Smells good. I'll get the luggage in a bit. I wanted to ask you a few questions about your dad."

That would be a short-lived conversation. "I don't really know much about what he did or didn't do other than he was deployed overseas and then was involved in undercover shit with the FBI."

Trent nodded. "That must have been tough on you."

"Sure, but it was harder on Dad, I think. Every time he was able to come home after an assignment ended, he seemed sadder, more distant."

"How did that make you feel?"

She was about to make a snarky remark about him acting like a shrink, but then she thought better of it. He was just being sympathetic. "Sad, but mostly for my mom. She really loved my father, but it was like she encased her heart in some kind of protective barrier after each episode to prevent further suffering."

His lips pressed together. "Your dad mentioned you did interior design work. What made you go into that field?"

Was he trying to put her at ease or figure out what kind of person she was? Maybe he thought she was some crazed artist who attracted the loons, and that the man after her had nothing to do with her dad or her mom.

She shrugged. "I didn't do very well at academic subjects. I'm not blaming dad or anything, but my mom and I were a bit distracted every time he left for work. We never knew if he'd come home again."

Trent's brows pinched. "That had to be difficult. What did the kids at school say?"

Her chuckle came out rueful. "We told people he was a salesman who traveled around the country a lot."

"I'm sorry."

"It sucked at times, but Mom and I grew closer because of it. She's an amazing artist. While I was never talented enough to paint, she taught me what looked good together. Eventually, I developed my own style of design. After my parents divorced, I wanted to stay near home for school. I studied interior design at the University of Virginia."

He nodded. "Vic mentioned you two didn't talk a lot."

That was a nice way of putting it. "Not for a long time. I was mad that he wasn't around when I needed him. Kids aren't very understanding. After the fire, he called me. He sounded different, so I agreed to meet with him."

"Different? How so?"

"He acted defeated, and I'd never seen that attitude in him before. I know you and Max Gruden, as well as the FBI team, helped bring down that terrorist cell, but I think my dad felt bad he wasn't involved as much as he'd have liked."

"Your dad was fighting for his life. He couldn't have helped physically."

"I know." She wished her father could see it that way.

"Just so you know, it was your dad who cracked the case. He had the evidence that led to the takedown."

She sat back. "He never mentioned it."

Trent shook his head again. "No, I suppose he wouldn't." He waved a hand. "Didn't mean to get off topic. Tell me how you repaired the relationship."

"I'm not sure I can say it is totally healed, but it's getting that way. When we met after his accident, I could see he was really torn up about how things were between us." She sniffled, determined not the cry. "I guess I wanted to give him another try at being a dad." She smiled, but her lips wobbled. "He's doing the best he can."

"He is at that. It was nice of you to take time off work to come here."

She raised her brows. "I think I've created more of a mess by doing so."

Trent drank his now-cooled cocoa. "If you hadn't, we might have focused on someone being pissed at your mom instead of a person aimed at hurting Vic's family."

Charlotte sat up straighter. "You think?"

"I can't be certain, but that attempt at your life made your dad look at other options."

She drank her cocoa, too, a bit calmer than before. "I hope so." This conversation had dredged up some guilt and pain. She set down her cup. "I'd like to help. What can I do?" She was referring to both figuring out who was after her dad, her mom, and her, as well as getting them settled. If he didn't find something for her to do, she'd have to focus on what made the hot detective tick.

"When I hear from your dad, I'll see if there's something I can have you research. Did you bring a laptop?"

"Wouldn't leave home without it." She'd promised her boss she'd work on some designs while she was in Rock Hard.

As bad as this seemed, if this mess brought her mom and dad back together, then getting shot at would be the best thing ever.

Chapter Twelve

ELLIE WASN'T THRILLED about sitting at Vic's office all day with nothing to do, but he said he needed his computer and files, which meant he had to go to the office. They stowed her suitcase in the trunk, phoned in a to-go order at a place called Italiano's, and headed to his work. The food would be delivered shortly.

As soon as they stepped into the reception area, Sharon placed a hand on her chest. She had her coat on and her computer shut off. Vic said the office closed at noon on Saturday and it was a little after that now.

"There you are. I was worried about you," Sharon exclaimed.

Vic glanced to the ceiling then back at her. "Shit. I'm sorry. I should have called in."

"Yes, you should have. I heard about the car wreck. My goodness, but you are an injury magnet. You sure you're okay?"

The two seemed to have a good rapport. Ellie was glad that after she left, Vic would have someone to watch over him.

"Just a few bumps and scrapes. Any calls?" Vic asked.

Did nothing faze him? What would it take to upset him? He probably told people that his burns had been a mere inconvenience.

"Nothing I couldn't take care of, boss."

Vic placed a protective hand on Ellie's back. "You remember El?"

"Of course." As Vic detailed the wreck, and then described the attack on Charlotte, worry laced her features. "That's terrible. What can I do?" she asked.

"You have your gun handy?"

Sharon patted the side of her purse. "I don't go anywhere without my Annie."

Annie? As in *Annie Get Your Gun?*

"Good. If I have to leave for whatever reason and can't take El with me, can I count on you to protect her?"

She opened her over-sized purse, withdrew a big ass gun, and waved it. "Don't you worry. I'll shoot anyone who comes through the door and threatens her."

"Good. I've got some calls to make." He faced Ellie. "You'll have to sit in my office since Sharon is leaving."

"I'll stay for a bit longer, boss," his secretary offered.

Vic smiled. "You sure?" She nodded. "Remind me to give you a raise."

Sharon laughed. "I tell you every week, yet I never see a change in my paycheck."

Vic chuckled. "How about a bonus then?"

Sharon gave him a thumbs up. He turned to Ellie. "I've got another room in the back that we use for storage. You mentioned you might want to paint back there, so take a look and see if it can accommodate you."

"Thanks, I will."

Vic leaned over and kissed her before heading down the hallway.

Sharon jumped up and dragged over a chair. "Have a seat."

She shrugged off her coat and Ellie did the same. "I don't want to keep you," Ellie said, never liking to inconvenience anyone. "I can stay with Vic."

"Nonsense, I have nowhere to go. I'd rather sit here and talk to you. As much as I've tried, my damned cat won't answer me back."

Ellie liked Sharon. "Well, thank you." They looked at each other for a moment, and the silence turned rather awkward.

"So, you and the boss back together?" Sharon raised her brows.

That was a bit personal, but the first time Ellie had come in, she could have frozen boiling water. Two days later, they were kissing. She probably would have questioned the change if she'd seen such a difference in two people. "Just trying to make the most of my time here."

"You go, girl. If I thought I had a chance with Mr. Hart, I'd have asked him out myself."

Ellie wanted to take the focus off their budding relationship. "Vic said you're quite the shot. Do a lot of women in Montana carry guns?"

"Some, but Dad wanted a boy real bad."

"So he decided to teach you how to shoot?"

"Yup. After I was born, the doctors said Mom shouldn't have any more kids—high blood pressure and all—so he kind of raised me like the boy he wanted. When I was barely old enough to pull a trigger, he took me hunting."

Ellie smiled. "That's rather sweet."

Sharon shrugged. "I guess, but a lot of men are a bit put off by it. That and the fact I'm large." Ellie could sympathize. "Dad tried to get me to wrestle in high school like he did, but I refused. Who wants to smell some pubescent male's armpit? No, thank you. Mom put her foot down, too. She went right out and bought me a kids' cook set." Sharon laughed. "If you know any men who can be swayed by a gourmet meal, let them know I'm available. Or at least I will be once Darryl dumps me."

He must be the new man Vic mentioned and the reason for the new blue-streaked hair. "Why do you think he'll dump you?"

She shrugged. "They always do. Besides, Darryl travels a lot. He'll find someone else, but I plan to enjoy all he has to offer, if you get my drift."

"I do."

The bell above the door chimed and Sharon's hand went straight to her purse. When a young man wearing a green and white-striped shirt entered, carrying a delicious smelling bag of food, Sharon relaxed.

"Delivery for Hart?"

"Yes." Ellie dug her hand in her purse and gave the young man a tip. Vic had already paid over the phone.

Ellie felt bad Sharon had to work overtime. "Why don't you head on home? I'll stay with Vic in his office."

"You sure?"

"Yes. Unless you want to join us. We have plenty."

"I'm good, thanks. Will I see you Monday?"

Ellie didn't want to think how long it would take to solve this case. Poor Wendy might end up covering her classes for another few weeks if Vic didn't get this resolved soon. Hilton might even have to do some work for a change. "Absolutely."

As soon as Sharon left, a sense of unease blanketed her. The front of the office faced the street and was mostly glass, making Ellie feel exposed. With food in hand, she rushed down the hallway and into Vic's office.

"Lunch is here," she said with as much cheer as possible.

"Does Sharon want to join us?"

"I asked. She said no, so I suggested she head home. She shouldn't have to wait around for you to work. I'll sit in here, if that's okay with you."

He grinned. "Are you thinking after lunch you can have your way with me? I know how much you used to like doing it on the kitchen counter."

She stared at him. "You're kidding, right? Did you forget what we just finished doing?"

"Yeah, so?"

"Women need a break sometimes."

"Oh, so you want to wait until tonight. Got it. No problem."

When had he turned into a sex machine? "Haven't gotten out much lately, have you?"

Vic reached for the food. "Let's eat."

The avoidance told her a lot about him. Perhaps women had been afraid of a man with a scar. Their loss.

He moved the files and other paperwork to the side of his desk and spread out the food. "It smells heavenly," she said.

"It should taste just as good. Italiano's is the best."

She dished up her helping of lasagna as did Vic. She nodded to the computer. "What are you working on?"

"My old boss just faxed me the names of all my cases. It was like going down memory lane."

"Did you catch all the men you went after?" If not, the person targeting her family might believe Vic was still an FBI agent, and the man might want to stop him from continuing the investigation at all cost.

"More or less. I first checked to see if any of the criminals were out of jail. Good news. None are. That leaves either an accomplice or perhaps a relative who would come after us."

"That doesn't narrow it down a whole lot."

He shrugged. "I've solved cases on less."

She liked to hear that. "How far back are you going?"

"I've looked at the cases since we split up. I figure someone from five years ago might know you were my wife. Hell, he might still believe we're together."

Ellie couldn't imagine the additional pain she'd have gone through if she'd learned Vic had been burned in a fire. "That's logical. You have any names?"

He pushed back his chair and picked up three pages from the printer. "Eat first then you can look at these."

She slipped them from his fingers as he sat down. "I can do both."

As she ate the delicious meal, she perused the list. "I remember this man, Stanton Neely, only because this was the last case you had while we were together."

He winced. "Yes. He stands out in my mind because of that, too."

Ellie studied the rest of the names, digging deep into her memory. "I got nothing here."

"Do any of the last names sound familiar? Could one of them have come into the gallery to browse or maybe buy one of the paintings under the guise of checking you out?"

"I'm not the best with names—other than Washington, Lincoln, and an occasional Benjamin Franklin, but I don't recall anyone even debating buying a painting who didn't seem into art."

"That's too bad. The hard part now will be researching the relatives of the incarcerated men, or possibly any cellmates who've been released."

"That could take forever since that could be thousands of people."

Vic finished his piece of lasagna. "You have a better idea?"

She decided against suggesting they go back to Washington and investigate, in case the man who took a shot at Charlotte was some hired hand rather than the criminal. "Not really."

Vic waited until she finished off the last of her food, and

then dumped the containers in the trash. "Since you seem dead set against having sex with me, what do you want to do for the rest of the afternoon?"

She laughed. "Will you stop with the sex talk, already?"

"I can't help it." Vic stepped from the other side of the desk and held out his right hand. She placed her palm in his and he helped her stand. "I swear I haven't thought about getting laid— at least not this often—until you walked in that door a few days ago. So, it's really your fault for looking so damn sexy."

"You are such a suck up. You want me to look like a bag lady?"

"Might help."

Before she could tell him he was being ridiculous, he wrapped his good arm around her waist and pulled her close. When their lips met, pure rapture spiked through her, and every objection to them being together evaporated. As much as she wanted to strip him naked and do him right there, she was sore.

Ellie broke the kiss. "For one thing, the front door's open, and secondly, we need to wait."

"I know. I was just testing you."

She lightly punched him in the chest. "Jerk."

"I have an idea about how to spend some fun time."

She could use some levity. "Does it involve ropes of any kind?" Vic seemed to have a one-track mind.

He narrowed his eyes. "I like the way you think, but no. We have an indoor miniature golf course attached to the bowling alley. The good part is that it's in a room with black light. The balls are painted fluorescent orange, as are the holes. It's dark in there, which means no one would try anything."

When they first dated, they used to play miniature golf all the time and had a lot of fun. "Sounds great."

After they donned their coats, they exited the front entrance and Vic locked the door. "I think it might be best if you park in the back next time."

"I didn't know there was a back entrance."

"There is. I use it because I don't need people seeing my comings and goings."

"I'll remember that next time." Not that she'd be in her car alone anytime soon.

Once in the car, Vic directed her the four blocks east. The bowling alley seemed packed, but it made sense since it was a Saturday afternoon.

"Looks like we might get some bad weather," Vic said, as she located a spot close to the front.

"Just what we don't need. Getting snowed in would be bad."

"I don't know about that. Warm fire, hot coffee, lots of snuggling."

She could only shake her head. Where had this man been when they were married? Leaving the FBI seemed to have been good for him. She was happy he appeared content.

They hustled inside as the wind was biting and the sky gray. The noise from the pins, along with all the chatter, assaulted her—as did the smell of beer, oil, and perspiration.

Vic paid and the kid behind the counter handed them the golf balls. "It's around the side to the left."

"Thanks."

As they walked toward the back, Ellie thought Charlotte should be here. She loved to bowl. "Do you think we can call Charlotte? I want to make sure she's okay."

Vic placed a hand on her back and led her to the section where they could pick out their golf clubs. "I know this is hard for you because it's really hard for me, but it's best if we don't contact her. Trent is a good cop. He'll make sure nothing happens to her."

"I know, but I miss her. What harm can one little call do?"

"Phones can be traced."

Damn. "You think this guy is that smart?"

"Some criminals are unbelievably stupid while others are rather bright. We don't know who or what we're dealing with."

She didn't want to do anything that would jeopardize her daughter's safety. "Okay."

Vic pulled out his phone and her pulse jacked up. "Speaking of being able to trace phones, I want to make sure I always know where you are. There's a location setting on your phone as well as mine."

Vic showed her how to change the setting on hers. "In fact, I asked Charlotte to do it to her phone a while back." Vic brought up her number and a map appeared. "She's in Seffner. That's about an hour from here. It must be where Trent's cabin is. When we finish playing golf, we can check it again. I bet she'll be in the same spot."

Ellie gave Vic a hug. "Thank you. That makes me feel better."

"Ready to get trounced?"

"Trounced? I don't think so. If you recall, I could hold my own in this game."

He shook his head. "Back then, I let you win so I could get into your pants."

She tried to punch him, but he stepped out of the way and laughed. "Come on."

Chapter Thirteen

ELLIE HADN'T EXPECTED it to be so dark inside the black light room. She held onto Vic's arm, waiting for her eyes to adjust. "Everything is glowing. How do you know where to start?"

"The first hole is over here." Vic clasped his hand over hers and moved slowly to the other side of the room.

Good thing he could see. From the laughter, and the number of florescent-colored balls rolling on the floor toward the cups, she guessed about six kids were there. That made her feel better.

Vic stopped then leaned close. "Here's hole number one. Can you see how the course bends to the left?"

By now, her vision had adjusted to the new conditions. "Yes."

"You go first," he said.

He probably just wanted to see how fast the greens were. As Ellie bent down to place the ball on the rubber mat, she gasped.

"What's wrong," Vic said.

She stood up. "Why didn't you tell me you could practically see my yellow bra through my white blouse?"

He grinned and his teeth glowed. "Why did you think I suggested this place?"

"You didn't know this would happen. If I lose this game it's because I'm self-conscious."

"No one cares. Look around. The kids are all too absorbed in what they're doing."

He was right, but she wished she didn't stand out like a neon sign. Refocusing on the task at hand, she tapped the ball. It ricocheted off the right hand wall and headed toward the hole. *Yes!* Just as she was about to raise her arms in victory, the damn thing sailed past its target, hit the back wall, and returned halfway back. Crap. It might only be a stupid game, but she wanted to win.

"Good try, El. Go ahead and put it in. I don't want to accidentally bump your ball."

When she bent over again to take her second shot, Vic dragged his club between her legs. She jerked up. "What are you doing?" she whispered, not wanting the kids to hear.

"Trying to distract you."

She stepped within an inch of his face and playfully grabbed the front of his shirt. "Oh, I get it. You're afraid of losing. Perfectly understandable since you know I'm that good." He laughed, damn him. "Now, can you be good for the next half hour while I play my way to a win?"

He wrapped an arm around her waist, and placed his lips to her ear. "If you promise I don't have to be good after we leave, I'll behave."

It was her turn to chuckle. "Win and we'll negotiate."

Vic stepped back. "Deal."

For the next thirty minutes, they battled. She'd get ahead for a few holes, and then Vic would edge forward. Her winning flow was often disrupted when they were forced to wait for a group of kids to finish, but Ellie admitted she couldn't remember when she'd had such a good time. Even though bad shit might be happening outside this building, inside, she was insulated against the danger.

In the end, Vic won by two strokes. Damn. Now she'd never hear the end of it. He raised his club. "Want to go again?" he asked.

The release of tension had actually made her tired. "I think I'd like to go back to the house and maybe take a nap. My sleep patterns have been interrupted." She cleared her throat.

He tapped his chest. "Don't look at me."

"Ri-ight."

They returned their gear and headed out. The sky had turned leaden, but so far, no snow had fallen. "Do we need to stop at the store for food?" she asked.

"We're good, assuming you can handle frozen dinners and canned food."

It wasn't her first choice, but she wasn't sticking to her food plan while in Montana. The trip to his place only took about ten minutes. While she'd been here after someone shot at Charlotte, Ellie hadn't been paying attention. Now she studied his house. The exterior of his one-story home was brick. Other than having more trees on a bigger lot, his house looked similar to the one they'd owned many years ago in Virginia. "You chose well."

"I'm glad you like it."

From the hope in his tone, she could tell Vic wanted to talk about their future, but she'd only break his heart if they did. There was a time when Vic was her world. Her love had been unconditional, but he'd proven time and time again that his job was his real love. Given all the stuff that was going on, Ellie wasn't ready to think about how much he'd changed. She had a gallery to run in the nation's Capital, not to mention all the good friends she didn't want to leave. While Rock Hard had its artist enclaves, it wasn't like home, and it could never be a match in terms of culture.

Vic opened the front door and led her inside then slipped the case from her fingers. "I'll show you where you can stay."

Really? She assumed he'd want her to be in his room, but she wasn't going to complain.

He nodded to a room on the left. "This is where Charlotte would have stayed had she been here."

He walked Ellie to the next room. "I'm putting you in the master so you'll have an attached bath."

Now he was being silly. "Where will you sleep?"

"Don't worry about me."

Frankly, Ellie was getting tired of his bravado. "How about if I can't help but worry? You always want to shoulder the responsibility for all things." She had no idea why her voice had risen, but all the shit that had gone down in the last few weeks was coming to a head. "What about me?"

His brows pinched. "What about you? I'm trying to keep you from stressing out."

"By blocking me out? I feel so alone." She shook, and it wasn't from being cold.

"Hey, tell me what's wrong." Vic led her over to the bed and sat down next to her.

"You don't get it. The only way I'm going to get through this mess is if you tell me everything. If we share this experience by talking about our feelings, I might be able to better handle what's happening."

He picked up her hand. "I haven't hidden anything from you."

"What about your fears?"

He glanced away. "I don't know what you want me to say."

She withdrew her hand from his grasp. "I want you to tell me you're afraid of losing our daughter. I want to know I'm not the only one who's dying inside. You've been run off the road, yet you act as if it was an everyday occurrence. You won't even wear your fucking sling." Tears tumbled down her cheeks, and Vic drew her to his chest. She clung to him for dear life—for her sanity.

"I'm sorry. I was trying to protect you. I didn't want to add to your burden." He leaned back. "Am I afraid? Fuck yeah. In fact, I'm petrified I'll lose Charlotte or you. I want to keep you two safe so badly that I've had to put on this brave front. I'm scared shitless that when the time comes to stop this maniac, I might not react the way I should if I let my true feelings show." He looked away but the water in his eyes convinced her he meant every word he said. "I, too, want us to be a team, to get through this together. If I promise to try harder, will you forgive me?"

Ellie never expected him to admit to any vulnerability, and here he'd laid open his soul. "Yes. And thank you."

Vic nodded and stood. "I know you wanted to take a nap. I'll let you rest."

As he turned away, she grabbed his hand. "Stay with me?"

He didn't respond with his usual sexy, snarky comments. Instead, he kicked off his boots and removed his pants without saying a word. She did the same, but he finished undressing before her. Vic pulled down the spread.

"May I finish taking off your clothes?" he asked in the softest of voices. "I have so much to learn about being a good person. I've been trained to keep my emotions in check, so I'm not sure I know how to show them anymore."

"Wanting to change is half the battle." She wanted to tell him she didn't expect him to change overnight, but any explanation now would break the spell between them. Vic truly seemed to understand what she'd told him, and that meant to world to her. "I'd love for you to help me." Whether it was to take off her clothes or keep her from breaking down.

He knelt on the bed and lifted the sweater over her head. "You are so perfect."

The old saying that beauty was in the eyes of the beholder certainly held true. If he liked what he saw, who was she to argue? It would serve no good purpose. "Thank you."

Vic dropped his butt onto his heels. "I want to make love to you. Slowly. Gently. If you'll let me."

Vic never asked permission. He was the type to take what he wanted. Ellie wanted to show him that she needed him more than anything. She got up on her knees and slid her palms up his shirt, his warm skin pure heaven on her palms. She yearned to love every inch of his body until they both exploded with such an intense passion that they couldn't think from all their lustful feelings. Was she capable right now of taking her time and not rushing? She doubted it, but she wanted to try. Vic placed his hands over hers.

"Kiss me," she said.

Instead of the usual hard capture, the pressure was soft and tentative, almost as if every insecurity he'd ever possessed had leaked out of his body. With his right hand, he cupped her face and nibbled on her lips before dragging his kisses up to her eyes. "I'm sorry," he whispered so softly she almost missed the words.

She lowered her head. "I'm the one who should be sorry. I don't want to change you. I just can't be alone right now."

Vic lifted her chin. "I promise you won't be."

He hugged her close then nipped at her earlobe, sending shivers of pleasure up and down her spine. He leaned her back until she had to uncurl her legs. Without a word, Vic kissed the crests of her breasts above her bra. Using his thumbs, he lifted the material above her tits and cool air pebbled her nipples.

"I want to love them all night long." He dragged his tongue

across one nipple and then lavished his attention on the other. Pleasure bubbled.

She reached out and grabbed his cock. "I dare you to last more than an hour."

"Damn, girl. A man can dream can't he?" His words held a bit of bravado, but they were also laced with pain.

"I believe he should try." Today, he'd opened his heart and she wanted to enjoy it for as long as she could.

Vic dipped his head again and sucked each tip as if he was paying homage to her breasts. The slow movement ratcheted her desire.

"How about taking off those briefs?" she said. "I want to see my reward."

"You got it."

Vic continued to tease each nipple while he removed his boxer briefs with one hand. She glanced down at his erection and licked her lips. Soon, he'd be hers.

Vic palmed one breast while tugging on the other pert tip. His slow, seductive movements electrified her, but she didn't move, loving the care he was giving her. It was just what she needed. He nibbled, sucked, licked, and loved each nipple.

"Let's take this off," he said as he reached around her, unhooked her bra, and tossed it to the end of the bed.

He slid to his stomach, and instead of tugging off her panties, he licked his way down her belly. The hairs stood up straight as anticipation swept through her. She clutched the spread to keep from grabbing him again. As much as she wanted to suck on his dick, Vic was now in charge, and she didn't want to disturb the loving moment. This was the old Vic, the one she'd fallen in love with so long ago.

He inhaled deeply as he slid lower. "I love how you smell."

She had to think if she'd put on any perfume since showering. She hadn't, so it must be her freely flowing juices that had scented the air. Vic had a unique way of touching her that set her body spinning. Heat began at her core and spread upward and outward.

"Lick me," she panted.

"My goal is to make you come so many times, you'll beg me to take you."

"You can try."

She was close to that point already. Keeping his palm on her rounded belly, he slid lower and nibbled his way from one thigh to the other. She planted her feet on the bed and scooted nearer to him. He pressed down harder to keep her still.

"Be good. I want to take my time."

That would be hard for her. "When can I take my time on your cock?" She had yet to taste him.

"Soon."

Vic slid off her panties, and then ran a thumb over her clit. She bucked at the intensity, straining for more. Her womb coiled tight, in need of some friction. When he slipped one finger into her needy hole, her yearning grew more demanding. "That all you got?"

She couldn't help but toss out some sass. It was the way to his soul—or so she hoped. He threaded a second finger inside her and wiggled it around, banging it against her G-spot, and causing her climax to go off before she was ready.

Ellie closed her eyes and let the pleasure wash over her. It served as a brief respite from his tormenting. "Now, it's only fair to let me have a chance at you."

Vic slid up next to her and rolled onto his back. "Go for it."

Really? "You won't stop me?"

"Never said that. Remember, I'm in a weakened state."

She smiled. "Payback's a bitch."

Chapter Fourteen

V IC NEVER SHOULD have allowed El to suck on his cock. He
wasn't kidding when he said he was weak around her, but
he remembered it was one of her favorite things to do. Who was
he to deny her that pleasure? If only he could last long enough
to delve into her sweetness, he'd be content.

She lifted onto her knees and leaned over him. Dear God in
Heaven. Her tits swayed and her pussy glistened. He reached up,
and when he brushed his palms against her distended nipple, his
cock jerked.

She smiled then licked his cock from base to tip. He'd been
strong when those thugs had beaten him right before the
burning plank fell on him—but he sure wasn't now. He probably
wouldn't be able to keep from coming if she used her wicked
tongue on him.

El drew her lips around the head and grabbed his dick.
When she pumped her fist fast, he took hold of her wrist. "Be
careful or he'll explode."

"Don't worry. I know when to stop."

She always did have that knack. El scraped her teeth down-
ward, pressing hard enough to nearly set his climax in motion
but not too hard to break the skin. When the head of his dick
banged against the back of her throat, he closed his eyes to keep

from spiraling out of control.

Stay strong.

It was when she grabbed his balls and rolled them in her palm that all the previous memories of their lovemaking swamped him. He wouldn't last. With a swing of his leg, he was able to move away from her sexy mouth and land on his knees. "Bend over."

Gone was his ability to exercise control. He had to have her. Now. El got up on her elbows and spread her knees wide. Her offering nearly undid him. Vic placed his cock at her entrance and eased into her wetness. When the slick walls welcomed him, he let out a groan. Leaning over her back, he palmed her tits as his cock worked his way down her pussy. Her wet sheath hugged him tightly.

"I want to fuck you all night."

She laughed. The woman knew what she did to him and that was a dangerous thing, but he couldn't help himself. Everything about El was right. When he reached the end, he pulled out and plowed right back in again. He might have been able to dip into her many more times had she not pressed her hips back and clamped down on his cock at the same time.

"Jesus, El."

She lowered her head into her palms and pumped her hips back and forth. The rhythm, the friction, and her moans, along with her glorious breasts were too much for him.

El lifted up onto her palms, and increased the pace of her thrusting hips. When she stilled and yelled out his name, he, too, lost it. His balls drew up and he climaxed fast and furiously. Vic wrapped his arms around her waist and just held her. Being one with El was the ultimate high.

When their breaths calmed, she collapsed onto the bed, forcing him to pull out. After he helped her clean up, Vic crawled next to her and held her, hoping to provide some comfort for all that had happened.

WHEN ELLIE WOKE, bright sunlight streamed through the bedroom windows. She squinted and reached behind her to see if Vic was awake.

"Vic?"

When he didn't answer, she rolled over. He was gone and the sheets were cold. How long had he been up? The man always had been an early riser. She guessed some things didn't change. Only then did the rich aroma of coffee reach her. So that was where he was. The allure of caffeine was enough to get her out of bed.

She tossed off the blanket then immediately drew it up again. She was naked and the room was cold. Damn. Because the clothes wouldn't walk their way over to her, she steeled herself against the unpleasantness and dashed across the room, opened her case, and pulled out everything warm. With a speed that even surprised her, she was dressed in layers of fleece in under a minute.

After brushing her teeth and splashing cold water on her face, she headed out toward the divine smell. Vic was at the stove making eggs, looking quite manly being domestic.

"You're up," he said, without turning around. She hadn't been that loud and even had on her wool socks. How had he heard her?

"Yup." She moved behind him and was about to wrap her arms around his waist when she stopped.

That was what she used to do when they were married. Leaving would be harder if she fell into that habit again.

"Hope you still like scrambled eggs," he said.

"I do. That coffee I smell?"

"The black mug's yours. I already added a drop of cream."

Aw. He remembered. Ellie moved around him, picked up the cup, and brought it to her lips. The first taste was divine. "Perfect."

Outside, the sky was a cerulean blue, and the ground was covered in a few inches of clean white snow.

Vic looked over at her. "If you want, we can go out and play after breakfast."

"Play? I'm not getting naked in the snow."

He burst out laughing. "I've really fucked things up, haven't I? You must think I'm just a horny old man."

"If the shoe fits." She raised her brows.

Vic growled. "Watch it. I can still take you down. I only need one hand to tickle you."

Yikes. She was so sensitive. The slightest finger wiggle and she was a mess. "Trust me, I remember." She sipped her coffee and walked over to the kitchen table that was already set and sat down. "What time did you get up this morning?"

"Five."

"Why so early?"

"Couldn't sleep. I wanted to go through the names of the men I'd pissed off to see if any were potential suspects. Trust me there were a lot."

Ellie leaned her elbows on the table and made herself at home. Even though someone wanted to harm them, it didn't diminish the peacefulness of this morning. "Find any possibilities?"

"After breakfast, I'll show you the most promising names."

She didn't hold much hope, but she'd look anyway. Vic brought over the food on a platter. She helped herself, relaxing for the first time in a long while. "You really think you'll capture him?"

"Yes. Criminals slip up eventually. If it is the same person doing all of this, I'm a bit impressed that he'd travel from Virginia to Montana." Vic ate his eggs, washed it down with coffee, and then set his fork down. "Here's the thing. I get the sense he didn't want to harm you in Virginia."

"I was thinking about that. The only purpose of scaring me would be to drive me to you, but I didn't come for you. No offense."

"None taken, which makes me think this guy isn't very thorough—just pissed and obsessed with what I've done."

Ellie hadn't wanted to ask, but she needed to know. "Do you think he missed Charlotte on purpose because he thought it was me?" Her palms sweated.

"I don't know."

So they were back to square one. After they finished, she cleared the dishes while Vic retrieved his laptop.

"Take a look at these four men. I've narrowed it down the best I could. They've all had a known address in Virginia at some point in their life and were related or associated with the men I've put in jail." Vic turned the computer toward her.

She studied each man, trying to imagine him with or without a beard, with or without glasses, and even with different colored hair. "Sorry, I don't recognize any of them. Can you forward these to my phone? Perhaps something will come to me later."

"Sure. I'll keep looking."

Ellie didn't know why she was so disappointed. Had she really expected it to be that easy? Part of her wanted to believe it would be. Then again, if she could point to the man, Vic would have arrested him, and she'd have headed home. The thought of returning to her life should excite her, but somehow it didn't.

"Want to build a snowman?" Vic asked.

"A snowman?"

"It's easy. Make a snowball and then roll it into a big ball. Repeat three times."

"I know how to make a snowman." They'd made many of them when Charlotte was little.

"Or we can do a snow woman if you want to be gender unbiased."

She laughed. "I can't imagine what you'd use for nipples."

"Coal?"

She didn't want to get into that discussion. She seemed to be taking after Vic since her mind had gravitated toward something sexual. Had they been this active when they first met? She mentally shrugged. That was so long ago she couldn't remember.

"Works for me." Ellie pushed back her chair. "Let me suit up. I'm not used to the cold like you are."

Vic followed her. Only then did she remember she was in his room. She pulled on her jacket, hat, gloves, and boots. Vic did the same.

"Remember when Charlotte was really little, we had to fight with her to even play outside?" Vic asked. "She hated the cold."

"She seems to relish it now." Proof that people could change. "I remember when you started making a snowman, Charlotte watched you from the window. She wanted to help so badly, she finally gave up her fear and joined you." Ellie leaned back with a smile.

"I remember. What do you say to making more memories?" Vic asked.

"Sure." As dangerous as those might be.

Ellie and Vic stepped outside, the reflection of the sun off the snow nearly blinding her. She shielded her eyes and studied the surroundings. While there were a few homes nearby, basically they were out in the open with the majestic mountains in the background. "It's so quiet," she said.

Vic nodded. "That was the first thing I noticed about this state when I came out here—its vastness and its serenity."

While it was cold outside, the lack of wind made it pleasant. "How about a contest?"

Vic shook his head. "You don't learn, do you? I'm going to win. What will be my reward?"

"Nothing sexual."

"Spoilsport."

She laughed. "The loser has to give the winner a foot rub."

"How does that not lead to sex? You know a good massage is foreplay."

Ellie blew out a breath. Poor Vic. "If this is the way you treat your dates, it's no wonder you're alone."

He pinched his brows together. "Ouch. I'll have you know I could have any woman I want. I just haven't found anyone in Rock Hard that has excited me."

"Say it a few more times and you might believe it." She was getting off track. "Will you promise to be an impartial judge when you see what I build?"

"Absolutely. Is there a time limit?"

"Yes. Whoever finishes first gets to call time."

"Deal."

Ellie really hadn't thought this through. She had initially thought she'd build a snow woman, but that was too common. She was an artist and creativity was her game. While Vic began rolling snow to make a ball, she decided to go with an ice-fishing scene. Getting on her hands and knees, she began to dig a hole that would represent where a person would fish, and then she'd craft a fishing pole of sorts next to it. On the side of the hole would be a pail and some fish.

"Do you remember the one Christmas when we took Charlotte sledding?" Vic asked.

She was about to say they'd taken their daughter sledding only one time together, but it hadn't been his fault he couldn't be home. With a few exceptions, Vic had called to wish them a happy holiday.

"Yes. Charlotte mentions it from time to time."

He blew out a breath. "Yeah, I bet she does because it was so rare for me to be there for her."

The pain in his voice tore at her. Ellie didn't want to turn the day into remembering all the sadness. With the hole dug, she made a pole. She next fashioned a fairly large fish with his mouth open. If she had time to scrounge up some stones for the eyes, she would add them. Next came the pail. She thought she was done, until she studied the fishing pole. Damn, but she needed a line.

Ellie sat on the ground and unlaced her boot. She then stuffed the eyelet in the end of the rod. She glanced over at Vic who seemed to be making excellent progress. Ellie needed to find those stones for the eyes. They'd add a lot to the finished product.

Vic placed the head on his snowman. Darn. She needed to delay him. She made three snowballs. If he looked over, because she'd stacked them, he'd think they were part of her design.

When he wasn't looking, she heaved one at him and hit him squarely in the back. He turned around.

"You want to fight? I'll show you a fight."

Vic rolled a handful of snow into a ball and tossed it at her. It didn't have a lot of force, which enabled her to step out of the way. "Missed. Ha, ha."

As he bent down to make another snowball, she picked up two from her arsenal. Just as she rushed closer to make sure she wouldn't miss, Vic pounced on her and stuffed the snow down her front.

She froze both literally and figuratively. She patted her chest to help absorb the cold, but that only made the snow turn to liquid and drip down to her waist. "That wasn't fair."

His eyes widened. "Fair? Who threw the first snowball?"

"I did, but you should have confined the fight to throwing not stuffing."

"Really?" Vic was now standing inches from her, but she could tell he was baiting her to do something else.

"Really."

"Nineteen years of marriage and I didn't think you would stoop so low." He nodded to her chest. "You need help getting warm?"

By now, her body had heated the wetness. "What do you think you could do?"

"Lick it dry?"

When had he turned so ridiculous? And fun. And charming. "I think we should judge our work now even though I'm not quite done."

"Okay, I'll look at yours and you can look at mine." He grinned.

"We are talking about our sculptures, right?"

He laughed. "Certainly, I'm not sex crazed."

"Uh-huh."

With her head held high, Ellie walked past him and studied the lopsided snow person. "Why is the head bigger than the body?" It was the strangest snowman in the world.

"That's an imitation of me. I have a fat head."

"Meaning you are a fat head?"

"Yup."

This was becoming rather strange. At least he'd given the figure feet and a nose. He hadn't found any objects to make the eyes or mouth yet though. "You gave this snow person ab-dominals?" She'd never seen a snowman with rippled stomach muscles. "Snowmen are supposed to be round, not flat."

He said nothing. She walked back to where he was staring at her work. "Is something wrong?"

"No. It's remarkable. How did you think of this?"

The awe in his tone pleased her. "I am an artist, remember?"

"A painter, not a sculptor."

It wasn't that good. "So do I win?"

"Hell yeah. One foot massage coming up. I can't wait. Let's go."

Somehow, she had a feeling Vic would not limit the touching to just her feet.

Chapter Fifteen

"WHAT WOULD YOU like to do for the evening? Cards or a board game?" Trent stood in the living room at a cabinet filled with games.

Charlotte sidled up next to him. "How about chess?"

All day long, Trent had acted like she was fifteen and he was some old man. She wanted to show him that while she didn't excel at math or science in school—or any subject other than art for that matter—she wasn't dumb. Just disinterested.

"You really know chess?"

When her father had been home, the two of them liked to play and Dad was really good. His mind worked about ten moves ahead. "Why don't we try and see?"

"Okay." Trent set the board on the coffee table between them. "You can have white."

That meant she'd go first. Her standard opening involved moving her pawn in front of the knight.

"Hmm. What should I do?" Trent mimicked her move.

The start of the game was often the same. Next she put her bishop in the spot where the pawn had been, thus protecting her rook from being captured by a sneaky bishop.

"I see you have played before."

She liked the grudging respect. Trent moved another pawn.

She wasn't sure of his strategy, but she methodically marched her pieces forward. While Trent moved quickly and decisively, she managed to capture his King. "Checkmate!"

Victory never tasted sweeter.

He blew out a breath. "I have to say I misjudged you, Charlotte. Care to try again?"

They had nothing else to do. It wasn't as if he'd suggested they have wild passionate sex by the fireplace or anything. If he had, she would have answered the same. "Sure."

They ended up playing four games. She won two of them, though on the last game, she suspected Trent purposefully lost. Maybe he thought a happy prisoner would be easier to deal with.

Even though she wanted to stay up and chat with him, she was unable to stop yawning. "Sorry. It's been a long day. I'd like to take a shower and hit the hay."

Trent nodded. "It's not every day you get shot at." He dumped the chess pieces back in the velvet bag and stored them in the closet. "I'll say one thing, Charlotte."

"What's that?"

"You are one cool chick."

Cool, as in he liked her? Or cool in that she hadn't freaked out after possibly dying? Given that Trent was her bodyguard, she decided he meant the latter. "I guess I take after my dad in that department."

"Remind me to thank him." He smiled and her insides gushed. Damn, but he was one good looking man. What a shame, he was only her bodyguard.

Trent said he wanted to read a bit before going to bed. She suspected the real reason was to give her some privacy in the bathroom since they had to share one. He'd already shown her where his dad kept the extra towels, shampoo, and conditioner in case she hadn't brought any. She debated locking the bathroom door, but she was curious what Trent would do if she didn't.

After she undressed and stepped into the shower, the reality of what could have happened had she not stumbled backward began to sink in. Sure, she'd overheard her parents talk about Dad getting shot at, but she never really thought about how it might make a person so scared afterward. She shivered just thinking about her father beaten to the point of unconsciousness and then burned. What turmoil had he gone through after almost dying? She couldn't imagine why anyone would willingly put himself in danger like that.

Dad always claimed it was to keep the country safe. Her respect for him grew, but it also petrified her. What if, after this person was caught, more crazies came after him? Or her? Her father probably had a ton of people who hated what he did.

Stop it.

This wasn't helping to calm her, and if she didn't get some sleep, she'd be a basket case by morning. At least she was safe here with Trent, but what would happen when she went back home? Would she be looking over her shoulder all the time? Would she need counseling for almost dying?

Charlotte's stomach twisted. Dwelling on what happened wouldn't help her mental state. She washed her hair and scrubbed her body hoping to erase all trace of that terrible man. Not wanting Trent to run out of hot water when he needed it, she shut it off and dried. Crap. Her pajamas were in her room. Hmm.

Wrapping a towel around herself, she checked the hallway, and then tiptoed to her room. Part of her was a little disappointed that Trent had kept his distance. Then again, he was a cop. If her dad had been a bodyguard for anyone, he wouldn't have seduced the person.

Sometimes nobility sucked.

Once in her bedroom, she put on her pajamas and climbed into bed. She could only hope that sleep came quickly.

✧　✧　✧

SOMETHING WOKE CHARLOTTE from her restless slumber, but she wasn't aware of what it was exactly. A door handle rattling perhaps? A dog barking? She didn't know, but as long as she was awake, she might as well get up and pee. She checked her cell. It was 3:24 a.m. God, but it was early.

Rubbing her arms to ward off the cold, she stepped into the hallway. Light glowed near the kitchen. What was Trent doing up at this hour? She inhaled to see if maybe he was making coffee or heating up some food. It smelled like whatever he was doing was burning. Had he left something on the stove and fallen asleep on the couch?

Charlotte turned toward the kitchen and yawned. "Trent? What are you making?"

No answer.

As she neared the kitchen, only the lights from the stove display glowed. What the hell? As she turned to go back, lights flickered outside the living room window. A car's headlights? Her heart beat madly. What was going on? Trent had drawn the drapes so she couldn't see outside. Then came sounds of something scratching and being scraped along the ground.

Okay, that wasn't good. What should she do? If she screamed, whatever was outside would hear her. Rather than peek her head out from behind the curtains and chance getting blown to smithereens, Charlotte decided to rouse Trent. Her heart pounded as her fogged brain finally woke up. "Trent? Wake up," she shouted as she raced toward his bedroom.

If this were a false alarm, she'd apologize later. But some shit was happening. His door sat ajar and she barged in. As if she'd entered a time warp, things stood still. His light was on and Trent was in the process on putting on his jeans—commando style. She'd seen men get dressed before, but none that looked as amazing as he did. His cock was hard, probably from being roused out of his sleep, but that only made her stare.

As he finished zipping up his jeans, he turned and faced her. "What's wrong?"

The words stuck in her throat. "Someone's here. It smells like fire."

Trent's face hardened. He rushed to his dresser drawer and grabbed his weapon. "Stay here."

She wanted to tell him to put on shoes and a shirt, but he raced on by before she could say anything more. Charlotte was tempted to follow him, but what if that madman was out there? She glanced around to see if there was some place to hide. His bedroom was situated in the back of the house with windows on both the west and north sides. Most likely, they'd be locked. If they weren't, she wasn't about to climb out and be captured. The closet door sat open, but it was too small to hide in. Shit.

Noise sounded outside, as if Trent had gone out to investigate. Then the front door banged closed, but she didn't want to peek out for fear of giving away her location. Damn. She wanted to stay calm, but her pulse was racing and her mouth had turned dry. She pressed her back against the wall and looked around for something to use as a weapon if whoever was outside got by Trent. Other than his suitcase on the floor, there was nothing heavy or sharp to use.

Before she could come up with a strategy, the bedroom door opened. "Someone set the porch on fire, but I used the fire extinguisher to put it out. You okay?"

Okay? How could she be okay when her heart was in her

throat? There'd been a fire? The light she'd seen must have been the flames. She inhaled, and could now smell the burning wood.

"Yes. I think so. What happened?" That was a stupid question since he just told her the porch caught fire.

"Someone knows we're here."

Charlotte's legs gave way and she slid down the wall. She choked out a gasp. "How did he find me?"

"I don't know, but he'll make a mistake, and I'll get him. Fuck. Someone sure must be pissed at your dad if they'd go to this extreme." He pulled out his phone and pressed one button. He paced as the cell rang. "Hey, it's me. Got a problem." Trent explained about the front porch fire, and then detailed how all the hedges along the front of the house had caught fire, but that he'd put it out before the flames reached the wooden windows. "I'm at my dad's place in Seffner." He turned his back to her. "I'd say about an hour." Trent gave him the address then disconnected.

"That wasn't my dad was it?" He'd probably call in the National Guard once he found out.

"No. That was Max Gruden, Rock Hard's Fire Marshall and arson investigator. How about coming into the kitchen. I need some coffee." He grabbed hold of the doorknob and held it open.

"How about putting on a shirt first?" She didn't need the distraction of his amazing body. His face and chest were a bit red, which she figured was from the cold. "And some socks, at least. You must be freezing."

A small smile lifted his lips. "I hadn't even noticed. Sorry. Might I suggest the same? No telling who Max will bring."

She looked down at her flannel pajamas. While her nipples weren't protruding, she'd feel better dressed. "Good idea."

❖   ❖   ❖

TRENT TOSSED ON a sweater and some wool socks before heading to the kitchen to make coffee. He needed something to perk him up, and he bet Max would, too, when this was all done. While Trent was capable of doing the forensic work—checking for tire markings and asking questions, he didn't want to leave Charlotte. Poor girl was beginning to crack, and an absent bodyguard wouldn't help her state of mind. He had to hand it to her, though. At least she hadn't panicked. No telling what would have happened if she'd stepped outside to investigate. Cripes.

As much as he didn't like rousing his boss at this hour, Trent trusted the RHPD a hell of lot more than he did the older-than-shit Seffner sheriff, who at this moment, might even be sleeping off a hangover in his own cell. Craig Duvall was a great guy, but since this tiny town rarely had crime, he wouldn't have the manpower or the equipment to do the job right.

Trent called Dan Hartwick. His boss answered on the first ring. "How's Charlotte?"

Nothing got past that man. "Don't you sleep?"

"Some."

"We had an incident tonight." He explained the situation.

"I'll send up a few men. I might even show up myself. I'd like to meet Vic's daughter. She might be the key to all this."

"Could be, but remember Vic was run off the road. The fact his ex-wife was stalked, makes it look like he's the real target."

"Who's covering the hit and run?"

"Not sure. I've been busy with the shooting and now the fire."

"I'll check it out. Catch you soon." He disconnected.

Trent was busy with the coffee when Charlotte came in. Her eyes were red, looking as if she had been crying. His heart ached. He finished putting the grounds in the machine then sat across from her at the kitchen table. "Want to tell me exactly what happened?"

She wet her lips. "Can I have a beer?"

He chuckled. "At four in the morning? Sure. You can have anything you want, sweetheart." Shit, he hadn't meant for that endearment to slip out.

Trent jumped up, not wanting her to see the heat racing up his face. If he hadn't believed he was the best person to watch over Charlotte, he wouldn't have volunteered. She might be pretty, but it was her attitude that he liked. She was someone who seemed to know what she wanted and had no problem going after it—like being a success in the interior design field and getting her dad back. He grabbed a beer, twisted off the cap, and handed it to her.

She tipped back the bottle and drank. Letting out a deep breath, she set it down. "Okay. I wasn't sleeping very deeply when I heard a noise."

"What kind?"

"I don't know. I had to use the bathroom and was in the hall when I noticed light flickering near the kitchen. I went to investigate, thinking you might be in here getting a drink. That's when I smelled something burning. My addled brain couldn't put the pieces together. When I neared the living room, lights flashed from the outside and I thought it was headlights."

"It probably was. Did you see flames?"

"The drapes were closed and I didn't want anyone to spot me looking out." She looked up at him, her chin lifted.

"That was smart."

It would take Dan about an hour to get his crew together, but Max might get here sooner. Regardless, once the men arrived neither of them would get any sleep. "I think I'll make some scrambled eggs and some of those cinnamon rolls you bought."

"Yum. I love those."

Having her keep busy would help prevent a possible break-down. "You want to work on the rolls while I do the eggs?"

"I can do that."

To his surprise, Charlotte seemed to find everything with ease. To top it off, she was efficient with her time, setting the oven first before making the rolls. Her clear-headed actions told him she was handling this new situation as well as anyone could.

"Can I ask you something?" She placed the rolls in the oven, set the timer, and came over to the stove.

"Shoot." He whipped the eggs and added some milk.

"Weren't you afraid to be outside with an arsonist?"

He hadn't really given it much thought. "He's not after me. Besides, I didn't want the house to burn down."

"Why set the house on fire in the first place? There's not much that could burn. Was he hoping to draw you outside then shoot you? With you dead, he could rush in and take me."

Trent poured the eggs into the hot pan. "Excellent point. If I'm out of the way, he could do what he wished with you." He kept his voice light, hoping to ease her fears, but it seemed to backfire. He changed his tactics. "Perhaps I need to teach you how to shoot a gun so you can defend yourself."

She chuckled and the sound delighted him. "What makes you think I can't shoot a gun?"

She was right. Her dad had been an FBI agent. Vic would understand his job could result in harm to his family. "I wasn't thinking. You any good?"

She shrugged. "Not really, but I have my concealed weapons permit."

"That's a start, but one can never get too much practice."

"You're right."

He stirred the eggs, and when they were done, he dumped

them on the plate. Just as he carried them over to the table, the oven timer dinged. The rolls were ready. In companionable silence, they ate a very early breakfast. Trent was more curious about Charlotte than ever before, but it would be best for both of them if he didn't learn more about her. Keeping his distance was the only way to keep her safe.

She devoured all of her eggs and two cinnamon rolls. Impressive.

"You're quiet," she said.

"Been thinking."

"About what?"

"You."

Chapter Sixteen

CHARLOTTE WASN'T SURE she liked the tone of Trent's voice. "What about me?"

"After what happened, we can't stay here. Not only does it smell bad, but what's to stop the guy from trying again?"

Damn. "You're right. Want to come live with me in Kalispell?" She laughed to make sure he knew she was kidding. Actually, she was only half kidding.

"After I speak with the Fire Marshall and my boss, I want to call your dad and discuss an option with him."

She noticed the lack of direct response. "What kind of option?"

"I'll let you know when it's decided."

That wasn't very nice. He was cutting her out of the decision making process. Fine. "I guess I should gather my things then, not that I've unpacked much." Charlotte pushed back her chair. "Will you be coming with me?" She held her breath.

"Possibly not."

Her shoulders slumped. She searched his face to see if that made him happy, but she couldn't tell. Well, damn. Now things had gone from bad to worse. The whole fire thing still didn't make sense. They were missing some big puzzle piece, as her dad used to say. Why not wait until they had to leave for groceries or something or get some fresh air and then take her out? Could it be this man was trying to lure her dad there? Was his plan to get all three of them together and then start firing?

Her stomach almost heaved. Rushing to the bedroom, she gathered her gear. As soon as Trent finished with the fire person and his boss, he'd want to take her away. Again. If he wouldn't stay with her, would she be safe?

Speculating would only cause more anxiety. She'd learn her fate soon enough.

When a knock sounded on the front door, she jumped. Her nerves were clearly shot. She snapped her suitcase closed and wheeled it out to the living room. Trent said they needed to leave once he spoke with the experts. A tall man, about ten years older than Trent, was in the kitchen. Charlotte stepped in.

Trent smiled, and her heart lightened. "This is Charlotte, Vic's daughter. Charlotte, this is Max Gruden, the man who will hopefully figure out who did this."

They shook hands. "I'm well acquainted with your dad. I'm sorry this has happened."

She shrugged. "Dad has spent his life trying to make our country a better place. I guess it's not surprising there might be repercussions."

Max smiled. "I see he's rubbed off on you."

"I guess he has."

Max turned back to Trent. "Rich is outside taking pictures of the area and collecting samples of the ground, checking for an accelerant. Given how much burned, I'm thinking it was arson."

"That would be my guess, too," Trent said.

Another knock sounded, and a stately man entered. He was dressed in a suit, which seemed a bit odd, especially at this hour.

Trent straightened and nodded to the man. "Dan."

Ah, Trent's boss. Dan faced her. "You want to tell me what

happened?"

✧　✧　✧

VIC WAS CURLED up next to El, dreaming of their early years together when the jarring sound of his phone roused him. He didn't want to wake her, so he grabbed his cell and slipped out of bed. The display indicated it was Dan Hartwick. Oh, fuck. This couldn't be good.

He hurried to the hallway. "What's happened?"

"Sorry to disturb you. Charlotte and Trent are okay."

Vic reached out and steadied himself against the wall. The hits kept on coming. "Tell me."

Dan told him about the fire; how Trent had quickly put it out. "Trent wants to speak with you."

Vic made his way into the kitchen and flipped on the light, his anger building.

"Vic? I want to move Charlotte."

They couldn't stay where they were. "Good. Where are you thinking?"

"I have a cousin in Billings who's a cop. In fact, her whole family is cops. She's tough and good. I just wanted to check with you first. I can't be sure I'm focusing all that well. If Charlotte hadn't woken up and seen the lights, I don't know what might have happened."

Fuck. "Dan said your house was brick. It wouldn't have burned much."

"Not unless the roof caught fire, but Charlotte's theory is that this person wants you to come up with Ellie to see if she's okay. If all three of you are in the same place, he can take you out."

Vic had to be the target. "She might be right. Go ahead and move her, but can you give her a burner phone so El can speak with her? She's going crazy with worry."

"Absolutely. I'll let you know when we're settled and give you the number."

"Thanks." After Trent hung up, Vic grabbed a beer. It was five in the morning and probably time to get up anyway.

"Vic? Did I hear you talking with someone?"

Shit. He hadn't meant to wake her. El was in her wool socks and gown looking beautiful as ever. "Let's get back to bed and I'll tell you."

She clamped a hand on his arm. "What is it? I can see something's wrong."

"It's cold out here." He was barefoot and shirtless. "I can think better in bed." This time, he wasn't making up an excuse to make love with her.

"You don't drink unless something bad happened."

El was too damned perceptive. He led her into the bedroom and insisted she crawl under the covers. Vic set the bottle on the nightstand then turned off the light.

He needed her warmth and her loving body. Gathering her in his arms, she placed her head on his chest. "That was Trent." She stiffened. "Don't worry. Our daughter is fine."

"Vic. Tell me." Her words pierced him like sharp nails.

He detailed the fire. "Only the porch and some plants burned. The snow prevented most of the damage."

She lifted up on her elbow. "I want to speak with her."

"I need to get you a burner phone. Trent's getting Charlotte one. He knows you'll want to speak with her to make sure she's okay."

El hugged him tight. "I'm scared, Vic. It was one thing when someone was after me, but to attack my family, I won't stand for it."

He kissed her forehead. "Good, but let's see what Max

comes up with. He figured out who'd tried to kill me before. Maybe he can do it again."

El didn't say anything for a while. "Do you think Charlotte is really okay?"

Vic stroked her cheek. "Trent said she's doing well. He's moving her to Billings as we speak. She'll be staying with a family of cops."

"That's all well and good, but I meant emotionally. How do you think she's holding up? First she learns you've been hurt, only to have someone shoot at her. Then her safe house is set on fire."

Vic tried to smile. "This is Charlotte we're talking about. We, or rather you, raised her to be resilient. If anyone knows how to get through a difficult situation, she does."

El nodded. "I hope you're right, but she's young." She ran her hand up and down his chest. "I just hope this ass doesn't figure out where she's gone."

"He won't. Trent will take extra precaution."

She lowered her hand closer to his cock. Did she have any idea how much he needed her right now? His whole life was unraveling. El and Charlotte were the most important people in his life, and he was helpless to do a damn thing to keep them from harm. "I wish I had the answers."

El lifted her head and glanced up at him. "Do you think I'm safe?" Her voice shook.

"I want to say nothing can harm you, but right now, I don't know what to think. This guy seems to know our every move, but we will get him."

"When?"

"Soon."

She cradled her head on his chest again, and when she sobbed, Vic's heart cracked. He rubbed her shoulder, trying to soothe her.

El sniffled. "Make love with me, Vic."

He stilled, his mind going a million miles an hour. Pain emanated from her, and then entered his body. He needed the loving as much as she did, but he feared he might do something to ruin the fragile bond that existed between them.

Stop analyzing. She needs me. Just say yes.

"It would be my pleasure."

She rolled onto her back and pulled him on top. "Make me feel again. I've been dead inside for a long time, but when I'm with you, I come alive. I probably should be pacing the floor with worry or ranting and raving, but then I'd go crazy. I need some normalcy right now. Some goodness. Some loving."

Despite his own soul shattering, he smiled at her words. "You're a poet."

"I'm just an artist."

He wasn't worthy of her. El was so good and he'd failed her many times, but if she'd find comfort in his arms, he wouldn't deny her.

With as much tenderness as he was capable of giving, he feathered kisses on her lips, her cheeks, her eyes, and her forehead. "I want to be one with you," he whispered.

He wanted to add the word *forever*, but he didn't dare. This wasn't about El loving him. It was about her banishing demons and finding safety in his arms. He would do anything to give her what she needed.

El pulled down his head and returned his kiss, only she wasn't delicate. Her need came out strong. "I won't break, Vic. I want to feel passion. Desire. Desperation. Make me believe I'll shatter without you."

Jesus, but those words seared holes in his heart. If only she meant what she said. He had enough passion, desire, and desperation for the two of them, but he worried if he showed his true side, she'd realize how much he loved her. Right now, that love was killing this family.

He unbuttoned her flannel gown. "I thought about turning on the lamp but then decided I'd rather explore your body inch by inch with my tongue and my hands."

"Promises, promises." She grabbed his cock through his flannel bottoms. "How about taking these off so I can love you the same way."

Her mood had suddenly changed, but deep inside she was most likely grieving. El had learned over the years how to push back the bad in life and grab hold of the good. From the way she had a grasp on his cock, she was going for the gusto.

He chuckled. "Gotta let go of it for a moment."

She did. "Be quick."

He rolled off her. As he slipped off his bottoms, she slid out of her gown. By now, his eyes had grown accustomed to the darkness, and the scant light from the hall outlined her delicious breasts. "You are truly amazing to look at."

"You can't see me."

"I can. I'm Superman and have X-ray vision." Damn, now wasn't the time to joke, but the words had slipped out. It was what Charlotte had called him when things were good between them.

"Okay, Superman. What am I doing now?"

Damn. He couldn't see. "You tell me."

"I'm playing with myself." She was trying to drive him insane. Fortunately, she was back to teasing him, and he could handle that emotion better.

"That's *my* job, or did you forget?" he asked with more levity than he felt. If she shot him down, he could say he was just playing.

"I must have forgotten."

"Would you like me to show you what I can do for you?"

She raised her arms. "Hug me first?" Her voice cracked. Gone was the temptress. In its place was a scared woman.

The need to embrace her ran deep in his soul. He crawled on top of her again and gathered her in his arms, leaning heavily on his right elbow. Her breasts pressed against his skin, her nipples burning holes in his body. He lowered his hand and gently sucked on her neck, and then dragged kisses down to her shoulder. To take the pressure off his injury, he rolled onto his right side and slid down so that his lips were close to her breasts. He ran a tongue across one nipple as he placed his palm on her belly. Her stomach fluttered and she wove her fingers through his and squeezed.

Without any words, he understood her need. El was floundering, hurting for her daughter. Vic wanted to take his time, but with each lick, his need grew.

With her free hand, she grabbed his head and pressed hard. Her breaths increased with each swirl of his tongue. This was the woman he'd fallen in love with—the one who reacted to his every touch. He leaned across her body, seized the other nipple, and pulled it taut.

"Yes!" El's head dropped back. What this woman did to him.

If he didn't taste her, he'd expire. As slowly as he could, he crawled between her knees and slid down. Dragging his lips from her belly to her pussy, he reached up and strummed his thumb across her nipple. The delicate tip puckered. El was everything he wanted in a woman. Too bad, she'd never be his again. He'd abandoned his family too many times. He doubted she'd believe him if told her he never would again.

When he dipped his tongue into her sweet honey, she bent

her knees and lifted her hips. "Vic, please."

Wanting to keep the wonderful connection alive for as long as he could, he was hesitant to take her too soon. Touching her was the ultimate high. It washed away the horrors of what he'd seen in his life and made him believe—if only for a moment—that life could be good again.

Vic plunged a finger into her hole and swirled it around. El bucked and thrashed, groaned and moaned. At this moment, she was his to love and to have. He crawled on top of her and nudged his cock into her opening an inch.

"I want you," he whispered.

Leaning over, he captured her lips, tasting, devouring, claiming. She wrapped her arms around his neck and pulled him even closer. Then she broke the kiss and dragged her lips to his ear. "Fuck me now or you'll pay."

Chapter Seventeen

V IC ALMOST LAUGHED at the way El growled at the end of her plea. Using every ounce of restraint, he eased in, loving the way her pussy fit him like a glove. It was as if they were meant for each other. Wanting to last as long as possible, he edged his way in as he nibbled on her ear. She grabbed his arms, and he couldn't help but flex his muscles.

"How about putting some of that strength into pounding me hard? I need the release now," she begged.

"Demanding, aren't we?"

"Damn right I am."

El lifted her hips and his cock drove straight to the end. Jesus, what she did to him. He fucked her hard and fast, just the way she wanted it.

"Vic, yes. Don't stop."

She opened her mouth once more and drew him in. He wanted to pretend all her hot passion was because she loved him again, but he knew better. Their scare tonight had brought them together—but for how long? Vic sparred with her, dipping and plunging as he drove into her velvety smoothness.

El raked her nails down his back then broke the kiss to scream her release. When she tightened her hold on his cock, he let go, and his hot seed spurted. He dipped his head to her neck, trying to memorize the elation coursing through him. Not wanting to put too much weight on her, he rolled off and rested, waiting for his heart to calm.

"Let me clean you up," he said as soon as he was able to talk.

Vic walked into the bathroom and when he returned with a warm cloth, El was already dressed in her gown. He couldn't blame her. It was cold in the room, but he planned to warm her up very soon.

✦　✦　✦

ELLIE NEVER SHOULD have turned to Vic last night, but she'd needed him. To be honest, she seemed to be doing that a lot lately. Could it be that he'd changed? Or was the pressure getting to her? She liked to think it was the latter. Vic had a new life here and she was just starting hers in Virginia.

"Ready?" Vic asked.

It was time for them to go to work. "Sure. Do you think I can ask Sharon to go shopping with me for some paints? Sitting all day isn't my style."

"We'll see what she has to do, though she might be able to protect you better than I can. While she probably sucks in hand-to-hand combat, she won't let anyone get a drop on you." If he hadn't smiled, she'd have been worried.

"It's broad daylight. You think he'd try something?"

"No."

She wanted to believe him.

When they arrived at his office, Sharon looked up and smiled. "You're here! Glad no more tragedy happened over the weekend." Papers were strewn on her desk, looking as if she might be busy for the rest of the day. Darn.

"Actually, our daughter had a little incident, but I'll let El fill you in. I have a lot of research to do in light of the fire." He leaned over and kissed El on the cheek.

The casual way he did that told her things had gotten a little out of control. Vic was no longer tentative around her. While she enjoyed the relaxed time with him, she didn't want him to believe they were back together.

"Fire? Holy shit. Sit down and tell me everything," Sharon said with renewed energy.

Ellie wasn't sure she wanted to relive her fears, but perhaps retelling it might not make what happen seem so bad. "I don't know all that much, except that the person after us tried to burn down Detective Lawson's cabin—with them inside."

Sharon sucked in a breath. "That's horrifying. Are they okay?"

"Yes. No one was harmed. Just scared."

"I bet. Does Vic think it's the same person who tried to run him off the road and who shot at Charlotte?"

"He won't comment except to say your Fire Marshal is on the case."

"Ah, hunky Max Gruden. He used to be a cop, you know."

"Vic never said." Ellie wondered what else he never mentioned. She pushed back her chair. "I should get out of your hair. Looks like you have a lot to do today."

"Nah. These are old papers. Makes the boss think I'm doing something."

Ellie laughed. She needed that. "Would you be up for a little shopping then?"

Sharon's eyes widened. "What are you looking for?"

"Since I have no idea how long I'm going to be here, I'd hoped to get some Acrylic supplies. Vic said I could use the back room for my art."

Sharon grabbed her purse. "Let's go. I'll just tell Vic we're headed out."

That was easy. "Thanks."

Once Vic gave his blessing, they were on their way. This small town was such a far cry from Washington, D.C. with all its congestion and one-way streets. "Is this rush hour?" she asked. It was eight-thirty, yet not many cars were on the road.

Sharon laughed. "Rush hour? Rock Hard wishes it had a rush hour. Pretty much the streets look like this all the time, unless it snows. Then people wait for the snowplows before doing anything." She headed down Second Street and pulled in front of Charley's Crafts. "Here we are. I'm not sure how much he carries."

Ellie really didn't care about the quality or the color selection of the paints. Creating art was her way of reducing stress. First, she looked around inside to make sure there wasn't anyone she recognized. She'd yet to figure out if the person after her was someone she'd met before. Just women milled about and Ellie calmed. Sharon followed her to the art section and Ellie found just what she wanted, including a cheap easel. "This is perfect."

"Great," Sharon said. "What are you going to paint?"

"I'm not sure but something will strike me."

They paid and headed back to the office. Sharon carried the easel and Ellie grabbed the bag with the paints, brushes, and canvases. When they walked in, Detective Trent Lawson was there with Vic.

"There she is," Vic said with a smile. "Get everything?"

"Yes." What was the detective doing here? Her throat seemed to close up. Did he have news of Charlotte?

"Since Trent was headed back to town, I asked him to get you a burner phone so you could call Charlotte. I would have picked one up, but my chauffeur was out shopping."

"Funny man." She turned to Trent. "Thank you, but why aren't you with her?" Had he sent her off by herself? She couldn't think straight anymore.

"Don't worry, Ms. Hart. She's with my cousin, who's a cop. Charlotte is perfectly safe."

She shook her head. "You said that before."

His face colored. "You're right, but at least she wasn't harmed."

Damn. "I'm sorry. I'm still upset over everything that happened."

"I understand." He reached into his pocket and pulled out a number. "You can reach Charlotte here."

Just having the ability to speak with her daughter helped lower her blood pressure. "Thank you."

Vic pointed to the back room. "Why don't you call her now? You'll feel better."

"I will."

Ellie hurried to the back, her hand actually shaking. She closed the door for privacy and dialed the number. When her daughter answered, tears welled in Ellie's eyes. "Charlotte?"

"Mom? Is that really you?"

There weren't any chairs in the storage room, so she sat on a small file cabinet. "Yes, it's me. How are you holding up? I heard you saved the day."

Charlotte groaned. "Me? No. Trent put out the fire. He was amazing. I saw some lights outside the window and I called his name. He was like Superman. He was dressed and out the door so fast, I didn't have time to hide."

Superman—Charlotte's favorite hero. Ellie wasn't sure she liked the way her daughter seemed to idolize this cop. It didn't matter she probably would never see him again. "Did you call him Trent?"

"Yes. He's only like nine years older than I am."

"Only?"

"Dad's five years older than you."

She was about to say that she and Vic were older but then remembered she'd met her future husband when she was only twenty-one and he was a very mature twenty-six. "So you like the detective?"

They used to have these kinds of conversations in the past, especially when Charlotte was in college. The familiarity was nice.

"Haven't you seen him? He's hot."

She stilled. "Did something happen between you two in the cabin?" Charlotte sounded too happy.

"Mo-om. No. Though if he'd been interested, I'm not sure I would have turned him down."

It was Ellie's face that heated. "Just so you're okay. How's his cousin?"

"She's nice. How are you and Dad holding up?"

Ellie recognized the change in topic. "We're good now that you're safe and out of harm's way."

"Just good? I can hear something in your voice. Ooh. Did you two hook up?"

Charlotte had always dreamed of being a family once more, but Ellie had no desire to discuss her chances of getting it. It would only lead to disappointment. The image of Vic carrying a young Charlotte on his shoulder surfaced and she smiled.

Then she changed direction and pictured the two of them together where he used to cuff her to the bed and tease her unmercifully. She worked to banish that erotic image. No good could come of it.

"I'm not sure what you mean by hooking up, but we're not fighting, so that's good." There was no way she'd tell her daughter that she and her father had been having out-of-control sex.

"Uh-huh. Oh, Mom. I'm sorry. Gotta go. Annetta is calling to me."

Thank you, Annetta. She must be the cop. "You can call me anytime on this line."

"Okay. Love you, Mom."

"Love you, too, sweetie." Ellie hated to hang up, but it was for the best. She wasn't ready to admit even to herself that Vic was getting under her skin.

Voices sounded in the main entrance near Sharon's desk, implying the detective was still there. As long as she had some time, Ellie wanted to check in with Wendy and then Hilton. She better use her regular phone or Wendy might not answer. Her friend would be working at her old art store at this time and not answer an unfamiliar number. Given the time difference, Wendy might even be at lunch, which would allow them to talk in private.

Ellie dialed and Wendy picked up right away. "Ellie? How are you?"

"I'm fine." She gave her friend the rundown, leaving out nothing but her growing attraction to Vic. She knew what Wendy would say—go for it.

"Oh, my Lord. How is Charlotte doing?"

"I can't really tell. She seems quite taken with her bodyguard and not all that thrilled to have moved once again. I'm sure it will hit her soon that her life was in danger not once but twice."

"Does Vic have any leads?"

"Not yet, but he's working on it. How's class going?"

"Good, but Cal called to say he wasn't coming for a while. Something about an emergency. To be honest, I'm kind of glad. He creeps me out."

Ellie tried to count the days to see if Cal could have followed her to Montana. He always complained that he was broke, so she doubted he'd spend the money to fly there. "Did he say what kind of emergency?"

"Nope, just that he wouldn't be back for a while."

"Okay, thanks. How's Hilton doing? He's not used to manning the store." A small smile lifted her lips. "I wonder if he even knows how to use the credit card machine."

"Funny you should ask. He, too, said he had something he needed to take care of."

She didn't like the sound of that. "Who's at the gallery then?"

"He asked Ronnie Maloney to come over."

Ugh. "I didn't know they'd patched things up." Hilton had first asked Ronnie to go in with him to start the gallery, but he'd turned Hilton down.

Her friend groaned. "I know nothing, and I ain't asking."

Wendy was smart. "I appreciate the input. I won't keep you but call if something new comes up."

"Will do. I miss you."

Ellie smiled. "You have no idea how much I miss you, girl. Hugs."

"Stay safe."

As soon as Ellie hung up, a heavy weight sat on her shoulders. She had to tell Vic about Cal's and Hilton's disappearing acts. She thought they'd already crossed both names off the list, but after what Wendy told her, the possibility existed that one of the men was her stalker. Just when she believed it couldn't get much worse, this had to happen.

When she stepped from the room, Trent had gone. Sharon looked up. "Everything okay? You look pale."

There was no reason to give Sharon all the details. "I'm fine. I need to speak with Vic for a minute. Is he free?"

"Yup. Go on in."

When Ellie entered his office, he was seated, wearing glasses. She hadn't seen him in them before, but he looked good.

He looked up. "Something wrong?"

"I didn't know you wore glasses." That was a dumb thing to say, but she was still trying to figure things out.

He took them off. "Only need them for reading. How's Charlotte?"

Ellie pulled over the wooden chair. "She seems fine, though I think she has a little crush on Trent."

Vic's jaw tightened. "Did he try something?"

He always was protective. It was one thing she admired about him. "No, but our daughter wished he had."

Vic leaned back in his chair. "That's good."

"No, it's not." This wasn't why she'd come in here. "We'll talk about this later. I spoke with Wendy and she said both Cal and Hilton gave excuses as to why they had to go out of town."

Any semblance of cheer left Vic's face. "That's not good. I'll see if I can get a handle on where they went."

"How can you do that?" As soon as the words left her mouth, she realized her mistake. Amy, of course. "Never mind."

"No. It's a good question. I plan to ask Ted if he can check flight manifests to see if either one booked a flight to Rock Hard."

He was amazing. "You don't work for him anymore. Why would he help?"

Vic shrugged. "He's a nice guy."

It would be smarter to accept what Vic said. "Neither man has motive to harm me."

Vic cocked a brow. "Sex is a powerful motivator. And you weren't harmed, I was. And Charlotte almost was."

His mind always seemed to go to sex. "This isn't about un-requited love. If it were, I can see him taking you out, but harming Charlotte makes no sense."

"Don't sound so blasé about my possible demise."

Sometimes, Vic tried too hard. "I'm not. Sorry."

"He might have thought Charlotte was you. If he knew the difference, perhaps he believed if your support system disappeared, you might seek solace from him."

That was a horrible thought. "Well, doesn't that suck?"

Chapter Eighteen

V IC NEEDED TO get to the bottom of this. "It does suck, but when a man fixates on a woman, he can do strange things—like harming the person he cares about."

"Are we talking about Cal or Hilton?" Her body language looked identical to when she'd first come into his office, but it couldn't be helped.

"Both. I need to know—not as your current lover, but as your private investigator. Have you slept with either man?"

She sat up straighter. "Hilton, but only once. I realized right away that I had made a mistake."

"Describe mistake."

"Why are you doing this? To embarrass me?"

Fuck. "No, El. Don't you see?"

"No."

He was messing this up royally. "Hilton might have been ashamed if he had a performance issue. He'll want to prove to you he's a real man. There are a ton of reasons. Men are basically stupid creatures." He threw that last bit in to appease her.

"He doesn't have a performance issue."

That had been his best theory. "Did something happen?"

She shrugged. "We were celebrating the opening of the gallery and went out to dinner. I might have had a bit too much to drink. Hilton drove me home and stayed. It was a rather slam, bam, thank you ma'am kind of thing."

Vic smiled. "He didn't love you right. I get it."

She glanced away. "Don't flatter yourself." Humor tinged her tone.

Vic chuckled. "Then what happened?"

"Hilton asked me out a week later, and I had to tell him I thought it best if we kept our relationship professional. Business and pleasure don't mix."

Vic begged to differ, but he wisely kept quiet. "He wasn't pleased I take it?"

El glanced to the ceiling. "No."

"Did he remain upset?"

"Not really. He tried a few more times but finally got the hint. We were back to normal within a few weeks."

Vic found it odd that Hilton, a widower, would give up so easily. "You said you dated a man by the name of Brian. How did Hilton respond to that?"

"Is this relevant?"

Perhaps he'd pushed her too far. "It could be. Both Hilton, and the one you describe as your creepy student, have left town. You don't find it odd that they are conveniently away just when someone tries to run me off the road and shoot Charlotte?"

"I don't want to believe it."

Now they were getting somewhere. "I understand." He'd do more research before asking additional questions about the wealthy Hilton Davies, though Davies asking his first-choice partner to take over the gallery the moment El left town seemed more than a little coincidental. "What about Cal?"

Her eyes widened. "He asked me out several times, but I never acted on it. I told him it wasn't appropriate."

"I trust he wasn't happy either?"

Her lips thinned. "No."

"I'm sorry, El, but I really want to get this guy. It's possible our stalker is from Virginia, and when he failed to frighten you, he decided to come after your family."

She dragged a hand under her eyes. "I know you're only trying to help."

Vic pushed back his chair and came over to her side. He held out his hands. "El, look at me." She glanced up and placed one hand in his. He drew her to her feet. "I'm sorry. I wasn't trying to pry."

A fleeting smile lifted her lips. "Yes, you were."

Damn, but she knew him too well. "Okay, I was a wee bit curious, but you wouldn't have come to me in the first place if you didn't think one of them could have been your stalker."

"You're right."

"Why don't you go paint and I'll continue to investigate. Tonight, what do you say to a nice romantic evening at Rock Hard's best steak house?" Hopefully, she still loved her medium rare steak.

"I thought you were concerned about your high cholesterol."

How sweet that she cared. "I am, but I haven't been to the Steerhouse in months." She hesitated. "Come on. We need a break. It'll help me think better."

He finally received the smile he'd been waiting for. "Okay."

ELLIE HAD BEEN angry at first with Vic for asking all of those personal questions, but she soon realized he had to look under every rock. Neither knew for sure how long she'd have to stay there. While it was nice not to work all the time, she was getting a bit antsy. After putting on her coat for their date, she headed toward the front door.

"You parked in the back, remember?" Vic asked.

She halted. "I forgot." Sharon had driven her to the store because her car was in front and Ellie's was in back.

She turned around. At the end of the hallway was a door that led to the back lot. While she didn't mind driving, as soon as Vic's arm completely healed, she hoped he bought another vehicle. Not being familiar with the roads made her a little nervous.

"Relax. Nothing's going to happen," he reassured her.

"You don't need to placate me, Vic. I'm a grown woman. I know it's dangerous for us to be out, but I do appreciate the freedom—no matter how temporary."

She hoped she wasn't giving him hope of a future with her. Her problem was that she couldn't keep her hands off him. Once he was naked, she seemed to lose all thought. *Stupid libido.*

As Vic held open her car door, he looked around. She decided not to ask him who he thought he might see. Tonight she wanted to forget. Her goal was to direct the focus on Vic. Let him sweat for a change.

As they headed into town, he told her where to turn. Because it was a Monday night, they thankfully found a spot close to the restaurant entrance. Vic escorted her inside. She had to admit, being in the upscale, cozy place made her feel as if she were back home. "This is nice."

He smiled. "I'm glad you like it."

Once they were seated, their server took their drink orders. "I'd like to hear the details about the incident that caused you to give up your life's work," she said.

"You mean this?" He touched his scar.

"Yes."

"It's not very interesting."

She leaned forward. "Don't shut me out. Again." That was

part the reason why they'd divorced—that and the fact Vic believed someone might target her or Charlotte.

The waiter brought their drinks. She'd ordered wine, while Vic wanted a beer. "You're right. I'll tell you. You should know. While I was in Washington, I was researching illegal arms deals. Long story short, we suspected the large amount of guns destined for Rock Hard were some kind of stockpiling for a terrorist group. Ted and I decided it would be best if I went undercover. We had a team here for a while, and they needed to shake it up a bit. By posing as a homeless man, I could listen to the chatter without drawing attention. After a few months of living outside during the day, I learned that things were happening at a particular warehouse."

"A warehouse owned by Ed Hanson, I think you said?"

He smiled. "Yes. You always were a good listener. I was there about a month when I got wind of a possible attack, although the details were sketchy."

"What did you do?"

"I pick-pocketed one of the higher ups. He had a flash drive that described the terrorists' plan. I had intended to get the drive to my team as soon as possible. I believed I was in the clear but was unfortunately spotted and had to ditch the drive."

"I remember you saying you gave it to a young woman by the name of Jamie." She snapped her fingers. "Max Gruden's wife."

"Yes, only they weren't married at the time. I still feel bad about that, but I had no idea I wouldn't be able to retrieve it later in the day."

"What happened?"

He tipped back his beer. "Someone saw me give it to her, which then made her a target. When they realized I wasn't some hapless bum, they grabbed me that day and dragged me into the warehouse."

She wasn't certain she wanted to hear the rest of the story, but Vic had gone through something horrific, and maybe he needed to talk about it. "I take it that didn't go well?"

He chuckled. "Hardly. As I lay broken and unconscious from the severe beating, they set the wooden structure on fire. When I woke up, I was in the hospital. I was lucky that the assistant Fire Marshal happened to be driving down the street at one in the morning and spotted the flames. He called it in."

She hissed in a breath. "Weren't you scared?"

"I was scared that I wouldn't see you or Charlotte again."

Ellie studied his face to see if he was just saying that for her benefit, or if he truly meant it. She believed him. "Was the pain intolerable?"

"I was drugged up a lot. In all honesty, those days are still a blur—proof that I was in bad shape."

"Yet you still wanted to stay with the FBI?"

He shrugged then finished his drink. "Deep down, I knew my career was over."

If anything happened to her hands and she couldn't paint, she wasn't sure she'd have been as brave.

The waiter stopped by and they ordered their meal. She asked for a steak with a warm red center, while Vic had the salmon.

"Do you miss the job?" Ellie wasn't certain why she wanted to know. Perhaps she wanted to convince herself that he wasn't the man for her. Too bad every answer seemed to be what she wanted to hear.

"Yes and no. I like bringing the criminals to justice, but I don't like the fallout. Clearly, someone wants to harm what I hold dear."

"Or someone wants to harm what I hold dear," she said.

"You mean Charlotte?"

And Vic. She nodded. "Do you think you'll ever find him?" Too many damn possibilities existed. She didn't want to consider a woman was responsible. Even though Wendy answered the phone and talked about what was going on in Virginia, she could have been in Montana.

Stop it. Wendy is my friend.

"All criminals make mistakes. It's just a matter of time."

"I'm not sure I can wait around that long." The server brought their food, and her stomach grumbled.

"What are you saying, El? You plan to leave if I don't fix this within the week? Or are you giving me a month?"

A month? She'd be bat shit nuts if she had to sit in his back room all that time. "I don't know."

Vic reached out and clasped her hand. "I know you want to get your life back. I don't blame you. You think I like knowing someone tried to harm our daughter? Twice?"

Guilt swamped her. "I know you're doing the best you can, but I have a gallery to run."

"I know. Give me a few more days. Please."

"Okay."

He smiled and her heart did that flip-flop thing it always did when Vic exposed his soul to her. All she'd ever wanted was a connection with him—to know that she was important. Heaven only knew she'd put him first for so many years.

"Good. Let's eat and agree not to talk about the case for the rest of the evening. It's stressful enough."

She blew out a breath. "I couldn't agree more."

All through dinner, Vic asked questions about the gallery. "It seems as if you really love your job."

She smiled, happy he understood. "I do. I did need financial help from Hilton, but I had a vision of how it could be. We're just beginning to get a name for ourselves."

"I'm happy for you, El."

"Thank you. You seem happier in Rock Hard than I've ever seen you."

"I am."

They finished their meal, and both of them pulled out their credit cards at the same time. Some things would never change. "It's my treat, Vic. If you hadn't known me, and I'd hired you, would you be paying?"

His lips twisted. That was enough of an answer. "Perhaps not, but I do have money saved up." Once more, he reached out for her hand. "But you aren't just a client. You are the woman I dream about at night."

Ellie didn't need this. It would rip her heart in two when she explained why she couldn't stay. "Vic, don't. Please."

He let go. "No pressure. I just thought that while you're here, we could enjoy each other."

She laughed. "Enjoy each other?" She leaned forward, not wanting the entire restaurant to hear their conversation. "You mean have wild sex all the time? We're already doing that."

His grin dimpled one cheek. "I've never heard you complain."

"You are hopeless."

"Wait until we get back home, and I'll show how hopeless I can be."

Chapter Nineteen

O N THE DRIVE home, Ellie told herself she wasn't going to make love with Vic again. It caused too much anxiety. Every time they were together, she fell for him more. His touch seemed to alter her insides. This had to stop. When she was finally able to go back home, the separation anxiety would be bad. Charlotte would bug her, but Ellie had to stay strong.

When they entered his house, she faced him. "Dinner was wonderful. Thank you, but I'm tired. I'm going to shower then hit the hay."

"Sure."

He stepped into the kitchen and opened the fridge. Hmm. That was a bit odd. Usually, he made up some excuse as to why he needed to take off her clothes and ravish her. Perhaps he, too, had realized that no good could come of it.

In the past, he used to seek out his alone time. Maybe he was trying to figure out what came next.

Once in the bedroom, she undressed and placed her clothes back in her suitcase. If she had to stay another week, she'd need a few more things. She'd only brought one top that she wouldn't mind getting paint on. Perhaps she could ask Sharon to take her clothes shopping during their lunch hour tomorrow.

Bolstered by that thought, Ellie grabbed her nightgown and

stepped into the bathroom. If she could finish and crawl into bed before Vic came in, he might be convinced she was asleep. Truthfully, Vic wasn't always the one who initiated the lovemaking. She was equally at fault—or should she say, equally weak.

Vic's kisses were familiar, comforting, and quite wonderful. They reminded her of the days when love was in the air, before he joined the FBI.

Ellie let the water warm then stepped in, the heat soothing her muscles and helping relax her mind. Nothing bad could happen while she was here. Vic wouldn't let it. She had washed her hair and was lathering her body when the bathroom door opened. She stilled. Without thinking, she covered her breasts with her soapy hands.

"Vic? What are you doing in here?"

"What do you think I'm doing? Sharing a shower. I thought you could check my back to see if it's good."

"You are so full of shit. A mirror can tell you that."

He laughed. "Can't twist that far."

Apparently, he wasn't going to take no for an answer. Without waiting for her approval, Vic stepped in the large stall and moved next to her, sending the spray in every direction. "I'm not having sex with you," she announced.

"Sex? Did I mention sex? You have a dirty mind." He held up a hand. "Now, if you really want to make love, I won't turn you down." He winked.

He was too much. Ellie chuckled and shook her head. "Let me rinse, and then you can have the shower to yourself." She dropped her head to finish cleaning her hair.

He wet his body and stepped back. Casually as could be, he rubbed the bar of soap over his pecs and down his abs. "You look incredible, all soapy and wet and enticing," he said, never taking his gaze off her.

She was about to say her hips were too wide and her belly was too flabby, but then he'd want to show her how much he desired her. Hell, his cock was growing by the second. Damn man had to go and pick up his dick and rub it. If she asked exactly what he was doing, he'd say he was getting it clean.

Stepping away from the warm flow, she motioned it was his turn. "If you give me the soap, I'll do your back."

As he handed the bar to her, he smiled. *Resist!* She rubbed his back, once more enjoying the dips and valleys between his spine and his flared lats. Vic was honed, strong, virile, but sleeping with him every time they were together made her appear weak. Who was she kidding? She was weak.

Spotting no more redness around the cut, she touched his stitches, but he didn't flinch. "This is healing well." The gash on his forehead didn't even need a bandage anymore. "How's the shoulder?"

Without turning around, he lifted it parallel to the floor then lowered it. "Good."

"Liar."

He raised his left arm above his head. He didn't groan, but she bet he was in pain. "Satisfied?"

"Turn around and do it again." Oh, damn. That was what he wanted.

He did as she asked and then grabbed his cock with his left hand. "You just want to look at this, don't you?"

Step out of the shower now.

"No. Are you finished? I need to rinse." *Just as soon as I soap up again.*

Vic moved out of the way and she stepped past him, but not before he grabbed her by the waist and pressed her against the wall. Water hit her leg. She wanted to tell him not to kiss her, but her lips refused to comply.

"I can't resist you, El. I've never been more alive than when I'm with you. We're good together."

It would be a lie to say she didn't enjoy his company. "It's too soon."

"Too soon? I've waited five years to get my life together. Now that I have, I want you back. We're good for each other. We have fun, right?"

The words were ones she'd dreamed of hearing—back when they were married. "This madman has forced us together. This isn't normal. If I'd moved out here, we wouldn't be naked in a shower right now."

"Perhaps, but I'm glad we are. Can't you feel our passion growing?"

Yes, but she wouldn't admit it to him. "Let's see what happens after you get this guy, okay?"

"Deal."

Instead of stepping back, Vic dragged a thumb across her nipple, and it was as if he'd plugged in her virtual electric cord. Damn him. Despite the heated steam, the tip puckered. "What are you doing? I need to get out." Didn't that sound forceful? Hardly.

"Don't you like it in here?" He leaned forward, dipped his head, and tugged on her nipple.

She pressed her palms against the wall in an attempt to stop the streaks of pleasure from eating away at her willpower. "We can't...keep....doing...this."

"Yes, we can. We're consenting adults. There is so much darkness out there, and we deserve a little light. What can one more time hurt? Huh?"

That was the problem. If she gave in now, she might never stop. The second his hand slid between her legs and pressed on her pussy, her willpower dissolved like water on hot asphalt. Aw, fuck.

Her tiny button throbbed and she wanted more. Vic stepped back, grabbed the showerhead off the hook, and aimed it at her, one breast at a time.

"Don't move, or I might have to arrest you for obstructing justice."

She laughed. "What justice?"

"I deserve to enjoy that sweet pussy of yours, and if you try to stop me, I'll have to take you in."

He always did have a sense of humor—at least in the beginning. "I'll try to be good, officer."

"Good girl." Vic lowered the spray. "Open your legs. I want to make sure you're clean."

He grabbed the soap and swiped it across her slit. After he set the bar down, he dragged his palm across her opening, making sure to dip his finger in her pussy over and over again.

"I think I'm clean," she panted.

"Not yet. You keep leaking."

"Ew. Am not. If you want to stop that from happening, don't keep turning me on."

He grinned. "I'm exciting you?"

"A little." She'd had enough of his flirting and grabbed his cock.

He lifted her hand off his shaft. "Not yet."

He turned the nozzle upward and aimed the water right up her pussy. It tickled and excited her at the same time. She shrieked and he stopped.

"Turn around and plant your hands on the wall," Vic commanded. "I want to play with your tits."

The angle would be better anyway. Besides, she liked it when he took her from behind. There was more friction and her climax was more intense. Ellie turned around, stuck out her butt, and wiggled her hips.

"You're asking for it."

"As long as I'm going to hell, I might as well enjoy the ride down." She'd pay for this slip in resolve at some point, but Vic was right. Life was fragile and she needed all the goodness she could grab.

His palms cupped her breasts, and when he rolled her nipples between his forefinger and thumb, shards of bliss shattered her. How could his one touch undo her like that?

Am I falling in love with him again?

Ellie didn't want the answer to be yes. Vic was a complicated man. Once the danger passed, he'd go back to his workaholic self, and she'd be forgotten. And Charlotte? Now that he'd won her back, how much time would he give her?

Pleasure was fleeting, so she needed to take it when and where she could. That would be her new mantra until she left for Virginia.

His cock slipped between her legs and Vic's chest plastered against her back. "I need you."

Over the roar of the water, she couldn't be sure, but she thought his voice cracked. She prayed Vic could let her go when the time came. His slid a palm down her belly and teased open her pussy lips.

He slowly massaged her opening but didn't give her the release she desired. Needing to urge him on, she reached between her legs and grabbed his dick. His pecs tightened on her back.

"You're tempting fate," he said.

"I'm trying to tempt you into giving me that big cock of yours."

"Don't you worry; I just want to make sure you're ready for me."

She was already teetering on the edge. After being together for so many years, he knew she was easy. What he might not know was that she was that way only with him.

She pumped her hand up and down and would have suggested she suck on his cock had he not pinched her nipples and short-circuited her brain. The delightful surprise made her loosen her grip enough for him to slide out of her palm.

Vic nudged her legs wider and pressed on her back so that she was level with the floor. He reached between her legs and strummed her clit.

"Vic!"

"Just seeing if you were paying attention."

"Damn you. Give me that cock."

"Patience."

Not going to happen. She'd finally agreed to give into her desires and now he wanted to torment her? Ellie twisted around and flattened her back against the wall.

"What are you doing?" Vic looked crestfallen.

"This." She grabbed his cock, leaned over, and drew him into her mouth.

"Jesus, El. You don't want me to go off, do you?"

Why was it okay for her to be on the edge and not him? "You're the soldier. Suck it up."

She went back to work, rolling his balls and dragging her tongue down his length. Because she could only fit half of his dick in her mouth, she clasped the lower half and pumped her fist again. He groaned and grabbed her wet hair and tugged.

"I forgot how wicked your mouth was."

She smiled and lost suction. Damn. This was her chance to bring him to his knees. She bet every criminal Vic ever brought to justice would line up to see him beg. And beg he would. Five years was a long time, but some things she'd never forget—like how to drive him wild with need.

Using every technique she'd ever learned, she dragged her tongue up and down his length, swirling it around and sucking hard. The tension on her scalp increased. She was loving this. From his moans and the hint of cum on her tongue, he was about to lose it. It would almost be worth it to have him blow.

"Enough," Vic gasped. "I have to have you."

"Patience."

Vic withdrew from her grasp and lightly tapped her nose. "Patience, my ass."

He pressed her against the wall, aimed his cock at her pussy, and drove up into her. Explosions detonated everywhere. Sparks flew. Oh, my fucking Lord. Ellie cupped his face and kissed him with more passion than she ever had before.

His hands roamed over her hips and up to the sides of her breasts as he pounded into her over and over again. She couldn't get enough of him, and only broke the kiss when she needed air. He plastered his chest against hers and as his cock exploded, he dropped his head on her shoulder, taking her over the edge with him. It was as if they were holding hands in a free fall.

The power, the lust, and the emotion were so strong that her mind blanked. He held still and eventually the pulsing slowed.

Vic withdrew and stepped back. "Okay, maybe I'm too old for this. I think that took five years off my life."

Ellie didn't know why that was funny, but she laughed and couldn't stop. Vic joined in, and side-by-side they planted their backs against the wall then slowly slid down to the floor.

"Aren't we a pair?" she asked.

His picked up her hand and kissed each knuckle. "That we are."

Chapter Twenty

E LLIE WAS IN the back room painting when Sharon knocked. "I finished my work. You said you wanted to go clothes shopping?"

"Fantastic. Yes." Ellie had already gotten a paint stain on this shirt, and she needed a few more tops she didn't mind messing up. "Let me rinse my brushes and then tell Vic we're doing a girls' day out."

"Cool."

Ellie used the bathroom sink to rinse her brushes, and then wiped the porcelain clean. This setup wasn't ideal, but it worked. After she returned her supplies to the back room, she gathered her purse and coat and headed into Vic's office.

He looked up, smiled, and took off his glasses. She wished he'd keep them on as he looked scholarly, but he said he was self-conscious. Men. Go figure.

"Sharon and I are going to do a little clothes shopping. I don't imagine we'll be too long."

"I'm glad you're making friends here."

She bit her tongue. He was trying to make her see she could have a life in Rock Hard. While that might be true, she also had a job and friends in Virginia. It was the only place she'd ever known. "I'll text you when we're done so you don't worry."

"I appreciate it. Just keep your phone on."

She remembered that he could always locate her because of her phone. That comforted her. "Will do." She shoved her hand in her purse and extracted her keys. He hadn't asked to borrow her rental even though his shoulder had healed enough for him to drive. She didn't want him stranded should something come up. "Just in case." She dropped them on his desk.

"Thank you." He winked. "Be vigilant."

"Always am."

Ellie left with Sharon, ready to enjoy a day out. Sharon drove, not only because she'd parked in front, but also because she knew the roads.

"I'm thinking we'll head over to Dayton. They have a nice mall."

"How far away is it?"

"Thirty minutes, tops."

Ellie wasn't sure Vic would want her to be so far away, but Sharon did have her gun. "As long as you park close to the entrance, I don't think Vic would mind."

Sharon reached over and clasped her hand. "You're safe with me and Annie."

Ellie laughed. When they arrived at what Sharon called The Mall, Ellie said nothing. Ten single-story stores in a row wasn't her definition of a shopping mecca, but for now, it would do. One consolation, it would be hard for anyone to sneak up on them. As long as they'd come this far, Ellie was going to enjoy shopping.

✧　✧　✧

VIC WAS MAKING good progress on the potential candidates when his cell rang. He smiled. It had to be El telling him she was on her way home. She'd been gone a few hours already. He wasn't worried, though. He'd checked her location several times. They were in Dayton. Not his first choice for haute couture, but what did he know about women's clothing?

The call wasn't from El's phone. He didn't recognize the number. Tension rippled through him. "Hello?"

"I have your daughter." The voice came out distorted.

His heart nearly exploded. *Stay cool and think.* Vic had checked on Charlotte's location when he'd looked up El's. His daughter was in Billings where she was supposed to be. Trent said he was calling his cousin every few hours to make sure all was okay.

"What do you want?" He'd play along. It didn't help that his heart wouldn't stop banging against his chest, which made it very hard to talk.

"I want you in exchange for your daughter."

It wouldn't be the first time a criminal had asked for such a swap. "Let me speak with her."

"I'm sorry. I can't do that."

That was because he didn't have her. Vic wanted information about this guy. "Were you the one to set the garage on fire?" He knew damn well it was a porch, but maybe this clown didn't.

"Nice try, Agent Hart. It was Detective Lawson's front porch. And, yes, I did."

Bile raced up his throat. "Who are you?"

"Meet me at the picnic tables at Harmes River Park in thirty minutes. Bring the cops and Charlotte dies." He disconnected.

Vic's mind raced. The stalker was the only one who could know so much, yet there was no way he had Charlotte. Damn. He immediately dialed Trent's private number, hoping this creep hadn't somehow figured out where Charlotte was.

"Hey. Can I call you back?" Trent asked. Noise sounded in

the background.

"No. The stalker called. He said he has Charlotte. Is that possible?" His words rushed out.

"No."

"You sure?"

"I just called Annetta. Charlotte is at the station house in Billings. What did he say?"

Vic told him then checked his cell for the time. "I have to leave now or I won't make it in time."

"Fuck. I'll organize everyone on my end. When you get there, stall if you have to until we arrive. He doesn't have your daughter so there's nothing he can do even if you come in with a squad of cops, guns blazing."

"I want this fucker alive. I want to know who he is and why he's targeting my family."

"We'll meet you there, and we'll get him. I'll have every exit sealed off if he attempts to run for it."

Vic blew out a breath, appreciating that Trent had his back. "Thanks."

As soon as he disconnected, Vic shrugged into his vest. No telling what this fucker had in mind. He slid on his gun belt and added an ankle holster for his knife. Vic was certain he was missing something. Since his retirement from the FBI a year ago, he had softened. Mentally, he raced through how he wanted to do this. He debated going in the back way and hiking in the last mile, but that would take too long. However, since this guy did not have Charlotte, what difference did it make?

Logic intruded. The difference would be the stalker might go after El next, and that would be horrible. After he donned his jacket and hat, he headed out the back. Ellie's car was parked in the second row. With each step, his anger built.

Only when he'd gone ten feet did the sound of snow crunching behind him enter his brain. As he spun around, something hard smashed him in the side of the head and he dropped to the ground, his vision black.

✧　✧　✧

"WHAT DO YOU think of this top with these jeans?" Ellie said, as she modeled her outfit for Sharon.

"They look great together."

"I don't look too fat?"

Sharon laughed. "You're asking me, Miss Skinny?"

Ellie really enjoyed Sharon's company. She was a no-nonsense woman who didn't seem to take shit from anyone. "I am."

"I'm sure the boss will think you're hot."

"That's not why I'm buying it."

Sharon rolled her eyes. "Keep telling yourself that. I can practically smell the chemistry between you two. I've never seen the boss so happy."

She didn't need to hear that. Vic did seem happy despite all the crap that was going on in their lives. She'd admit that a large part of his good cheer might be from having her back—if only for a little while. "Me neither. But enough about me and Vic. Tell me about your new beau."

"Darryl isn't really a beau. He travels too much, but when he's passing through town, we do have a good time, if you know what I mean." Sharon smiled, looking like Charlotte used to in high school when a boy she liked paid attention to her.

Ellie decided she'd take both the top and the jeans and slipped them off. "Got a picture of this hot man?" Women loved to share.

"I think I do." Sharon pulled out her phone and scrolled through the photos. "Here he is. I love when he wears a suit."

She grinned and held up her cell.

Ellie took a quick glance. "Nice." She'd planned to look away, but there was something familiar about the guy. "How old is he?"

Sharon laughed. "Now you sound like my sister. He's thirty-eight."

"Sweet." Ellie dressed back in her clothes. "As long as he treats you well, that's all that matters."

"He sure does. I've never met a man who's more interested in me and what I do. I couldn't have asked for anyone finer."

Vic's words came back to her. He'd found four men who were relatives of the criminals he'd put away. "Sounds like Vic. Let me see if he tried to call. He's is such a worrier."

Ellie wanted to find a way to check her phone without looking obvious. The photo of Darryl seemed familiar. She pulled out her cell and scrolled through the pictures. When she reached the third one, Ellie's legs weakened.

"What is it? You look like you've seen a ghost."

"I have." She handed the phone to Sharon, hating to disappoint a woman she'd come to like. "Who does this remind you of?"

She checked out the picture. "How did you get a photo of Darryl?"

Ellie wished she remembered what this guy's name was. "These are my possible stalkers. They have relatives who Vic put away."

"Motherfucker. I'll kill the SOB."

Ellie held up a hand. "Let's not be hasty. It might not be him." But she was pretty sure it was, though. "Can I see the picture you have again?"

"Sure." Sharon handed it to her.

"Oh, shit. I remember now. That's the guy I met in the bar. I might have had too much to drink, but I do remember he said he sold some kind of energy-efficient windows and that he was married with three kids."

"He has a wife? Son of a bitch. Why me?"

She could think of a few reasons. "Could it be he wanted to learn about Vic's habits?"

"Shit." She balled her fists. "If this is true, I'll never forgive myself."

"It's not your fault. You didn't know. I'm calling Vic and telling him. The good news is that Darryl might be our stalker. Identifying him is most of the battle." Ellie pressed the call button. It rang. And rang. "He's not answering."

The machine picked up. "Hello, this is Hart's Investigations. I'm unable to answer this call so please leave your name and number and I'll get back to you."

Ellie wasn't certain what to do. The beep sounded. "Vic. It's me. My stalker is Darryl...ah." She looked over at Sharon.

"Grainger."

"His name is Darryl Grainger. Please call me back."

Sharon opened the changing room stall and rushed out. "We need to get back to the office."

"Right." Instead of taking the time to buy the clothes, she left them at the check-in counter. "Can you hold them? I'll be back."

They ran out. The next half hour was the longest thirty minutes Ellie had ever experienced. She wanted to yell at Sharon to drive faster, but the poor woman looked possessed by the devil as it was.

When they reached Vic's office, Sharon slammed the car into park, jumped out, and ran to the door. Ellie was right behind her. "Locked. Vic must have gone out." Sharon fished around in her purse for the key and finally got the door open.

Ellie rushed passed her. "Vic?" No answer. "I'll check his office." Her stomach tumbled at the thought something bad might have happened to Vic. He never would have put his phone on vibrate.

She ran down the hallway to the darkened room. He wasn't there, but maybe she could learn where he'd gone. She flicked on the light and her gaze shot straight to the brightly colored object on his desk.

No. This couldn't be happening. Not again. Ellie screamed.

Chapter Twenty-One

SHARON PRACTICALLY RAN into Ellie as she rushed in. "What is it?"

With as much control as she could muster, Ellie stutter-stepped over to Vic's desk and picked up the dark pink Gerbera daisy. "It's him. My stalker." A sob escaped. "He was here. He wants me to know." Her hand shook so hard, Ellie had to set down the flower, and then fisted her hand.

Sharon moved next to her. "What does he want?"

She faced her new friend. "I don't know, but Darryl might have Vic." Just because Vic wasn't in the office didn't mean something bad happened, but her gut told her it had.

"Oh, fuck." Sharon's jaw tightened and her eyes darkened, almost as if she was preparing for battle. "I'll check out back and see if your car's still there."

Thank God, one of them was thinking clearly. All Ellie could do was nod. The blood in her body had turned to a heavy sludge that made thinking and everything else next to impossible. The back door opened and then slammed shut. A long minute later, footsteps pounded.

Slightly out of breath, Sharon ran in. "Car's still here, but there's blood on the snow next to the driver's side door." She leaned over and planted her palms on her knees. "I'm so sorry."

Vomit rolled up Ellie's mouth; she sped to the trashcan and threw up. "Oh God."

Sharon rubbed her back then handed her a tissue from Vic's desk. "It's okay, sweetie. I know Vic. He'll be okay."

"I hope so." She had to find him.

✧　✧　✧

TRENT HAD EVERY available RHPD officer ready to take down Vic's attacker. He'd sent ten men to block all main park exits. The problem was that the woods bordered a vast National Park that would be impossible to monitor if this man chose to go out on foot.

He and fellow detective, Thad Dalton, rode together because, not only were they friends with Vic, Trent needed a sounding board, and Thad was as level headed as they came.

The picnic area sat along the riverbank about a mile into the park. The long drive added to their vulnerability. No telling if this crazy man would be waiting in a different spot hoping to attack Vic, or expecting the cops to come. When Trent arrived, the lot was vacant. A sign said the area was closed until the spring, but someone's vehicle should be there.

"Where are they?" Thad asked.

Trent's sixth sense shot into overdrive. "Something's off. We couldn't have beaten Vic here. He left his office before we took off, and his place is closer."

"Maybe he switched locations," Thad said.

"Anything's possible." Trent pulled to a stop.

The rest of the men, all in unmarked cars, drove in behind them. Without a word, they parked in different locations and exited their vehicles, guns ready. They knew what to do. A sniper, along with several other men, had orders to hide on the other side of the river, ready to take out this man on Trent's signal.

Lieutenant Donovan was technically in charge of the operation, but he was willing to give Trent the temporary command because he was already working on Vic's case. Donovan and some of his officers were stationed at the various exits.

Static came over Trent's ear bud. "Have you spotted your target?" Donovan asked.

"Negative. Thad and I are heading down the trail now."

"Let me know what you find."

"Roger that." On high alert, they followed the path toward the tables. Trent pointed to the pristine snow and mouthed "no footprints."

Thad shook his head as he scanned the area. When the tables came into view, the area was empty. "Shit. Were we duped or did something bad happen?" Trent asked.

Thad shrugged. "Beats me. Want me to call Vic?"

"Let's not take the chance. He might be lying in wait to see what the guy will do. In case he didn't turn off his cell, it could give away his location. Trent tapped his mic. "Sir, no one's here."

"Damn."

Trent's cell vibrated. "Hold on, sir. Incoming call. It might be Vic." He swiped his cell, but didn't recognize the caller's name. "Lawson."

"Trent, it's Ellie Hart. Something bad has happened to Vic. I know it." She choked out the words.

Adrenaline filled his veins. He motioned for Thad to follow him back to their cruiser. "Take a deep breath and just tell me what you know." He hadn't spent much time with Vic's wife, but she'd always appeared strong.

"Darryl Grainger is my stalker."

"Who's Darryl Grainger?"

"Does it matter? He has Vic. We saw blood. He's at—"

"Detective Lawson, this is Sharon, Vic's secretary. We checked on his GPS and he's at the McDonald's old place. We're heading there now."

Oh, fuck. "We're at least forty-minutes away. Don't do anything when you get there." His stomach ached. Everyone knew about the hot-headed Sharon Dumont. At least she was good with a gun.

"Hurry." She then disconnected.

He turned to Thad. "Someone by the name of Darryl Grainger has Vic. He's at the abandoned McDonald place." The name Grainger rattled in his brain as they both dashed back to the car. As soon as he hopped in the driver's seat, the first name registered. "Ed Hanson had a stepson by the name of Darryl. Could be him." He wished he'd asked Ellie Hart for more information.

Thad yanked out his phone. "I'll contact Hartwick to see if he can scrounge up some information on the guy."

"Good thinking." Trent told Lieutenant Donovan what he'd learned, and then turned on the siren. He sped down the park lane toward town. Forty-minutes would be an eternity. If Sharon and Ms. Hart got there first, no telling how many casualties Rock Hard might have.

VIC CRACKED OPEN his eyes, the pounding in his head worse than he'd ever experienced in his life, and that included the beating last year that had nearly killed him. After the car accident and now this, brain damage was a real possibility.

The putrid smell hit him first. It was a mixture of hay and rotting flesh. He hoped the second odor wasn't coming off his body. Light streamed in through a crack in the wall across from him. Vic was sprawled on the floor of an old barn. If he didn't know better, he'd think he was in back in Hanson's warehouse—a structure that no longer existed.

He tried to look around but moving his head increased the pain to an unbearable level. Something dark crossed in front of him.

"I see you're awake."

Vic didn't recognize the man's voice, so revealing anything about himself would be stupid. "Kind of."

Vic tried to rub his face, only to find his hands tied. Fucker. He wiggled his wrists. When the clank of metal didn't sound, he inwardly smiled. Plastic ties could be broken if one used quick, hard force. Right now, he didn't have the energy.

"You aren't going to ask who I am?" The stranger's voice was laced with irritation.

Vic tried to focus but couldn't. "Sure. Who are you?"

"I'm Ed Hanson's stepson."

As if someone poured a bucket of ice water on his body, he pushed up on his bad arm and winced. "His son? Oh, yeah. Darryl." Vic couldn't recall the man's last name, but he'd discounted him since he had no record and worked at a good job as a banker—in Virginia. Fuck. "What do you want?"

The man moved closer, and only then did Vic spot a gun in Grainger's hand. "I want to see you suffer like I've suffered."

The concussion must be messing with his head. "I never hurt you."

Darryl moved quicker than a scared jackrabbit. The kick to the ribs came from someone a hellava lot stronger than a bunny, though. "You ruined a man I cared for."

Shit. Vic's ribs ached and the contents of his stomach threatened to come up. Thank God for the vest or they'd be broken for sure. He debated whether to go with the truth or try to placate his abductor. It probably wouldn't be wise to engage him in a conversation he didn't want to hear but too bad. Vic's nice filter had disintegrated.

"Your father not only had me beaten and set on fire, he was a terrorist, ready to take down hundreds of innocent lives because he didn't like something our government was doing."

The feet edge closer and Vic tightened his muscles to steal against the next blow. "My. Father. Was. Innocent." Darryl spit on the ground.

Don't egg him on. "I wasn't the one to point the finger at him. The FBI arrested your dad."

"You testified."

"To pickpocketing a flash drive that incriminated your father. I was not on the jury. His peers were."

Darryl's eyes narrowed. "It's a lie. All of it. My father was an upstanding citizen and a good man."

This wasn't getting him anywhere. Darryl was clearly delusional. Vic pushed up again and this time succeeded in sitting up, but his ribs violently protested the movement. "Then appeal. Gather the facts to prove he wasn't involved. Your dad admitted to letting a group of men use his warehouse. Perhaps the terrorists lied to him about what they were doing."

Not a chance in hell.

Vic wasn't going to mention that the FBI had found a stockpile of guns in Hanson's house as well as payments from his bank accounts to many of the known terrorists. Hanson was their leader. Of that, Vic was certain.

"My father took in my mother when no one else would. He also built homes for needy people." He inhaled. "If it hadn't been for your snooping, my mother wouldn't have left him."

Imagine walking out on a paragon of virtue. Vic suspected Hanson's acts of kindness were all for show. As for the mother, he applauded her good sense. "Have you spoken with him since the trial?"

"Fuck, yeah."

"Did he say I framed him?"

Darryl paced. This argument seemed to be getting to him. "Not exactly, but you brought the FBI down on him."

"I did not." That was the truth. "I was in a coma in the hospital. Ask your dad." Darryl's eyes flickered. "Didn't know that, did you?"

"I see you got burned, but that didn't mean Dad was involved."

Vic would never be able to convince Darryl his father was anything other than a good man, but the longer he kept him talking, the more time Vic had to recover. "Someone gave the orders to beat me, dump me in your father's warehouse, and set the building on fire."

"It wasn't him. If you had the flash drive, they had to take you out."

Was he now on the side of the terrorists? Was he one of them, too? Vic didn't think so. Darryl was confused and hurt. "Possibly, but if your father was innocent, he had nothing to worry about that flash drive." Darryl's arm hung by his side as he paced in front of Vic. While he appeared somewhat distracted, Vic wanted to ask him if he was the one who shot at Charlotte and stalked El. "You live in Virginia, right?"

He stopped moving and clenched his hand. "Used to. How did you know?"

To bluff or not to bluff? "Actually, you said you visited your dad in Washington. It was a guess. What do you do for a living?" Vic wanted confirmation that his sources were correct.

"I'm a banker. Or at least I was until they let me go. I spent too much time at dad's trial so they gave me the pink slip. The real truth was that the fuckers just didn't want a banker around who had a father in jail."

More than likely, he sucked as an employee even before his father was arrested. Vic put on his most sincere face. "That's got to be tough on you. When I got the boot from the FBI, it was hell. I drifted for a while, feeling lost and betrayed." Not the case at all, but Vic was good at sympathizing with criminals.

"I know what you're doing. Stalling for time. I bet you called the cops after I talked with you. Didn't you?"

"Yes." No use lying.

Darryl smiled, but the cheer didn't reach his eyes. "That means they'll be running around Harmes River Park for quite a while." Darryl ran his fingers up and down his revolver, probably intending to scare Vic. "Pretty wife you've got. Or rather, hot ex-wife. I'm looking forward to hooking up with her after you're dead. She took to me at the bar."

The pieces fell into place. He was the younger man in the gray suit who was sitting next to El. Adrenaline and hate slammed through Vic's veins. He popped up to his knees, ignoring the slashing agony rippling over his body, and stood. With a short, quick burst, he snapped the plastic to free his hands.

Darryl's gun cocked. "Don't move."

If Vic thought he could win the battle, he would attack. The ass deserved to die.

"You won't get away with this," Vic warned.

"We'll see about that."

Chapter Twenty-Two

AS MUCH AS Ellie wanted to reach Vic and help him, she didn't think it was a good idea for the two of them to go to this farm without the cops. Sharon might own a gun, but they'd be no match against a man like Darryl Grainger. "What exactly are you going to do once we get there?"

"Take down the jerk. He lied to me. I won't stand for that." Sharon slapped her palm against the wheel.

This wasn't good. Sharon wasn't thinking rationally. Ellie's stomach burned and her throat had turned dry about six miles ago. "This isn't about a woman scorned. Darryl Grainger is a dangerous man. He tried to kill my daughter and ran Vic off the road."

"All the more reason to shoot his ass."

Holy Mary, mother of God. Did Vic know his secretary was a loose cannon?

Sharon took the next turn too fast, slamming Ellie against the door, banging her head against the window. "Ouch."

"Sorry." Sharon sounded sincere, but this woman was crazier than Darryl.

"Sharon. Ah, we need to think about this. You can't just go in half-cocked and storm in there with your gun. He could shoot you."

"I've thought about it plenty." Sharon jerked the car off the road onto a dirt drive. "He'll be too shocked to see me to get off a clean shot."

"He might be shocked, but it's against the law to run in and kill him."

"Not planning on killing anyone. Just want to hurt him. A lot."

Sharon hadn't thought this through. "You'll go to jail. You want that?"

"I'll do what I have to in order to protect the boss. Besides, it might be worth it to see Darryl squirm and cry." She drew up behind a large tree halfway down the drive. What was once a nice house was now in sad disrepair. An equally forlorn looking barn and corral sat in back. A few of the barn slats were missing, as was part of the roof.

"As soon as I park, you hide in the back seat. I won't do anything stupid, I promise—assuming he's even there. Darryl won't hurt me. He's a coward."

He wasn't a coward when he'd shot at Charlotte or tried to burn down a house. Then Ellie keyed in on the part about Vic possibly being alone and a trickle of hope seeped in. "You think he might have left Vic in the barn?" His cell phone implied he was there, but a chance existed that Darryl had taken Vic's phone. She refused to think the reason why.

Sharon slowed. "Won't know until I get in there." She cut the engine. "Now get into the back and keep down." Sharon tossed the car keys to Ellie. "Just in case I don't make it out."

This wasn't good. Ellie opened her door and leaned out. "Hey. I see a car on the side. It's a black sedan."

"Shit. That's the kind Darryl drives."

Ellie couldn't tell if Sharon was worried or pissed. "Tell me your plan."

"My plan is to look through one of those missing slats and see where he is. Then I'll rush him."

Sharon might be a good aim, but Ellie bet it was only when Sharon was trying to hit a paper target or a tin can—not a human. "I'll come with you. Not inside, but I'll look, too."

"No, you stay here and let the cops know I'm inside."

This was stupid. "When they see another car, they'll proceed with caution. You want me to call Detective Lawson again? He'll figure we got here first."

"Don't bother. He'll tell you to stay put."

That was because Trent was a smart man.

Sharon whipped out her gun from her purse and started toward the barn. Ellie didn't want to be stuck in the back in case things went south. She slid over to the driver's side, shoved the key in the ignition, and rolled down the window an inch in order to listen for the police.

Sharon had gone no more than a few feet when a shot sounded. Ellie ducked. *Holy shit.* Her heart pounded so fast she thought it would jump out of her chest. A few seconds later, Sharon tapped on the passenger side window and Ellie unlocked the door. Sharon slid in.

"Was he shooting at us?" Ellie asked.

"Don't think so. Door didn't move and unless he was watching us drive in, he wouldn't know we're here. My engine's quiet."

Her stomach heaved up bile. "Do you think he shot Vic?"

"I'm about to find out. Wish me luck."

She was going out again? Was she insane? Before Ellie could come up with a good reason why Sharon should stay put, her friend pushed open the car door and zigzagged her way to the old house. For a larger woman, Sharon sure could move. When her friend was halfway between the house and the barn, Ellie called Trent Lawson. She wanted nothing to do with a possible murder.

✧   ✧   ✧

"No need to get excited, Darryl. I ain't movin'," Vic said, working to keep his voice calm. The shot had hit the dirt about three inches from his foot. Vic held up his hands and widened his stance, ready to charge. It was hard not to wince given his ribs and head ached. "Tell me what you want."

"You know what I want. To see you suffer. Sit down."

"Sure thing. Give me a sec. Ribs might be busted." Vic huffed out some long breaths to make it look as if any movement hurt. He was only half acting. Holding his side, he eased down to one knee. Darryl's rage seemed to have been festering for a long time, and Vic wanted to give him time to calm down. Vic looked up at him. "I'm suffering a lot right now."

"You're about to suffer more."

Just as Darryl leveled the gun at Vic's chest, the barn door burst open, and Darryl pivoted toward the sound.

Go. Now!

Vic leapt up to his feet, using the last of his energy. When Darryl returned his focus to Vic, Vic dove to the ground, and three shots sounded in rapid succession. The order was a bit blurred, but he sure as hell felt the pain in his calf as Darryl's shot found its mark. Fuck, that stung.

Vic landed with a thud as Darryl screamed in pain, grabbed his gut, and dropped to his knees. Just as he let go of the weapon, Vic's vision blurred from the jarring aches stabbing his body from every direction.

Gotta get the gun. Gotta get the gun. Nothing else mattered.

He crawled three feet, each inch wreaking havoc with his ability to function. Finally, his fingertips touched the handle. *Just a little farther.* The pain was excruciating, but he stretched a bit more and nabbed the weapon. *Yes!*

Vic tried to secure the gun, but a wave of nausea assaulted him, forcing him to stop.

"You asshole." Sharon loomed over Darryl with her gun aimed at his crotch.

"I can explain," the whimpering fool said, blood pooling over the man's fingers.

Not only was Vic shocked that his secretary was here, she'd taken down the man who tried to kill him. Vic was having a difficult time putting those two thoughts together. Using his left hand, he placed his palm over the bleeding hole, forcing himself to remain conscious.

"You used me." Venom dripped from her voice. "And you shot at me."

"You didn't have to shoot me in the gut." Darryl's eyes rolled back in his head, and he passed out.

Sharon's demeanor instantly changed from hatred to concern just as sirens sounded in the background. Vic wanted to smile and thank her, but his lips wouldn't lose their grimace.

"What are you doing here?" he asked as she rushed toward him.

"Is that anyway to say hello?"

She was right. "I promise to give you a raise." She'd like that better than a thank you.

"Now you're talking." She slipped off her jacket. "Move your hand."

It took him a moment to realize what she planned to do. "Don't ruin your good jacket. Help is on the way."

"Nonsense. Can't have you dying on me; I need the job." She smiled.

He wouldn't die from a shot to the lower leg. He almost laughed, but then nodded toward the nearly closed barn door.

"How about waving in the cavalry first?"

Her mouth slackened for a second before firming. She held up a finger. "Right. Move your hand." Sharon balled up her jacket and pressed in on his wound. "Keep pressure on this."

She then jumped up and dashed to the exit. Easing the door open a bit, she stuck her hand out and waved, possibly fearing they'd open fire. Smart thinking.

Darryl groaned, but he still appeared to be passed out. Good.

The next thing Vic knew, El was by his side, and the pain seemed to disappear until the worry descended. "Hey. You shouldn't be here," he grunted.

"I know, but I am, so lay back and rest." She placed a hand on his shoulder and gently pressed. Once his head hit the straw, she removed her jacket and placed it under his head.

He wanted to wave her off, but it took too much energy. "How did you find me?"

"Your GPS."

"I mean, how did you know something was wrong?"

Two paramedics, Stone Benson and Drake Longworth, tapped El on the shoulder. "Ma'am," Stone said. "We need to look at Vic."

Her brows pinched. Vic hoped someday she'd learn that Rock Hard was a small town, and that people looked out for each other. El stood and moved back. "We'll talk later."

Trent and Dan Hartwick were with Sharon. From the way Dan was scowling, Sharon was in for a tongue-lashing. Vic wasn't worried. If anyone could handle the head of the RHPD's detective unit, she could.

"Ouch." Vic looked down at the IV in his arm.

Stone shook his head. "Don't be a baby."

"Baby? I was hit over the head with a metal object, kicked in the ribs, and shot."

When he'd mentioned the head smashing, Stone's demeanor hardened. "You black out?"

"Yes."

"Not good, buddy." Together, he and Drake slid him onto a backboard, and then lifted him onto the gurney.

As they wheeled him out, El ran up to them. "Where are you taking him?"

"To LACE hospital."

She looked confused at the acronym, so Vic helped her out. "It's where I was taken after the hit and run."

"Oh." Lips twisting, El glanced over at Sharon. "I wonder when they'll be finished with her."

"Not for a while, I suspect." He handed her Sharon's jacket. "Tell her I'll buy her a new one. You stay with her. You know where I'll be."

The paramedics wheeled him out. He was shaking, probably from the loss of blood. When they left the barn, the cold air didn't help his chills or his mood.

The saddest part of this whole event was that after this attack, Vic would never be able to convince El that he led a fairly safe life. It didn't matter that Darryl was possibly the last of the vengeance seekers from his past life. He couldn't be sure it was completely safe for El to be with him, which meant he had to let her go—again.

The only good news about Darryl's capture was that Charlotte could now get on with her life.

✦ ✦ ✦

WHEN THE PARAMEDICS rolled Vic outside on that stretcher, Ellie's heart broke. She wouldn't wish what he had been through on her worst enemy, yet her ex-husband only seemed concerned with her welfare. Vic Hart was a one-of-a-kind good man.

A second stretcher left the barn, this time carrying Darryl Grainger. Adios, asshole. To think she sat at the bar sharing drinks with him, not having a clue he wanted to harm her family. Sheesh. If that didn't make her stop drinking, nothing would.

After she picked up her jacket, Ellie edged over to where two police officers were questioning Sharon, but remained quiet, not wanting to disturb them. She couldn't wait to hear what had actually happened. Sharon had accomplished what she meant to do and hadn't been injured, but that didn't mean she wouldn't land in jail.

Trent came up to her. "Are you glad it's over?"

She jerked out of her reverie. "I haven't had time to think about myself. All I can think of is Vic. The blows to his head alone worry me."

Trent rubbed her shoulder. "He'll be fine."

What else could he say? "What happens to Charlotte?"

"I'll call Annetta and have her drive Charlotte down here. I'd go myself, but I've got a ton of paperwork to fill out."

Ellie couldn't wait to see her daughter. "I understand. Thank you."

Sharon held up a hand and motioned for Ellie to come over. "What's up?"

"Can you drive my car back to Vic's?" Sharon asked.

"Sure, but I'm not sure how to get back." Ellie had been too scared to pay attention to the street names.

"Use the GPS on your phone."

Christ. "Of course. Why don't I drive it back to the office? My car's there."

"Given the blood next to your vehicle, I'm afraid it might be where the abduction took place. They'll want to process the scene."

She'd forgotten about the blood—Vic's blood. Yikes. "Okay, but what about you?"

"They need to question me at the station."

Worry raced through her. "Are they going to arrest you?" She'd come to care for this woman.

"No. Darryl shot first, but he missed." She smiled. "I didn't."

Good old Sharon. "Would you have shot him if he hadn't fired at you?"

"We'll never know, will we? Go home and for God's sake put on your jacket. It's freezing in here."

Ellie had been so upset about Vic's injuries that the cold hadn't even registered. Sharon, too, was probably cold, but her jacket had blood over it. She handed it to her. "Vic said he'd buy you a new one."

"He'd better." She grinned.

"Call if you need me to pick you up."

"I will." Sharon leaned over and hugged her. "Thanks for figuring it out."

"Vic was the one who gave me the four suspects, and you showed me Darryl's picture." Ellie didn't think she'd helped much at all.

"But you put the pieces together."

True. Trent came over. "Everything okay? Want me to drive you home?"

"I have Sharon's car. I'll be fine. I want to head to the hospital to see Vic."

"Keep that man of yours from tearing up the hospital. He's going to be a bear for a few days."

Trent had Vic pegged. "Will do."

Ellie bundled up, and as soon as she rushed out the barn door, the cold air slapped her in the face. Brr. Winter was coming. To her, it signaled Christmas, which meant the rush at the gallery would be intense. People loved buying paintings and artwork for their big parties. The question was whether she'd get back in time to help.

Or if she really wanted to.

Chapter Twenty-Three

V IC WANTED TO go home. The surgery to remove the bullet
went well and the pain was now minimal—at least in his
leg. His head still ached and a few of his ribs were sore, but there
was no reason for him to stay in the hospital. Sure, the physical
therapists wanted him to work out the leg, but he assured them
he was capable of walking around on his own.

He glanced over at El, slumped in the chair with her eyes
closed. She'd been by his bedside since the shooting. While his
love for her grew with each passing minute, he knew he had to
let her go. She was born to work in the gallery, and the big city
life fit her. Besides, he couldn't guarantee that someone else
might not want revenge and harm her.

He shifted in the bed, and the rustling of sheets must have
roused her. She looked over and smiled. "You're awake. How
are you feeling?"

"Good. Do you think you can find the doctor and ask him
when I can get out of here?"

She narrowed her eyes. "I asked him last night. He'll tell you
when he thinks you're ready."

"I'm ready, now."

She laughed. "Next you'll be telling me you want to go back
to work."

He smiled. "You know me too well. I wish it was business as usual, but I actually need help at home. For starters, I don't have a car."

Why am I asking her to stay? Because I want her here, even though she'll need to leave soon.

As soon as he bought a car, he'd put her on the next plane to Virginia and cut the cord. If Charlotte didn't have to be back at work, he might have asked her for help.

Yesterday, Trent had brought his daughter to the hospital, and the reunion was quite tearful, especially on El's part. Vic really hadn't wanted Charlotte to see him lying in bed, but as Trent explained, Hart's were stubborn creatures. Charlotte had insisted.

"I'll be happy to stay for as long as you need me," El said.

While her smile was warm, she looked tired. "I appreciate it. Have you been in contact with Hilton to see how things are going at the gallery?" It would show her level of concern and interest in her work.

"I called him last night. His sister had a stroke and he'd flown up to see her, but he's back now. That's why he's been out of town. He said Ronnie Maloney did a great job tending to the gallery." She sighed.

That was an interesting reaction. "Why the long face? Afraid Hilton will want to buy you out and ask this Ronnie fellow to take over?"

She laughed. "He wouldn't dare."

Guess that settled it. El's comment implied she was eager to return, but at least she'd stay a bit longer. While he recuperated, he planned to enjoy her all that he could. Christ. Just the thought of making love with her again had his cock twitching.

El stood. "Since you seem so determined to leave, I'll see what the doctor has to say about your release."

Vic waved a finger. "Don't go suggesting I stay here a few more days."

"I would if I weren't so tired and needed a good night's sleep."

Poor El. She deserved better than a burned, beat up old man like himself.

It seemed to take a good hour before his surgeon rolled in. They shook hands. "Ellie tells me you want to go home."

Didn't every patient want to get out of there? The food sucked and the nurses stopped by throughout the night to prick and probe him. "No reason to be here."

"Let's take a look at that calf."

Vic swore the man tried to break open the incision with all the prodding and pushing he did on the wound. Vic didn't groan, but he probably winced a few times. "How does it look, doc?"

"You'll be good as new in no time. I spoke with Dr. Harrison. He wants you to come back in a few days to check your vision. Concussions are tricky creatures."

"Sure thing." His vision was fine. Vic would say anything to escape one more night there.

His surgeon, Dr. Gutna, looked over at El. "Can I count on you to bring him back?"

Christ. Did the whole town think he was unable to take care of himself?

"Absolutely."

Dr. Gutna nodded. "Let me do some paperwork, and then we'll send you on your way."

✧　✧　✧

AFTER MANY HOURS of waiting, the hospital finally released him. No surprise, El fussed the whole way home. Then she insisted he sit on the sofa while she fixed dinner. Vic wasn't an invalid. He'd been shot before. It wasn't that big a deal.

"Need help?" he called out.

"I'm good."

Damn. Being useless was driving him crazy. After a few minutes of hearing her bang around in his kitchen, he rose and limped in to join her. His headache was almost gone and his ribs were healing nicely. His calf wound would take a bit longer to heal, assuming he didn't overdo it.

El planted a hand on her hip. "You need to sit down."

Vic pulled out a chair at the kitchen table and dropped onto the seat. "There. I'm sitting."

She rolled her eyes. He dragged over another chair and propped up his leg. While she worked, he wanted to talk about their future—or lack thereof.

"I want to apologize for getting you involved in all this," he said.

"Vi-ic."

"Let me finish. As soon as I realized it had to be someone from my past who was after me, and not you, I should have sent you home."

She whirled around on him. "Are you kidding? Darryl, if that's his real name, would have targeted Charlotte even more. He already shot at her and set fire to the house where our child was sleeping."

"I don't think he wanted to harm either of you—at least not yet. He was filled with anger that he needed to get out. He believed his father was innocent. Besides, a brick house would be hard to burn down in the winter. He didn't use enough accelerant to do damage."

"Perhaps because he didn't know better." She wagged a finger. "If I hadn't been here, who would have saved you from that lunatic? I was the one who figured out it was Darryl, and don't forget Sharon shot the bastard."

Vic shrugged. "Point taken." He waved a hand. "But that's all in the past. I think we should talk about now—about us."

Her body stiffened as she pressed her lips together. Her face said it all. "Vic, there is no us. Don't get me wrong. Have you changed? Absolutely. You're a wonderful man, and I'm almost grateful to Darryl for bringing us together."

"But?"

"I don't know. I'm confused. I've worked so hard these past five years to start fresh. I've built a gallery into a thriving business—with Hilton's help, of course."

"I couldn't be more proud of you." He truly was.

"Thank you. It's not that Rock Hard isn't nice. It is. They have some great galleries, too, but I belong in Virginia."

"I totally understand." He was happy she was so content there. In fact, he was about to tell her she needed to move back, that she'd never be safe, or happy, with him.

She moved closer to him and placed a hand on his shoulder. "If you'd consider moving back to Virginia, we could see if it would work between us again. We could date for a few months. I don't want to jump into something this important after being with you for such a short time."

His heart nearly leapt out of his chest until reality reigned him in. "It's what I've always dreamed of, but I know myself too well. Everything would be ideal for a while, and then I'd get that one phone call. It would be my old boss asking me to help out with some case only I could handle."

She cast her gaze off to the side and her shoulders slumped. "And you'd have to say yes."

He nodded. "I'd get embroiled in the job, and some new danger would become my focus. I won't do that to you again, El.

I loved you enough to walk away five years ago, and I love you more now. I want you safe and happy. I'm not the right man for you."

At his profession of love, her chin trembled. "You are good enough, Vic. That's the problem."

No matter where he lived, his life would be fraught with danger. "Since we agree it's better if we part, how about making the time we do have together memorable?" He pasted on a smile, but, inside, his heart was breaking. Letting go of her again would be the hardest thing he'd ever have to do, but it was for the best.

El stepped closer. "Describe memorable?"

"How long before dinner?"

Her eyes narrowed. "Maybe half an hour. Why?"

He grinned. "I'm thinking that will give us just enough time for you to ravish me once more."

She laughed. "You want to have sex? Now? You're impossible."

He popped open his jeans and pulled down the waistband of his briefs until his cock sprang out. "What do you think?"

"You're injured."

"My dick's not. Since I can't press you against the counter and take you from behind, all the more reason for you to get naked and sit on my lap. I promise it will be a ride you won't forget." Vic moved his hurt leg off the chair.

She bit down on her lip, looking so adorable. "You sure I won't hurt you?"

"Nothing you could do would ever hurt me."

Other than not be part of my life.

"After sitting in that hospital for so long, I could use a good stress reliever." She set down the dishtowel and kicked off her shoes.

His mouth turned dry. All he'd thought about while lying in that hospital bed was making love with El one more time. "We can use the bed if you wish."

"Since when have I been conventional?"

"Good point." He and El used to make love in the oddest of places—closets, swimming pools, and even in a bar bathroom. He'd matured since then—or so he wanted to believe.

As much as he'd have liked to relax back and enjoy the show, he needed to undress, too. He toed off his shoes, removed his socks, and then slipped off his pants and briefs. Vic would let El remove his shirt. Having her fingers on his body would help brand her touch and scent into his skin forever.

Naked except for her panties, she walked over to his chair and stood next to him. "Want to take them off?"

His pulse skyrocketed. "More than you can know."

Vic slipped his thumbs between the waistband and her warm skin. He inhaled as he lowered the lacy material, inch by excruciating inch. His need to taste her almost made him hurry, but if this was the last time they'd ever make love, he wanted this experience to last.

"You smell so good," he said.

She smiled. "I hope I taste just as good."

Vic groaned. "Why are you tormenting me like this?" He looked up at her.

"Because it's what you like and what I need."

El always said the perfect words. "I do like to be teased and tempted, but only in small doses. I'm hanging on by the edge here. If I wasn't incapacitated, I'd haul you over my shoulder, toss you on the bed, and tie you down."

"You always did like to play fireman."

And a host of other things. He tugged the material lower until he exposed her delicious pussy. Vic leaned forward but was unable to gain access. "Lift your leg up and place it on the seat."

He scooted over, and she balanced by holding onto the table behind him. With her knee bent, he was able to lick her honeyed slit. At the first taste, he thought he'd died and gone to heaven. This was where he wanted to be. Unable to keep her forever made this moment all the more bittersweet.

When he nabbed her tiny pearl with his teeth, she squeaked and clutched his right shoulder. He loved her sensitivity. Using small flicks, he worked his way from her clit down to her wet heat. "You taste so damn good."

"How about you let me reciprocate?" she panted.

"In a moment." Vic leaned back and slipped two fingers into her.

She closed her eyes and gulped in air. "Yes. Faster."

What was it about this woman that made him want to sacrifice his life for her? He loved her ambition, her good heart, and her willingness to let go when making love. He removed his fingers. Exploring her tight, wet channel was too much to bear.

"You made a request?" Vic wasn't sure he wouldn't explode, but he sure would try not to. His woman was a goddess.

Grabbing the dishtowel she'd tossed on the counter a moment before, she folded it, and then dropped it at his feet. Keeping her gaze on him, she knelt in front. "Open your legs for me."

"That's what I always say to you."

"I know, but two can play at this game."

Only it wasn't a game to him. This was his farewell to her. His heart cracked, but he forced himself to put on a brave face. "Let's see what you got, lady."

Acting as if his cock would explode, she pulled his hard rod toward her, and her fingers nearly seared his skin. "Nice." She licked her lips.

"Devil woman." As she leaned over, he wound a lock of her auburn tinted hair around his finger, enjoying the silkiness. "So soft."

She looked up. "I can't say the same about you."

He chuckled. El was always good at comebacks. The first lick had him grabbing the seat—and she'd only just begun. He would not beg, though if he moaned enough, she might take pity on him. "Suck on him."

She chuckled, and then ignored him. Cupping his balls and rolling them in her palm, she continued to lick his cock. He grabbed a handful of hair at her scalp and tugged. Only then did she draw his stiff dick into her mouth. He closed his eyes, wanting to remember every lick and touch. The woman had a magic mouth. When he groaned, she increased the pressure. He'd have to stop her soon, or he'd shoot his wad.

El pumped her hand up and down while she sucked on him hard. Each stroke brought him closer to the edge. He tightened his grip as he leaned forward and touched her tit. Vic thought it would help him gain more control, but he was wrong. The smooth, supple skin nearly did him in.

"How about sitting on him, darlin'? I'm in a weakened state." Vic could smell El's arousal and figured she was close, too.

She looked up. "Can't take a little licking and keep on ticking?"

No use denying it. "No. Not when you're sucking on my cock."

When she looked up and smiled, he fell in love another notch.

Chapter Twenty-Four

ELLIE WAS DYING here. Vic was everything she wanted in a man—except his life was too dangerous. He'd even said it. It wasn't safe to be with him. But with Darryl in custody, they were protected—physically, at least, for a while and she had every intention of enjoying this last exploit. Of the few men she'd been with, Vic outshone them all. It was going to be damn hard to leave him, but leave she would—for Charlotte's sake, for Vic's, and for her own heart's sake.

Ellie stood then resumed her straddled position. "I want to see all of you."

She lifted his shirt over his head, hoping his shoulder had healed to the point where raising his arm wouldn't hurt. Pleased he didn't groan, she tossed the material onto the kitchen counter. "Much better."

Vic's body had become more muscular in the last five years. The scar on his shoulder and chin only bothered her because of the suffering Vic had gone through. Now that it had healed over, it gave him a rugged look.

"Are you going to stare at me all day, or sit on my cock?"

She returned her gaze to his face. "How about I do both?"

"Now you're talking."

Vic grabbed her waist and made her straddle his lap, his large cock dividing her pussy lips. Sliding a hand up her back, he drew her close, and when his lips parted, she took advantage of the offering. She clasped the back of his head and delved in, wanting to taste every inch of him. Ellie closed her eyes, inhaling his masculine, earthy scent and dueled with his tongue. As the need to possess him overwhelmed her, she could no longer catch her breath, but it was Vic who broke the kiss.

His lips were red and his eyes slits. "Let me make love to your tits."

He'd always had a fascination with them. Now that they were much heavier, he seemed even needier. Ellie arched her back and offered them to him. His teeth tugged on one nipple, sending chards of bliss straight to her pussy. He alternated from one to the other while he tugged on her scalp. Heated passion filled her veins. If he kept this up much longer, she wouldn't last. "I'm ready."

She lifted up and grabbed his cock. Vic groaned. "Fuck me hard, sweetheart."

She planned to do just that. Aiming the tip at her opening, she bent her knees and engulfed him. His dick slid in, stretching her wide, and pushing her closer to her climax. Ellie didn't move, needing time to gain her composure.

It didn't help when Vic twirled his tongue around her nipple again then sucked hard. The quick shot of pain morphed into delicious pleasure.

The sentiment nearly felled her. Who was this man? Vic had changed, but she couldn't ponder that now. Her hormones were in overdrive.

She lifted up and was about to drop back down, when Vic held her hips. "Let me love you the way you deserve."

With his good leg planted on the ground, he lifted up and drove into her, hitting her back wall. The friction alone was enough to topple her, but add in his mouth creating chaos on her breast, and she was helpless to stop the onslaught.

On his next thrust, she tightened her inner walls to keep him in place. His eyes widened. "You witch."

She smiled. He always called her that when she'd pushed him too far. As he plowed into her one more time, heat swamped her. Just as her climax swooped down and pushed her into the stratosphere, his hot cum filled her. Pulsing. Pounding. Stretching.

The rush swept her away to a place filled with amazing hope and joy. Peace then descended, and she blocked out everything else. Her legs eventually weakened, and she collapsed onto his lap. Leaning forward, she rested her head on his good shoulder. "Thank you."

He slid his palms up her arms, leaving goose bumps in their wake. "No need to thank me. It was my pleasure. Always know that I will love you, El, with my heart and with my body." As he stroked her face, her tears threatened to fall.

God, why did he have to be loving and caring now? Was he trying to tear her heart out? "Promise me something?" she whispered.

"Anything."

"Until I'm back in Virginia, you won't get mushy on me again? I can't take it."

"So it's working on you?" She sat back and punched his chest. Before she could retract her hand, he grabbed it and brought her knuckles to his lips. "I'll try to be good. It's for your own good to keep your distance, and while I can say the words, it doesn't mean I don't have to like them."

She glanced to the ceiling and sniffled. "Me, neither."

Not wanting to break down in front of him, she stood and grabbed another towel from the drawer. She cleaned up first then wiped him off. The oven timer dinged.

Vic smiled, but she could see he had to work at it. "We have good timing."

"We always did."

✦   ✦   ✦

THE NEXT FIVE days were hard on Ellie. Vic was a bad patient, not listening to her warnings about taking it easy. He kept moving about when it was obvious his leg pained him. While his shoulder had healed and his headache was gone, his ribs gave him difficulty when he moved too quickly.

With a lot of convincing on her part, Vic had cooperated and made appointments with both the surgeon and another doctor who checked his ribs and his eyes for any signs of damage from his concussion. Both said he was healing nicely and could go back to work whenever he wanted. That diagnosis should have thrilled her, but it didn't. While she was happy for Vic and excited to be getting back to her beloved art, leaving Vic would be hard.

The last obstacle to her departure had been him not having a car. Yesterday, they had found one he liked. With him now having transportation, she had no reason to remain in Rock Hard.

Their last night together had been a restless one. Depression seemed to have grabbed hold of both of them, but leaving was the right thing. Vic had said so, but it didn't make it any easier. Confirming her decision to leave tomorrow had been Wendy's phone call. Her friend had come down with some crud and wouldn't be able to teach the last two classes. Ellie had promised she'd catch the next available flight home.

All packed, Ellie never expected saying goodbye would be this hard.

Vic hugged her. "If you need a good private investigator, you know who to call."

"I do. I wish—"

Vic placed a finger on her lips. "Shh. Don't say anything, because if you do, I might cry."

He was only kidding, but it helped bolster her mood. "It might be worth tossing about a few love words just to see that." Vic never cried.

"No, it wouldn't. I'm an ugly crier."

She chuckled. Not wanting to delay the inevitable, Ellie leaned over and kissed his cheek. If their lips had touched, she might not be able to pull away.

"Let's go." Vic picked up her case and walked her to her car. He put her luggage in the trunk then opened her door. "Stay safe."

"I will." Ellie slipped in the front seat before she changed her mind.

Tears welling, she backed out of his drive. As she straightened the car, she glanced over at him. Seeing his slumped shoulders and brave face had the tears sliding down her cheeks. This was for the best. It was. It truly was. Then why did she feel like throwing up?

ELLIE HAD TO go to Kalispell to return her rental car. She'd spend the night with her daughter and then fly out the next day.

"How's Dad?" Charlotte asked as she escorted Ellie inside her house.

"Good. He'll get the stitches out of his calf in a few days. The doctors already gave him a clean bill of health and said he could get back to work."

"Did he ask you to stay?" Charlotte headed into the kitchen.

Ellie set down her bag and followed her in. All during the drive up here, she practiced what she'd say. Disappointing her daughter would add another layer of guilt about her decision. "Yes and no. Charlotte, sweetie, your dad and I have a lot of feelings for each other, but our lifestyles don't mesh."

Her daughter kept her back to her while she fixed coffee. "Don't you love him?"

"It's complicated."

Charlotte swiveled around. "Relationships are complicated, but either you love him or you don't."

Ellie didn't want to admit the truth to her daughter, but knowing Charlotte, she'd worm it out of her sooner or later. "Yes. I've never stopped loving him, but your dad fears someone else might come after me. He wants me safe."

"Well, I'm not going to stop visiting him just because some crazy loon could shoot at me again."

Was her daughter calling her a coward? That hurt. "I'm glad, but it would be different if you lived in Rock Hard."

"If I did move there, would you move there, too?"

Why was Charlotte asking her these hard questions? Ellie knew. She wanted a family—desperately. Ellie stepped closer and clasped her shoulders. "Even if I did return—and Vic let me stay—things would go back to the way they were in Virginia. Your dad admitted he's a workaholic. He could be gone for weeks at a time. You of all people should remember how he blocked us out of his life. It hurt me and it hurt you."

Charlotte shrugged. "Maybe, but that was when he worked for the government."

They'd rehashed Vic's actions to death already. "So tell me about Trent Lawson. Are you still high on him?"

Her cheeks colored. "It doesn't matter. I made a complete fool of myself on the way to his cousin's house. There's no hope now."

Too many scenarios rushed into her head. "Care to elaborate?"

"No, Mom. Some things are best left unsaid."

If Trent forced himself on her daughter, Ellie would bring up charges. "Did he do something you didn't want him to?"

"No! He was the perfect gentleman." The coffee perked and she poured two cups. "Let's sit at the table, but only if you agree not to discuss my lack of love life."

That was so Charlotte. "Deal, but only if you drop the subject of me and your dad getting back together. It's not going to happen."

Charlotte rolled her eyes, and Ellie laughed. She'd miss her daughter so much.

Chapter Twenty-Five

A S SOON AS Ellie walked into the Davies-Hart Gallery, Wendy came out of the back room, her nose red and a tissue in her hand. "Oh, my God. You're back!"

Her eyes sparkled, but her friend looked like shit. "I'd give you a hug, but I don't want to catch what you have," Ellie said. "You need to go home."

"I'm better than I was yesterday."

Now she sounded like Vic. No one was in the gallery since it was quite early. It was also snowing, but it was possible Wendy had scared them away.

Ronnie sauntered out from the back. "I thought I heard your voice. How are you, darling?" He kissed her on each cheek.

Wendy touched Ellie's arm. "I'll quarantine myself in the office. Happy to have you back."

"I'm glad to be home." She faced Ronnie. "How's Art World doing?" That was where Ronnie worked part time.

"Ugh. They are so gauche. Donald Everly is not a good administrator and he's a worse curator."

She laughed. "Be kind."

Ronnie placed a hand on her shoulder. "Oh, but I am. You and Hilton have exquisite pieces."

"Thank you. Since I'll need some time to get back in the

groove, I hope you'll stay around and help out."

During the trip back east, she realized that she'd worked too hard these past five years. Sure, she was successful and made good money, but the slower pace of Montana had gotten under her skin. She was almost forty-six. While not old, pushing herself like she had when she was twenty wouldn't help her live a long and productive life. Having another person to pick up the slack when she was researching other artists or teaching her class would be wonderful. If she could steal Wendy away from her job, too, life would be so sweet.

"That's very generous, but I'm looking to start my own gallery. When Hilton first asked me, I wasn't ready, but now I think I am."

She couldn't be more pleased for him. "I wish you luck. If we can help in any way, let us know."

"I will. Would you like me to stay for the day while you get back in the swing of things?"

"That would be great." The bell above the door chimed and a well-dressed woman came in. "I'll let you see what she wants."

Ellie wasn't up for dealing with someone new right now. She hurried into the back room, wanting to touch base with Wendy.

With a hot cup of coffee in her hands, her friend looked up. "I thought you might like to look at the artwork from your class."

"I'd love to." It was always hard judging a person's progress when she didn't see its evolution.

For the next hour, they poured over the paintings, discussing which artist had talent and which ones needed an extra push. It was wonderful to immerse herself in the art world again.

One of the pictures was a mountain scene, reminiscent of Montana. What was unusual about this one was the inclusion of a family of wolves. That reminded her of the wonderful artist in

Rock Hard. After extracting his card from her purse, she handed it to Wendy. "Here's someone you might try to land. His work is remarkable." Bringing in artists could help a person's career.

Wendy studied his card. "It says here, he's from Montana."

"Yup. I saw his work in a small gallery there. I'm thinking he could really be special."

"I'll check him out. He must have a website. Did you meet him?"

"No. I was thinking too much about my stalker, and besides, the owner told me he was out of town."

Wendy stashed the card in her purse. "I meant to ask, did the stalker ever say why he targeted you?"

"Not exactly, but he worked in Virginia." She'd already told her that his father was the man Vic helped put in jail. "We're thinking Darryl might have looked up Vic's name and found mine instead. We speculated he was trying to get the whole family in one spot so he could inflict more pain on Vic. By scaring me, we think he'd hoped I'd call Vic."

Wendy shook her head. "That's terrible."

"Tell me about it."

The bell above the door rang once more. "I guess I should see who that might be." Ellie nodded to the box of tissues next to Wendy. "Go home. Please. It's bad for business."

Wendy laughed, just as Ellie had wished.

"Okay, but as soon as I feel better, we're going out to dinner to celebrate your return."

That was the best offered she'd had all day. "You bet."

❖   ❖   ❖

WENDY HELD UP her wine glass and Ellie clinked hers against it. "To health, wealth, and happiness," Wendy said.

"Most definitely." Ellie had her health, and with the sale of a rare Feinberg painting two days ago, she was doing very nicely in the wealth department. It was the happiness part she couldn't quite grasp.

Wendy leaned against the leather booth at Magda's, a fine steak house in town. Ellie only came here when she needed to feel special. Unfortunately, Magna's magic wasn't working tonight.

"You don't look very happy," Wendy said.

Ellie shrugged. "It's been hard getting back into the stressful world of running a business. You being at the gallery two days a week has really helped me."

Wendy polished off her glass. "How long have we known each other?"

Her friend was too damned sharp. "Fine; I miss Vic."

"About time you admitted it."

She'd been back less than a week. Ellie had gone over her time in Montana about a hundred times. "It doesn't do any good. He won't move back here, and I don't want to leave the gallery."

"You do realize galleries can't hold you at night or kiss you madly."

She laughed. "For a thirty-five year old, you are rather wise."

"Thirty-four. I don't turn thirty-five for another week."

Ellie had forgotten about her birthday. Where was her head? "Thirty-four then. My point is that Vic fears for my safety. What if another person comes after him through me?"

"Really?"

"What?"

"You believed that line? He just said that because he's scared. It's the same for you. He was just nice enough to give you an out, but safety isn't the real issue."

The thought had crossed her mind, but she'd dismissed it.

"It's possible. He claims he loves me, but if he had to choose between me and his job, his work would always win."

Wendy's jaw slackened. "Seriously? From what you told me, when you were together this time, did he ever put his work above you?"

"I was his work."

"Are you sure he had no other jobs pending?"

"No. Fine. Perhaps Vic has changed. He's working for himself and can choose to do what he wants, but even he said it wouldn't last. Don't forget he crashed his car right after I arrived and then needed me to drive him around. He couldn't follow many other leads."

She chuckled. "You seemed to have been able to rent a car. Why couldn't he have?"

"His shoulder was hurt."

The waiter arrived with their steaks, and Ellie inhaled the delicious aroma. As soon as their server left, Wendy said, "Bullshit."

"You didn't see him. His shoulder was dislocated."

"You can't fool me, Eleanor Hart. I remember when I first met you and Vic. He was doing some undercover work, trying to unearth a drug cartel. Don't you remember when you found out he was in the hospital, that some thugs had jumped him, broken his nose, and cut his arm real bad?"

Ellie had pushed that out of her mind. "You have a good memory. That was such a terrible ordeal. Charlotte had freaked, believing her daddy was going to die. I couldn't get her to stop crying."

"Right? He was seriously wounded and was back at work in two days. Two days! Vic Hart can do anything he sets his mind to—like drive a car with an injured shoulder."

Ellie cut into her rare steak, watching the juices pool onto the plate. "So?"

"He wanted you nearby. That's why he had you drive, not because he was hurt. You even said it yourself—he's changed."

She set down her fork. "What's your point?"

"You are such a lucky woman. A man loves you. Go to him."

Ellie exhaled. "And chance that he'll become obsessed with work again?"

"Like you were obsessed with making this gallery the perfect place when you were dating Brian? How did you think he felt?"

"You're saying I'm like Vic?"

"In many ways. If you want a relationship to work, you have to want it bad enough, to make it a success."

Wendy wasn't exactly the poster child for working relationships, but what she said held merit. Sure, Ellie was ambitious, and she had thought of Brian as someone casual. "Vic and I had a child to raise, and he wasn't there for us. Can you honestly say that wasn't enough of a reason to work at keeping us together?"

"Vic was trying to keep his family safe by serving overseas. You can't fault him for that."

Maybe she had been hasty. "True, but when he returned, he wasn't the man I'd married. He didn't laugh as much." *Or hold me as much or want to make love with me all the time.*

"Those were sad times."

"I know. I could have been a better listener and a better wife. He was hurting, but I didn't know what to do."

Wendy reached out and clasped her hand. "You were a mom who had to put Charlotte first."

"That was what I told myself, but I think it was an excuse."

Wendy smiled. "You can do something about it now."

"No. He's happy in Montana and I'm good here."

"Fine, but don't say it's because being with Vic isn't safe.

You were in Virginia and had a stalker and got your tires slashed. How is that being safe?"

Ellie picked up her wine. "Can we talk about something else?"

"I'm sorry, hon. You're right. We're here to celebrate your return. I'm really not trying to convince you to go. I'd miss you too much if you did."

"That's better. So, any word from Cal?"

Wendy laughed. "Don't tell me you've set your sights on him?"

Ellie nearly spit out her wine. "Hell no. Just making conversation."

Chapter Twenty-Six

A KNOCK SOUNDED on Vic's door. He looked up and Sharon was there, hand on her hip. "Are you ignoring me?"

He had no idea what she was talking about. "No. Why would I?"

"I don't know, but I've buzzed you twice about a phone call, and even texted you the information, yet you haven't responded. Are you okay?"

"I'm perfectly fine."

She crossed her arms. "May I be frank?"

He chuckled. "When have you ever thought to ask?" He kept his voice light. Sharon was the best, and he never wanted to piss her off. Hell, if she decided to do him in, he would be dead in seconds.

"Since you haven't been yourself."

Vic had a feeling he wasn't going to like this conversation. "Shoot. Or rather should I say, tell me what's on your mind."

"Have you called Ellie?"

Shit. He didn't need this. "I texted her the day she left to be sure she arrived home safely."

Sharon stepped into his office and sat down in the chair across from the desk, something she rarely did. "And not since then?"

Ellie had been gone over two weeks. Contacting her would have been too painful for both of them. "No."

"Let me get this straight. After nineteen years of marriage and five years of being separated, your former wife comes in here looking for your help. You drop everything for her. In fact, you had me transfer two of your cases to your arch-enemy because you wanted to devote your whole time to her."

"Rich Sandringham is not my arch-enemy. I just think he's an ass and moderately incompetent."

She waved a hand. "Regardless, you put your life on hold for her. As soon as things turned good between you, the spark returned to your eyes. I'd never seen you so happy."

"I was happy." He'd told her that a few times, so he couldn't retract the statement now.

"And yet, you let the best thing in your life walk out." It came out a statement and not a question. Christ, she acted like he was just plain stupid.

Vic stabbed a hand in his hair. "Ellie has a life in Virginia—a gallery to run that she owns."

"That's more important than family?"

"To her it is." Ellie was used to fancy things, and he was good with pretty much anything.

"I know you love her. Are you afraid you can't satisfy her?"

He choked out a laugh. "Ah, that is way too personal—even for you. How about you leave my life to me."

Sharon stood. "Just saying. You're being an ass."

The damn thing was that she was right. She knew he'd never fire her no matter what she said. Shit. Seems the women in his life had him wrapped around their little finger. "I'll take that under consideration."

"You do that. You're not going to find a better woman than

Ellie Hart."

"I know, but she can do better than me." That was the truth.

Sharon shook her head and left. Vic pushed aside that conversation and went back to work on the Harold Evans case. He believed his wife was cheating on him, and it was Vic's job to find out with whom. He wouldn't find out sitting on his ass. Mrs. Harold Evans would be getting off work in a few minutes, and it was a Friday night. Harold said he had to go out of town and wanted to see what his wife planned to do. She'd been very secretive about something, sneaking off for the last couple of weeks.

Vic gathered his camera, bundled up against the cold weather, and headed out. Despite the snow covering just about everything, the streets were rather crowded near town. With Christmas but a few weeks away, people seemed to be busy with last minute shopping. After Sharon's brutal comment about him fucking up his life, even the Christmas decorations didn't cheer him up as they usually did.

He discreetly parked across the street from the bank and waited for Harold's wife to exit. It was some thirty minutes later that she came out in her faux fur coat and heels, hurrying to her car. After she was partway down the road, he pulled out and followed her. The residential area was on the outskirts of town, but she drove only six blocks and parked. Interesting. Perhaps she had an appointment with a divorce attorney in town.

As he checked the names of the establishments, he was surprised to see her dash into Fred Astaire's Dance Studio. Her lover must be inside.

Keeping the heat on in his truck, he leaned back and smiled, thinking about the first time he and El had danced. It was some silent auction event that his commanding officer suggested he attend. Having to wear a tux had been a nightmare, but having

El in his arms made up for it.

His wife had been such a graceful and talented dancer. Him? He could barely keep the beat. At least he hadn't stepped on her toes. For a split second, he considered going inside and taking a lesson or two. That way, when Charlotte married, he wouldn't look like a fool during the father-daughter dance.

Give it a try.

Vic pushed open his door, telling himself he was doing this as part of the job. If he could pretend to be a homeless man for a month, he could take a dance lesson or two and survive.

When Vic entered the small ballroom with a large mirror lining one wall and posters of famous dancers plastered on the others, he hadn't expected the sea of women to turn and look at him like a guppy in a shark tank. There were three men and about ten women.

Act casual.

An older woman he'd not met before came over to him. "Are you here for ballroom dancing?"

"Yes." His throat turned dry. "But I'm not very good."

She smiled. "All the more reason to be here, young man. I'm Millie by the way, and I will be your dance instructor."

Her lithe body spoke of someone who'd spent years on the dance floor, tapping out a beat. "How much are the lessons?" It didn't matter what she told him, but he wanted to act the part.

"Men get to come free. We have so few, we can't possibly charge them."

Oh, boy. "Where would you like me?"

She squeezed his arm. "A handsome man like you should know better than to ask an old lady a question like that."

His face heated. She was hitting on him? Dear God. "I'll stand behind the ladies and try to follow along." That way, he could watch Sandra Evans to see which of the three men she had her eye on, though none looked better than Harold Evans, stodgy though he might be.

"We're going to do the tango today," Millie explained.

He inwardly groaned. Millie, however, was an excellent teacher, taking the steps slowly. Vic watched Sandra while he tried to follow. Throughout the hour, Sandra barely made eye contact with any of the men. That was interesting. Perhaps her partner hadn't shown up tonight.

"Let's pair up." Millie went around the room putting the couples together—mostly women with women.

From what he'd observed, she put an experienced person with a novice. When it came time to pair him up, he ended up with Sandra. What a coincidence.

"Hi, I'm Vic."

She smiled. "Sandra. First time?"

"Yes. You?"

"I've been coming for almost three months now."

"That so?" Dumb comment, but his mind kept imagining him and El dancing.

She smiled. "Years ago, my husband used to dance professionally. The few times we went dancing, I couldn't keep up. He never said anything, but I could tell he was disappointed. This Christmas, he's booked us a trip to Argentina, and I know we'll be at a club where they do the Argentine Tango. I want to get out there and dance with him." Her eyes sparkled. "I realize the Ballroom Tango is different, but it's the best I can do on short notice."

"That's amazing and quite sweet." Not to mention, highly romantic. Boy, had he pegged her wrong.

"Thank you." So engrossed in her story, Vic stumbled. "Remember, it's right, left, right," she said in a helpful tone.

"Gotcha." It would take months for him to get good.

By the time the class ended, he'd been paired with three other women. When he left, he signed up for a month's worth of classes.

On the way home, he had to figure out what to tell Mr. Evans. There was no way he'd spoil the man's surprise. Sandra was a wonderful wife to sneak in dance lessons. He bet she'd like El, if they ever met.

El had made sacrifices like that for him all through their marriage, and yet, he'd done little for her. Damn. He had made so many mistakes.

As soon as he entered his house, he lit the fire and called Charlotte. He missed her. Hell, he missed El, too, but she was better off where she was.

"Hey, what's up? You call Mom yet?"

What was wrong with everyone? "We've been through this. I called to see if you wanted to come over for Christmas. I thought we'd build a snowman like we used to."

She laughed, sounding a lot like her mom. "I'm twenty-three."

So? He and El loved making one. "Fine, but come anyway. I'll have a tree."

"Sure. What can I bring?"

"Just yourself. When I know more, I'll let you know."

After he disconnected, he grabbed a beer, turned on the stereo and sank onto the sofa. Was he being an ass, like Sharon claimed? El wouldn't like Rock Hard, and he would never ask her to give up her career for him. His life was fraught with danger.

She'd already asked him to come with her, which meant she cared, but perhaps she was being polite. Why was this now so confusing? He'd told her to stay away. Shit. Had he made a mistake? Vic rubbed his eyes. Why couldn't he do anything right when it came to her?

Of late, things had become jumbled in his head—and it wasn't from the concussions. He'd totally believed the worst of Sandra Evans, and that wasn't like him at all. The facts pointed to her being a straight arrow, and the few people he'd spoken with had said she loved her husband, yet he wanted to believe the worst.

Something needed to change and fast, but he didn't know what.

✧   ✧   ✧

"I'LL GET US some coffee from across the street," Ellie said. "Be right back."

"Tell them to go light on the cream," Wendy called out.

"Don't worry, I remember."

Ellie bundled up, grabbed her purse, and left the gallery. With Christmas around the corner, business had become rather hectic. She'd convinced Hilton to take his turn at night, when the bigger customers usually stopped by, and yet she still was running ragged.

Outside, the air was brisk and the heavy clouds were about to dump its load. She stepped to the curb and waited for the light to change. She ran through her options of what to buy in the way of sweets. It was going to be a long evening. On Friday and Saturday, the gallery stayed open until ten.

The light turned red and the white walk signal lit. Ellie had taken about three steps when the sound of metal crunching ripped through the air, the loud crash startling her. Tires squealed and horns blared. As if time slowed, the car that had just stopped at the light was pushed into the intersection by the car behind it. Ellie froze, awaiting the impending disaster. A car entering the intersection from the right side slammed into the passenger door of that first car. Glass shattered and smoke puffed out from the engine.

Holy shit. Ellie wanted to rush to the woman, but it wasn't safe. More cars banged into the one in front of it. She whipped out her phone, dialed 911, and told them the location and nature of the crash. Drivers from as far as four cars back exited their vehicles and ran toward the site. Pedestrians stopped and gawked.

She wanted to help, but didn't know what she could do.

"What happened?" Wendy said, running out of the store.

"Someone slammed into a woman and pushed her into the intersection when the light was red. Oh, my God. I hope she's okay."

Less than two minutes later, sirens sounded. Wendy wrapped an arm around Ellie's shoulder. "Come back inside. We can get the coffee later."

Ellie nodded. Rattled, she followed Wendy inside. Still shaking, Ellie made her way over to the counter and sat down. "That poor woman. She was minding her own business and the next thing she's being slammed into the intersection."

Wendy shook her head. "Shit happens. You follow the rules, and bad stuff still goes down."

"You got that right."

Wendy shook her head. "Virginia just isn't safe like it used to be."

For the rest of the evening, those words resonated with Ellie. Maybe it wouldn't matter where she lived; some thug who'd never heard of Vic Hart could come after her. Wendy was right. Sometimes, bad shit comes when you least expect it.

A little after ten, Ellie locked the gallery doors, and then she stepped into the back room where Wendy was shutting down the computers. "I've been thinking," Ellie said.

Wendy looked up. "About what? You going to find out about that woman who was injured in the car wreck?" They'd watched the ambulance backboard the woman out.

"No. What do you think about me moving to Montana?"

Chapter Twenty-Seven

CHRISTMAS WAS IN four days, and yet Vic didn't have the energy to do much shopping. He'd ordered a few things for Charlotte, but he had yet to decorate his home. He figured he'd pick up a spruce tree at Lander's Lot tomorrow. By then, they'd be cheap.

A knock sounded on his door. He sighed. Hadn't he told Sharon just to walk in? "Come on in."

The door eased open and he glanced up. A woman in a trench coat, boots, and a hat pulled over her face strolled in. He stood. "May I help you?"

She raised her head and Vic's heart sputtered. "El?" Was she a mirage? She had to be.

"I wanted to wish you a merry Christmas in person."

"What are you doing here?" That didn't come out right. "I mean, I never thought I'd see you again."

She took off her hat and placed it on the chair in front of his desk. "You thought wrong."

He had a million questions to ask her, but he couldn't concentrate with her slowly undoing the tie around her waist. Once open, she slipped the top button through the slit, revealing nothing but skin. He didn't dare move and chance ruining this miracle.

"I sent Sharon home, by the way," she said. "We're all alone."

The ramifications had his cock threatening to jump out of his pants, but they needed to talk first. "How long can you stay?" Was this just a quick visit or had she decided she wanted to make a life with him?

Another button opened, exposing more bare chest. "I guess that depends on you."

He wanted her to stay forever. "What do I have to say?"

She laughed. "How about saying nothing and just watching before I lose my nerve?"

He pressed his dry lips together and held up his palms in surrender. "I won't stop you."

I might die or make a fool of myself before you finish, though. He adjusted his crotch, and then leaned against the desk to keep from tearing off that damned coat. She smiled and undid the next button. Only then did he notice her legs were bare and a bit red as if she were cold.

"Want me to turn up the heat for you?" He was sweating, but it wasn't from the room temperature.

"I was hoping you'd heat me up."

Kill me, now. She was a vixen, a temptress, sent by his maker to do him in. "I can do that." As he pushed off from the desk, she held up a palm.

"Stay there. I'll be done in a minute."

He licked his lips and rested against the corner. "I'm waiting."

Her hands dropped lower and she undid the next button. The lapels fell open to reveal naked breasts. Vic trembled. Could this be happening? He pinched his arm and she laughed.

"If you're thinking I'm not real, I assure you, I am."

"Good to know."

After undoing the last two buttons, the trench coat gaped open. Except for her knee-high boots, she was naked. Totally. Completely. Gloriously.

"May I help you out of that?" he asked with as much composure as he could muster.

She turned around. "Thank you."

Vic pushed off from the desk and placed his hands on her shoulders. He never wanted to move away from her. Her gardenia scent invaded his mind and his heart. Wanting to keep the tension high and the romance strong, he lowered her coat down her arms. Once free, he walked over to the coat stand and hung it up. Inhaling, he turned around. If someone walked in the room right now and shot him in the heart, he'd die a happy man.

"You're beautiful, but we have a problem."

Her smile disappeared. "A problem?"

"Are you aware that nudity in public is illegal in Montana?"

She shook her head. Vic strode over to his desk, opened the drawer, and extracted a pair of cuffs he'd used back at the Bureau. He'd kept them as a keepsake. Now they'd serve a different purpose.

Striding up behind her, he gently pulled her arms back and cuffed her. "You are under arrest for public indecency."

El twisted around to face him. "I'm so sorry, Agent Hart. Isn't there something I can do to make you change your mind? I have so much to accomplish and can't afford to go to jail."

He stroked his chin. "While I change, I'll think about it."

Attempting to keep a straight face, he ditched his clothes as fast as was humanly possible.

"You've lost weight." Concern filled her voice.

"I've missed you, El. So fucking much." He wouldn't break down. He'd gone through enough misery since she left to last a lifetime.

"Me, too. What are you going to do about it?" She tilted up her chin.

God, but he loved this woman. "Only thing I know—make love with you. I want you and need you more than you can imagine." He'd gladly spend the rest of his life fighting off any man who came near her if it meant he could have her by his side. He'd been stupid to let her go.

Vic stepped close and placed his palms over her tightly budded nipples. She needed to get warm, and he knew just what to do to help.

El dropped back her head. "That feels so good. I want to grab your cock."

"Which is one reason why you're cuffed. One touch and I'll explode."

Vic leaned over, wrapped one arm around her waist and suckled on her tit. Passion and ecstasy collided. He needed this woman like he needed to breathe, but he didn't want to assume she'd stay forever.

Once he licked and tugged on the other nipple, he swooped her up in his arms. She felt so right there. "What are you doing?" She giggled.

"Thought you'd be more comfortable on the desk." He set her on the edge then placed his laptop on the ground. The rest of the stuff he swiped onto the floor.

She laughed. "You do take your job seriously, Mr. Hart."

"That's former Agent Hart to you." Flirting and bantering did wonders for his soul. "Now spread 'em."

She scooted back to the middle of the desk and rested on her elbows. That position didn't look comfortable so Vic grabbed his clothes, folded them, and placed them under her arms and butt. "Better?"

"Much."

Vic pulled his client chair close to the desk and sat. "Now, for my feast. Don't think about coming, or there will be dire consequences."

She lowered her chin. "I bet if I were to suck on your cock, I could make you come."

"I won't lie. You could. Now lean back and let me enjoy you."

"Can you take off the cuffs? I want to touch you."

The metal cuffs couldn't be comfortable, but having her touch him right now would be bad. He jumped up, retrieved the key from his drawer, and removed them. Not needing her to take too much control, he strode over to the rack, slipped the belt from the coat, and returned. "Sit up."

"You're mean, officer," she replied doing as he asked with a delicious pout.

After he wrapped the material around her wrists, he tied it off in a bow. "Better?"

"Sort of. Once I pay my bail, you'll be sorry."

He laughed, the feeling so good he could taste it.

Dropping onto his chair, he slid forward and widened her legs. Her arousal lit up his libido to a dangerous level. As much as he wanted to bring her pleasure, his reward would be higher. His first lick had his dick turning to steel. How he was going to keep from coming, he didn't know.

"I love your taste. I can't get enough of you." Vic practically buried his face against her pussy, sucking, licking, swirling.

"Yes." She arched her back and groaned. "I need more."

Vic obliged by delving two fingers into her wet channel and curling his fingers to locate her most sensitive spot. As soon as he hit it, she writhed and slid closer. "That's it!" she crooned.

Heaven could never be this good. Her breathy pleas were too much for him. Vic stood. "I'm weak. I need you too much."

With a quick tug, he took off her restraint. "Your bail has been posted, but don't leave town."

"Promise, Agent Hart. I'm staying."

He wanted to shout for joy, but he had a few more pressing things to take care of. Standing between her legs, he drew her up to a sitting position and kissed the delicate plane of her neck then dragged his kisses up to her ear. "I'm glad you're here," he whispered.

"Show me."

Vic cupped the back of her head and kissed her with every ounce of passion and love welling inside him. She was the woman he wanted, and he made a promise to do everything in his power not to mess it up. Their tongues darted in and out, exploring each other as if this was their first kiss. His lungs tightened in need of air, but it was El who leaned back.

"Let me show you what I want."

The glint in her eye told him he was going to regret this. "Be my guest."

✧ ✧ ✧

ELLIE HAD BEEN so scared to pull off a stunt like this, but the more she thought about it, the surer she was that she was doing the right thing. If Vic loved her like he said, then she wanted to give this relationship a try.

She hopped off the desk. "How about you sit up there?"

"Your mouth is the match to my kindling."

She laughed. "I agree you might combust, but there's nothing small about your stick."

He cracked up. "Fine. Just be quick. I've been dreaming of having my cock in your pussy from the moment you told me goodbye."

"Is that all I'm good for?" She didn't really believe it, but his actions almost implied it.

Vic grabbed her to his chest. "No, sweetheart. You are my everything. It's easier for me to express what I'm feeling when we make love."

She leaned back. "Good, then let me express myself first."

He groaned then smiled. As if he hadn't been run off the road or shot, he sat on the edge, his feet touching the ground. "I'm ready for your magic."

Ellie shoved the chair out of the way and bent over. Using her fingers, she dragged them up and down his length, alternating between hard and light.

"Grr. Touch him or lick him."

"Patience."

"Remember, turnabout is fair play."

She rolled her eyes. "You can show me in a minute."

Because she was so needy, Ellie placed her mouth on his cock and ran her tongue under the edge of the head. Sweet. Vic cupped her breasts and desire pooled between her legs. He wasn't playing fair. Perhaps next time, she'd have to cuff him.

Drawing him into her mouth completely, she grabbed his cock hard. He hissed and squeezed her breast, sending chaos everywhere. Ellie had planned to take her time, to torment him, but in reality, she was the one who lacked discipline.

She stood. "Take me."

In a flash, Vic was off the desk and standing behind her. "I can't tell you how often I've dreamed of this moment in the last two weeks. I've relived every moment of lovemaking we've had over and over again."

"So have I. Now if you wish to add a few more to your playlist, fuck me hard."

He laughed. The joy in his voice stirred her deep love for him. She planted her palms on his desk and stuck out her ass. He rubbed each cheek with reverence. "Beautiful."

"Vic Hart. I'm warning you. There will be plenty of time later to look and touch. Right now, I need you to put that large piece of wood you possess into my fire."

"Yes, ma'am." He pressed his cock against her entrance and wedged his way in.

The stretching made her catch her breath. "He's grown."

"That's what pining for you can do to a man."

Their easy banter was one of the things she so loved about this man. After two deep thrusts, he'd stopped. It was as if he were lost in thought. Ellie pressed her hips back and it seemed to restart him. His fingers found her nipples, and they went to town twirling and twisting each one, giving her mega doses of pleasure. Each press and tug pushed her closer to the edge.

Only then did he thrust into her all the way, heating her body to volcanic temperatures. She lowered her head and absorbed all the loving, thrilled that he seemed as excited as she was.

"Yes, yes, more," she shouted.

Vic's chest pressed against her back and his lips found her shoulder. Between the nips and kisses, the way he was kneading her breasts, and his dynamic thrusts, Ellie was about to burst.

His cock slammed into her back wall again, and she lost it. Wave after wave of glorious ecstasy cascaded through her. Her scream sounded foreign even to her ears, but Vic's shout matched hers.

A second later, his cock pulsed and then exploded. Heat poured through her as his hot seed filled her. Blood pounding hard in her ears, she dropped onto the desk.

Vic brushed back her sweaty hair from her neck and kissed her. "I love you."

All she could do was nod.

Chapter Twenty-Eight

ELLIE HAD COME to Vic's office dressed and then changed in the bathroom. No way would she have even stepped outside nearly naked. After she'd received a big hug from Sharon, Ellie had gotten into her sexy outfit. Now dressed, she stepped back into Vic's office. He, too, had put on his jeans and shirt. The fantasy play had been better than she'd ever imagined, but now was the time to discuss the real reason she was there.

She glanced down at the coat in her arms. "We should talk."

"Okay." His voice came out a bit jittery.

Vic dragged his comfy chair from behind the desk and motioned she take the seat. He sat in the hard wooden chair opposite her. "Please don't tell me you only came to say goodbye."

She raised her brows. "You think I'm that cruel?"

"No. I just said that to make it easier on you in case that was your message."

Ellie stretched out her legs. She'd prepared what she planned to say the whole plane ride out here, but few of the words remained in her head. "I sold my portion of the gallery."

Vic sat up straighter, shock furrowing the lines jetting out from his eyes and around his mouth. "You did? But you love the gallery."

"I do, but I love you and Charlotte more. Family is more important than a bunch of paintings or the dream of being a famous curator." She leaned forward. "It was Wendy who reminded me that I can't hug a painting, and that a painting or piece of artwork won't be a comfort when I need some loving."

"Remind me to send her a Christmas card."

She chuckled. "I know you said there might be dangers, but there are no guarantees in life. I saw an innocent woman in a car get pushed into a busy intersection. I don't know the extent of her injuries, but I suspect they might have been worse than yours. What I'm saying is we'll deal with whatever comes our way—together."

Vic scooted his chair closer and picked up her hands. "Are you sure you want to live out west? Granted we have malls—and Starbucks—but the weather can be harsh."

"I can do harsh if I have you to keep me warm."

He shook his head. "What did I do to deserve you?"

"Well, you are hot in bed."

He dropped back his head and laughed. "So now, I'm just a hot piece of meat?"

In part, but she didn't think it wise to mention that. "If you play your cards right, you could play a more important role." She gave him her best shoulder shrug.

"You are too much. All kidding aside, do you think you can put up with me working late hours if I'm on a case?"

"As long as you tell me what's bothering you, I can handle anything."

"I can try, but what about you? I don't picture you sitting at home knitting."

"I've never knitted, or sewed for that matter, in my life." Vic was being silly.

"My point exactly."

She had considered her options. "I'll check out some of the local galleries. I make a pretty good sales person."

"Of that I have no doubt." He smiled. "Now that that's settled, Charlotte has agreed to come to my house for Christmas." He practically vibrated with excitement.

"She told me. She was thrilled you asked her."

"As if I wouldn't?"

Ellie leaned back. "You can be odd at times."

"True. Speaking of odd, some friends invited me to a party tomorrow night. I can cancel if you'd rather not go, but I've asked Charlotte to be my date."

"I'd love to meet your friends, especially now that I'm here for good, and I certainly don't mind playing second fiddle to my daughter."

"Fantastic." He slapped his forehead. "I wasn't thinking. You said you sold your gallery? To whom?"

"Ronnie Maloney. He told me he was ready to own a gallery. The timing was perfect, especially since Hilton and he are friends."

"That's wonderful."

"I figured it was the universe's way of telling me I need to be here."

He looked to the ceiling. "Thank you, universe."

✧   ✧   ✧

"SO TELL ME about these friends." Ellie turned her back to Vic so he could zip up her dress.

"The ranch we're going to belongs to Cade Benson. He's a detective who has worked with Trent over the years—who, by the way, will be there."

"So that's why you invited your daughter?" She turned around.

"Who me?"

Ellie slightly punched him. "You are such a romantic."

"Am not. Cade lives with Stone Benson and their wife, Amber. You've met Stone. He was one of the paramedics who took care of me at the barn."

"I'm afraid I was a bit preoccupied to notice anyone other than you."

"You say the sweetest things. The party is at Cade's house because they just had a baby. Trevor is about eight months old and Amber didn't want to leave him."

"I can understand that." Vic had mentioned that many couples were in a ménage relationship. It wasn't something she ever wanted to entertain, but if it worked out for others, she had no problem with it.

"Coming to the party besides Trent, is the other detective who was with him during my kidnapping—Thad Dalton. He'll be bringing his wife, Zoey, who's a therapist at the hospital, and their other partner, Pete Banks, who owns a construction firm."

She held up her hands. "Whoa. I'm already on overload. I'll never be able to remember their names."

He laughed. "Fair enough." Vic helped her into her coat. "Ready?"

"Yes."

They stepped into the living room where Charlotte was waiting for them. Her eyes widened. "You guys look awesome!"

Ellie walked over and hugged her daughter. "So do you."

"You don't think it's a bit too much?"

Her skirt was too short and the top cut too low, but she was an adult. "You look great."

Charlotte beamed.

"Let's go, ladies."

They piled into his truck and headed out to this Christmas

party. Vic went over who'd be there again, but there were just too many names to keep track of.

Vic glanced into the rearview mirror. "Charlotte, you remember Max Gruden?"

"The Fire Marshall?"

"Yes. He'll be there with his wife, Jamie."

Ellie was looking forward to meeting all these wonderful couples. When Vic turned down the drive, cars and trucks were parked as far as fifty feet back from the house. "This is some party."

"We Montanans like to do it up big."

She laughed. Vic never was one to socialize. He had changed. Once he parked, he wrapped his arm around both of their waists and escorted them inside. Ellie leaned over and whispered in his ear. "We should have brought something."

"I offered, but they said they had everything covered."

"That doesn't mean we shouldn't have brought a bottle of wine or a toy for Trevor."

"See why I need you?"

Vic was too much. "Yes."

A beautifully decorated lit Christmas tree sat by a large window with presents piled underneath. Stockings were hung on the chimney, and a table nearby was filled with more food than she'd seen at any Washington, D.C. event. "This is incredible."

"It is."

Charlotte clasped Ellie's arm. "There's Trent. What should I do?"

"Don't ask me, but if he comes over, please be polite and say hello." Ellie was glad her dating days were now over.

Trent made a beeline toward them. "Glad to see you all could make it, but I didn't expect you Ms. Hart."

Vic grinned. "El's come back to stay."

"Hey, that's fantastic. This calls for a toast!"

"No, please. This isn't about us. I just want to kick back and meet everyone."

"I understand." Trent turned to Charlotte. "May I get you a drink?"

Ellie couldn't quite get a read on her daughter, but she suspected it was a mixture of delight and mortification. "Sure."

Once Trent whisked her away, Vic took Ellie around and introduced her. It would take weeks, if not months, before she could keep people's names straight. They all seemed very interesting and nice. Most were either in the medical field, worked at the fire department, or at the Rock Hard Police Department. One exception was Alex Hendrix and his wife, Dina Banks. Alex owned a construction firm with Pete while Dina owned a boutique. She and Alex had just had a baby two months ago. The woman looked wonderful.

Between socializing and eating, Vic would have to carry her out to the car. Around ten, Cade gathered everyone around. "We have an announcement to make."

The group chatted, speculating about a possible second child for Amber. Instead of Cade or Stone stepping up, it was Max Gruden who moved to the front with his wife Jamie.

"I can't think of a better group of people to announce that Jamie and I are expecting our first child in April."

Several women rushed to her side and offered their congratulations. Ellie sighed. "My pregnancy was great until you had to go out on some top-secret case the night I delivered."

Vic spun her around. "I regret that more than you can know. I wish things had been different, but I can't change the past. All I can promise is that from now on, you and Charlotte will be my top priority." He kissed her slowly, tenderly, and with love.

"Gross. No daughter wants to see their parents kiss."

A bit embarrassed, they parted. "I'm sorry. You're right," Ellie said.

Vic leaned close. "How about we take this elsewhere?"

She laughed. "I think we should thank our hosts first."

"Of course."

Now that Vic had truly come out of his FBI shell, the times ahead were going to be interesting.

✧   ✧   ✧

CHRISTMAS MORNING WAS magical. A fresh layer of snow had fallen, and Vic was with the two most wonderful women in the world.

"Have a seat at the table. The eggs and bacon are ready," El said.

He'd fixed the coffee and Charlotte made sure no one had messed with the presents under the tree. Once they were all at the table, Vic lifted his mug. "Merry Christmas, ladies. You've made me a very happy man."

They both smiled. "I'm happy for the family I've always wanted," Charlotte chimed in.

El placed a hand over Charlotte's. "Better late than never."

"Amen," he added.

Vic told them about the text he'd received from Harold Evans, thanking him for keeping the most amazing secret in the world. They'd listened to his tale of misunderstanding last night, and were happy for the couple.

"Did he and his wife dance the tango then?" Charlotte asked.

"I'll be sure to ask him when they return from their Christmas vacation. How about you ladies clear the table, while I scrounge up one more present I forgot to put out."

They jumped up and rushed to get ready for the present opening. Vic ducked into the bedroom, pulled out his underwear drawer, and extracted the small gold case. His heart pounded. He kept telling himself this was the right time. They were ready. He stuffed the small box in his jeans pocket and went back to help the women in the kitchen.

The two of them seemed to be conspiring against him, taking forever to load the dishwasher. They insisted on scrubbing and drying each pot and pan. He wanted to shout at them to leave the dishes, but Charlotte seemed determined to make sure the kitchen was cleaner than when they started.

Finally, they all gathered by the tree. He'd already put the logs in the fireplace and the blaze was heating up the room.

While he should probably wait until after the presents were open before giving El her gift, he couldn't wait. When both women were seated, Vic moved in front of El. The first time he'd proposed, he hadn't dropped to one knee. He was too cool for that back then.

This time he did. Her eyes widened, hopefully in surprise and delight, and Charlotte squeaked.

"Eleanor Hart, you've made me the happiest man so many times—when you married me the first time, when you gave me the most wonderful daughter in the world, and when you came back after five long years of me wanting you."

Her chin quivered. He had to look away. If he didn't, he might cry. He had to shift on his other knee to tug the small case from his pocket. "I'm not sure if you still like this style of ring, but it was the best I could do on short notice."

When he flipped over the case, El gasped. "It's beautiful."

"I guess the only thing left to say is El, will you marry me?"

He hadn't expected the tears, but he sure enjoyed the hug.

"Mo-om. It's not official unless you say yes!"

They all laughed. "Then by all means I want to make it official. Yes, yes, and yes!"

All Vic knew was that the next fifty years were going to be better than the last.

THE END

MONTANA PROMISES (Full length contemporary)
Promises of Mercy (book 1)
Foundations For Three (book 2)
Montana Fire (book 3)
Hart To Hart (book 4)

ROCK HARD, MONTANA (contemporary novellas)
Montana Desire (book 1)
Awakening Passions (book 2)

PACK WARS (Paranormal)
Training Their Mate (book 1)
Claiming Their Mate (book 2)
Rescuing Their Virgin Mate (book 3)
Box Set (books 1-3)
Loving Their Vixen Mate (book 4)
Fighting For Their Mate (book 5)

Author Bio

Want a FREE book? Sign up for my newsletter and receive MONTANA DESIRE.

COPY AND PASTE INTO YOUR BROWSER:
http://eepurl.com/U1dm1

Check out my latest interview on You Tube:
youtube.com/watch?v=sQo5pyyVMDI

Not only do I love to read, write, and dream, I'm an extrovert. I enjoy being around people and am always trying to understand what makes them tick. Not only must my books have a happily ever after, I need characters I can relate to. My men are wonderful, dynamic, smart, strong, and the best lovers in the world (of course).

You'll find me most days on my chaise lounge with my laptop and my iced tea(unsweetened!) on the side table. I love to sleep in late and write into the wee hours. I also love FB, so you'll find me on there, too!

I believe I am the luckiest woman. I do what I love and I have a wonderful, supportive husband, who happens to be hot!

Fun facts about me

(1) I'm a math nerd who loves spreadsheets. Give me numbers and I'll find a pattern.

(2) I'm addicted to taking pictures (I taught high school photo for 30 years). I plan to periodically post some of my favorites on my newsletter [so sign up!].

(3) I also like to exercise. Yes, I know I'm odd. Not only do I walk with different women each week, I teach Pilates twice a week at a local rec center, and lift weights the other days.

I love hearing from readers either on FB or via email (hint, hint).

Social Media Sites

Website:
www.velladay.com

FB:
www.facebook.com/vella.day.90

Twitter:
velladay4

Gmail:
velladayauthor@gmail.com

Google:
plus.google.com/u/0/116041077486216602121/posts

Tsu:
https://www.tsu.co/velladay

www.ingramcontent.com/pod-product-compliance
Lightning Source LLC
Chambersburg PA
CBHW030252200626
46816CB00002BA/604